Serengeti Storm

The bitch is back, and nothing gets in her way. Except her own heart...

Shana Delray is hissing mad. The pride's Alpha has chosen a mate—and it's not her. Bred to be his consort, she's not going to let some runt of the litter take her destined place—no matter how much ass she has to kick in the process.

Her way back into the pride is Caleb Minor—her former lover, the Alpha's loyal enforcer...and the runt's brother. And if she has to go through Caleb to get what she wants, so be it. She'll do whatever it takes to pry the little usurper out of her way.

Caleb's familiarity with Shana's manipulative ways serves him well when he's assigned to keep the seething she-cat in line. A nearly impossible task, as he's forced to use his body—in more ways than one—to save her from herself. Now if only he can save his battered heart from the explosive desire that isn't as dormant as he'd thought.

Caleb's stronger now. Tougher and harder. And, to Shana's fury, he won't be used. The harder she pushes, the more she finds her heart yielding...and suddenly she wonders if she can somehow win back the man she spent a decade trying to destroy...

Warning: This book contains manipulations and power plays (in and out of the bedroom), a naughty kitten who deserves a good spanking, and a second chance at that first love.

Serengeti Lightning

Love can be a force of nature.

Mara Leonard is through hitting the snooze button on her biological clock. The Three Rocks Pride schoolteacher is ready to get serious about starting a family, and she needs a serious man to make that happen.

Regrettably, that means crossing less-than-serious Michael Minor off her list of potential mates. Michael is impulsive and passionate, but his spontaneity leaks into shapeshifting whenever his emotions run high—a tendency he should have outgrown long ago. As a sex buddy, he's delicious. Daddy material? Disqualified.

Michael is blindsided by Mara's rejection. Nine years separate them, and his genetic malady means no one in the pride treats him as an adult. But if she thinks he'll simply slink away to lick his wounds while she steps into the arms of another man, she has seriously underestimated him.

The tricky part will be convincing his over-analytical lover that he's more than a disposable sex toy. That real bravery means tearing up her damn checklist and following her heart. And doing it without letting their explosive sexual chemistry expose the Pride's secrets to the outside world.

Warning: This book features break-up sex, make-up sex, a lioness who's a cougar and a hot young lion who's grown up in all the right ways. Note: All electrical shocks are purely metaphorical.

Serengeti Sunrise

No strings? Try hopelessly tangled.

Zoe King is itching to get out of Three Rocks. Sure, the pride is more progressive with her brother in charge. She's just got a bad case of wanderlust...and an even worse case of the hots for Tyler Minor.

The pride's mechanic sets her senses on fire one second, then shuts down and walks away the next. Before she hits the road for good, this lioness decides it's time to bring their cat-and-mouse game to a satisfying end.

Twenty years ago, Tyler's father walked out and left him with a mountain of responsibility. Now that his younger siblings are settled, the last thing he wants or needs is another obligation. Which is exactly what he'll get if he screws around with the Alpha's sister.

When Zoe offers—more like demands—a no-strings affair, temptation wins and he finds his hands in places they shouldn't be, and his thoughts straying to words like his. But Zoe's got her own ideas about possessive, chest-banging males. And they don't include white picket fences...or letting Tyler keep her out of the danger zone when an outside threat to the pride's secrecy becomes all too real.

Warning: This story contains sexual relations, manipulations, ultimatums and two strong-willed shifters determined to be on top.

Look for these titles by
Vivi Andrews

Now Available:

Serengeti Sins

Vivi Andrews

SAMHAIN
PUBLISHING

Samhain Publishing, Ltd.
11821 Mason Montgomery Road, 4B
Cincinnati, OH 45249
www.samhainpublishing.com

Serengeti Sins
Print ISBN: 978-1-60928-445-9
Serengeti Storm Copyright © 2012 by Vivi Andrews
Serengeti Lightning Copyright © 2012 by Vivi Andrews
Serengeti Sunrise Copyright © 2012 by Vivi Andrews

Editing by Sasha Knight
Cover by Angie Waters

Serengeti Storm, ISBN 978-1-60504-875-8
First Samhain Publishing, Ltd. electronic publication: January 2010
Serengeti Lightning ISBN 978-1-60928-187-8
First Samhain Publishing, Ltd. electronic publication: September 2010
Serengeti Sunrise, ISBN 978-1-60928-454-1
First Samhain Publishing, Ltd. electronic publication: May 2011
First Samhain Publishing, Ltd. print publication: January 2012

Contents

Serengeti Storm

Dedication

A writer's life can be isolating. Most of our time is spent alone in front of a computer with only our imaginary friends for company. It's invaluable to have people in the trenches with you, sharing the highs and lows. So I'd like to dedicate this little story to my writing buddies, Kaye Chambers and Kelly Fitzpatrick, who work tirelessly to keep me (somewhat) sane. Thank you, ladies. You're priceless.

Chapter One

The jeep's engine coughed and sputtered as the wheels locked in place on the rutted dirt road.

Shana Delray swore and stomped on the gas. When the engine screamed in protest, she slammed the clutch to the floor in a last-ditch attempt to keep the damn thing running. The abused jeep just gave one last bone-jarring hack and died.

"Fuck."

She cranked the key, but got no response other than a pathetic whinny and a puff of smoke from the direction of the engine block.

"Double fuck."

So much for her majestic return to the ranch.

Shana breathed warm air onto her freezing hands and glared out the window. The winter night stretched cold and dark around her. Clouds heavy with the threat of snow hung low, almost completely concealing the moon and throwing eerie shadows across the plain.

Shana had never been afraid of things that go bump in the night. Hell, she *was* one of the things that went bump, a born predator, a lioness shape-shifter. But that didn't make the prospect of walking the two-plus miles to the ranch compound any more appealing. Especially not lugging her bags and her wounded pride.

She kicked the door open and stepped into the night, shivering even though it was barely a degree colder outside than it had been in the jeep. The heater hadn't worked for days.

The jeep she'd *borrowed* seven months ago had survived a

desert, a flood, and LA traffic, only to die within miles of home. The radio had met its maker at the county line, dying with a pathetic moan immediately after a report on the Blizzard of the Century about to hit west Texas. Throw in the flat tire she'd gotten a hundred miles back and it looked like the Almighty was bitching at her from on high.

If she believed in signs, she might take it as an omen that her current plan was ill-advised and reverse course.

Shana gritted her teeth. The signs could go suck it. She was here for revenge and she wasn't leaving until she got what was coming to her.

Flipping down the tailgate, she dug into her bags, shuffling things around. She'd take the essentials now and send someone back for the rest. There was no way in hell she was gonna show up carting all her possessions on her back like some damned beggar girl.

The icy wind shifted direction, swirling around her and teasing her nose with the familiar scents of the ranch. Earth and hay and that subtle, sexy musk of male lion... That scent...

Shana spun to face the wind, crouching defensively and snarling as she scanned the horizon. Her heart drummed wildly as a dark figure slowly straightened out of the tall grass along the side of the drive, no longer bothering to hide now that she'd scented him.

"Caleb."

She'd meant his name to sound like a biting epithet, but it caught in her throat, emerging on a hoarse whisper instead.

Why did it have to be him patrolling the land tonight?

Her memory had betrayed her. He looked even more edible than she remembered. Dammit.

Caleb Minor stalked toward her through the grass with a deliberate, feline grace belied by his extreme size. He was massive. Six-and-a-half feet tall with broad, heavily muscled shoulders. He could have easily looked like a gorilla, but the rest of his big body balanced the impressive strength so obviously on display in those shoulders. He was built like a Mack truck, but a very sexy, proportional Mack truck.

In spite of the cold of the night, he wore only a paper-thin, long-sleeved shirt that hugged the contours of his chest and a pair of khaki drawstring pants. The clothing was designed to be quickly discarded should he need to shift and fight. Shana dragged her thoughts away from other reasons he might need to get naked.

His hair was shaggier than when she'd last seen him, but still as dark and thick as a mane. It looked black in the night, but she knew when the sun hit it, or when he shifted into his lion form, streaks of red and brown would thread through the black, drawing the eye and making her fingers itch to bury themselves there.

He stopped in front of her, too close for human comfort, but still oddly distant for lions who traded touch so casually. She'd straightened slowly from her partial crouch as he approached and now met his gaze with a mocking arch of one eyebrow.

"Well, if it isn't little Shana. Back to cause more trouble, princess?"

Since that was *exactly* what she was back to do, Shana ignored the question as rhetorical. "Well, if it isn't big-assed Caleb. Still the Alpha's loyal lapdog?"

He bared his teeth on a hiss—no lion tolerated being called a dog. "At least I didn't run off in a pout because things didn't go my way."

Shana bared her own teeth. "I do *not* pout, Fido. And you have no idea why I left."

He snorted. "Oh, I have a pretty good idea. My baby sister married the man you were trying to wrestle to the altar and you ran off to lick your wounds. Stop me any time this starts to sound familiar."

"Marriage." She spat the word. "Such a ridiculously human word. Is your pint-sized sister too squeamish to claim Landon as her *mate*?"

Caleb folded his thick arms across his chest. "Actually, it was his idea. The Alpha's trying to humanize us. Didn't you hear his plan? Oh, no, that's right. You were too busy running away."

The look he shot her was icy with condescension. Scathing and contemptuous.

No man looked at her like that. Shana was a *goddess*. She was what all men desired but could never deserve, not some pathetic creature to be pitied.

She refused to explain herself to him. Goddesses did not explain.

"Get my bags, Alpo. It's cold. I don't want to spend all night listening to you embarrass yourself with your ludicrous theories."

"You think I give a shit what you want?"

She ground her molars. Men did not swear at goddesses. Even rough-edged men like Caleb Minor. It was time to remind him that she was not a creature to be pitied. She wasn't that lost little girl anymore, begging him to save her.

Hell, she could use that reminder herself.

Shana drew herself up to her full height. She would have towered over an average female, and most men, but she still had to tip her head back to meet Caleb's chilling gaze. She tossed her long, flame-red hair and arched her back, thrusting out her breasts and seeing his gaze flicker down for just a fraction of a second before locking again on her eyes. Caleb was all about discipline, but he was far from immune to her. She wet her lips and lowered her lashes, searing him with a sultry, melting look.

"You used to care what I wanted," she reminded him throatily, drenching the words in sex. "You used to beg to be allowed to please me." She traced one finger over the tightly flexed muscle of his forearm. "Don't you remember how good I can make it, lover?"

"You're a praying mantis," he growled. "I don't have that suicidal urge anymore."

She stroked down his stomach to brush her fingers across the rock-hard ridge growing beneath those drawstring pants. He may not be suicidal, but he definitely had the urge. "Oh, honey…" she purred, "…you know I'm always very careful with my teeth. I would never bite the head off."

His fingers closed vise-tight around her wrist, jerking it away before she could press against his erection like she wanted. "Still the slut, I see."

Shana flinched in spite of herself. Why did it always hurt when he said it? It was just a word. She'd been called worse and the words just bounced off, but that word, in Caleb's gravel-deep voice, and she wanted to run to her Momma and cry like a baby. As if her Momma wouldn't say exactly the same thing. And worse.

But she was going to change that. Claim her rightful place. The place of respect she deserved. Prove to her mother and Caleb and all of them that she was more than the camp slut.

"Still an asshole, I see," she mimicked acidly, jerking her wrist out of his hold, or trying to. For a heartbeat, Caleb held on, his strong fingers tightening fractionally around the fine bones of her wrist, as if to prove he didn't have to let her go if he didn't feel like it.

An unexpected jolt of heat shot down to pool at the base of her spine. She wanted to squirm with it, wallow in his possession and his strength, but she held herself regally still. It had been a long time since she'd been in the presence of a man she couldn't physically best—ever since she'd walked away from the ranch seven months ago, in fact—and she'd forgotten how much she loved the challenge of it.

As if he sensed her mounting excitement—the bastard could probably *smell* it—Caleb released her suddenly. He leaned away from her to put more distance between them and rubbed his hand on his pants as if she'd left her cooties on him.

In spite of his all-too-apparent disgust, his voice was still a little rougher than normal when he growled, "What are you doing here? Crawling home with your tail between your legs?"

Shana's lip curled in a silent snarl. Goddesses didn't crawl. "You'd like that, wouldn't you?" She let her nails shift into claws and stroked over his arm with the vicious tips. "You'd just love to see me on my knees, wouldn't you, Cale?"

"I'd love to see your ass..." he drawled, "...walking away from this ranch, never to return."

"Aw, honey, you don't mean that," she purred. "You'd miss this ass too much."

She patted the body part in question and his eyes tracked the movement of her hand hungrily. Oh, yeah, Caleb Minor would miss her, all right.

"Tell me what I can do to get you to leave."

Shana planted a hand on her hip and pushed her face into an exaggerated pout. "All this talk of leaving is going to hurt my poor wittle feelings, sugarbear."

"You don't have feelings."

The pout morphed into a feline smile. "You make an excellent point. But if I had feelings, I'm sure they'd be very hurt right now. I'd be poor, wounded Shana. Would you take care of me then? Protect me like the big, strong man you are? Or is your docket for damsels in distress all filled up at the moment?"

She reached to run her claws across his stomach again and he slapped her hand away. Shana didn't bother to pretend the smack had hurt. He wouldn't have been fooled. Maybe that was why Caleb had always been her favorite of all the asshole bullies in the pride. He'd never been fooled by her.

Or, more accurately, she'd only been able to fool him once. And that had been years ago, when they'd both been little more than cubs and too naïve to know better.

"Is some other hot teenage kitten sneaking into your bedroom every night?" she asked, calling up the memory of the time when she'd had him wound so tight around her little finger he'd nearly cut off the circulation.

He stiffened, his big muscles tensing deliciously before her eyes. Oh, yeah, he remembered. And the memory was apparently just as unpleasant for him as it was for her. Shana hoped it burned like a bitch.

"After you fuck her senseless, do you whisper how you'll do *anything* for her? How you *love* her and will protect her from the big, bad world?" Shana fought to keep the bitterness out of her voice. Cynicism was allowed. Cynicism was a barrier. Bitterness revealed pain and pain was a weakness.

Weakness was an anathema in the pride. Or at least it had been, before the dumbass Alpha had passed up his chance to make Shana his queen and taken Caleb's weakling sister, Ava, instead.

As she recalled why she'd come here—to take what she deserved back from puny Ava—anger and purpose washed away the insidious traces of bitterness and hurt. The anger was clean, powerful. She smiled viciously. "Or can you even get it up anymore? Did your master have his favorite dog neutered?"

He growled at her and Shana laughed. Men were so pathetically predictable. Attack their virility and all they want to do is snarl and bang their chests to prove their masculinity.

"I'm only going to ask you one more time. Tell me what to do to get you to leave quietly."

Shana pursed her lips and cocked her head. "That wasn't asking. That was demanding." She stepped forward until her front brushed his. "Lucky for you, I like demanding men," she purred. "Unlucky for you, I'm not going anywhere."

When he didn't immediately shove her away, Shana crowded closer, inhaling deeply. Goddess, he smelled fantastic. She wanted to wallow in his scent. Did all lions smell this amazing? Had she just been away from her kind for too long? Or was it him?

She leaned in, rubbing her body against his. It was a platonic gesture among the pride, the casual touching, cuddling and petting, but Shana's nipples were hard enough to cut glass and she was close enough to feel that Caleb's reaction to them pressing against his chest through two layers of cloth was far from platonic. *Hello, lover.*

"You're freezing," he growled, grabbing her by her upper arms and setting her away from him.

Shana was tempted to retort that she hadn't been freezing until he shoved her away. She'd completely forgotten about the cold, the impending blizzard. The world had narrowed down until it was just her and Caleb and heat. But admitting that would have been a confession too big to survive. So instead, she snapped at him.

"Yeah, well, some asshole is making me stand out here in the middle of a fucking blizzard when I could be at home in my nice, warm bungalow."

Fat snowflakes had begun to drift lazily down from the sky and she hadn't even noticed, though now she could see them melting on Caleb's cheeks as he glowered at her. Shana tipped her head back and stared at the sky, amazed in spite of herself by the display nature was putting on. It so rarely snowed here.

She'd always thought snow cold and wet and irritating, but now it fell so softly around her, it seemed the world itself was floating and she was floating with it.

"You don't have a bungalow anymore."

"Excuse me?" The floating sensation evaporated from one heartbeat to the next. Her gaze snapped down from the falling snow to land hard on Caleb. "What do you mean I don't have a bungalow? I will *always* have a bungalow. This is my pride."

Caleb shrugged carelessly. "You left."

Asshole. He was enjoying this. "If your pipsqueak sister has taken over my bungalow, I'm going to enjoy kicking her ass out of it."

He shook his head as if her mental faculties were disappointingly slow. "Ava lives with Landon now, Shay. That's what marriage means."

"Then who is in my fucking bungalow?"

At that moment, she almost wished he would say *he* had taken over her home, though she didn't care to examine why that thought was so appealing.

He shrugged again. "I don't know. Somebody. It's a nice place and it was empty. You know how things are in the pride."

Shana ground her teeth. She knew. Oh, did she ever know.

Possessions were community property in the pride. If you wanted something to be yours and yours alone, you had to be strong enough to keep it, fighting off all comers. Clothing, bungalows, mates—the best of everything went to the strong. At least, that's how it used to be.

"I thought your precious Landon was going to change our barbaric ways."

Caleb shrugged again. Goddess, how she hated that shrug. His fucking nonchalance. As if every shift of his shoulders was more proof that he didn't give a shit about her and never had. "We are what we are. Change is slow."

"So some asshole just *usurped* my bungalow?" Her shock was feigned, but her outrage was real. She'd had one of the nicest places on the ranch compound before she left, totally decked out, complete with a fireplace and a Jacuzzi in the bathroom. And she'd had to kick her fair share of asses to get it.

She'd known she was leaving it undefended when she'd stolen, or rather *borrowed*, the jeep and driven off the ranch. But, at the time, she hadn't planned on ever coming back.

Still, just because she'd walked away without a backward glance and hadn't been home for seven months didn't mean she was okay with someone else sleeping in her bed.

"You actually intend to stay?" Caleb asked.

"I have unfinished business."

And she'd been so lonely outside the pride she'd discovered that homesickness could actually make you physically ill.

This was her *home*. She wasn't about to let some undersized bitch and the undersized bitch's demented Alpha lover run her off.

Caleb must have seen her resolve in her expression. He sighed heavily, the poor put-upon Hercules, and turned to walk toward the ranch. "Come on," he called over his shoulder, not even glancing at the bags piled into the back of the jeep.

She grabbed the knapsack she'd packed with the absolute essentials and moved quickly in front of him, putting an extra little twitch in her walk just for his viewing pleasure. As she strutted toward the only place that had ever been home with the only man who had ever tied her up in knots marching along behind her, she thought she heard him mutter something under his breath, but she must have been mistaken. It had sounded a lot like, "Today's as good a day as any to commit suicide."

Chapter Two

Caleb had told her he wasn't suicidal, but there was no other explanation for what he was doing.

Shana was back. And he was taking her toward the ranch. Where she would be staying. Indefinitely.

He groaned aloud at the thought.

She looked like hell, but Shana looking like hell was still Shana—still hot enough to have him half-hard from the second he'd scented her in the night.

Caleb shot off a quick prayer of thanks to whatever unnamed gods were listening that he'd been patrolling in human form. Facing her for the first time in seven months stark naked after a shift was not an experience he ever wanted to have.

She sashayed along the rutted drive leading to the ranch's main compound, swinging her tight little ass. Her long red hair was loose, the ends flicking around her hips like tongues of flame. Most lionesses were blonde, their hair perfectly matching the color of their pelts, but Shana had to be different in every way. She stood out like a fire in the desert, unique and untamable. And dangerous as all hell.

The memory of those flame-red tresses tangling around him as they slept rose up in his mind, but he shook it away.

She was a viper. No matter how lush her body was. No matter how intoxicating her scent or how wicked the things she could do with her tongue.

Caleb barely bit back another groan. If only memories were as easy to fight as enemies.

She never once glanced back at him as they walked, but he knew she was aware of him. Unfortunately, the feeling was mutual. He'd always been hyperaware of her. His body had never cared that she'd become a soulless, manipulative bitch.

The entrance to the ranch's residential compound rose in front of them. There was nothing ostentatious or distinctive about the low, open gate bordered by a cattle guard. Nothing to indicate there was anything extraordinary about the group of families who lived and worked at this particular ranch.

None of the nearby landowners or businessmen in the small town twenty miles down the road had any idea the residents of the Three Rocks Ranch could take the shape of menacing predators. Through the constant vigilance of the pride and with the help of a few technological gadgets Caleb didn't pretend to understand, no one in their little corner of Texas had any idea fifty lion shape-shifters lived among them.

Fifty-one.

As Shana swung her ass through the gate, she turned her head toward the large tree where the gate guard would be perched in lion form. Caleb saw her flash a small feline smile in the guard's direction and give a little shimmy.

The sound of claws scrabbling for purchase on wood sounded from the tree a fraction of a second before a young male lion with his mane not fully grown in hit the ground with a thud.

Shana gave a low, wicked laugh that was like claws scraping up Caleb's spine. The juvenile male leapt back into the branches. Caleb closed the distance between himself and the troublemaker, making a mental note to talk to Landon about giving young Ryan a less critical post if he was going to be felled every time a lioness looked his way.

Caleb ignored the fact that he would have probably fallen out of the damn tree too, if he'd seen Shana walking through that gate again after seven months.

He caught her arm and nudged her toward the mess hall, where the rest of the pride was likely still gathered after dinner. The Three Rocks Ranch had originally been built as a summer camp and the communal dining arrangement worked well for a lion pride.

Shana slid her arm out of his grip and headed toward the hall. Caleb let her go, his fingers tingling from the touch of her bare skin, even as he wondered what kind of a fool wore a tank top in a snowstorm. Their body temperature might be a couple degrees higher than a human's, but that didn't make them impervious to cold. She could come down with hypothermia just as easily as the humans she looked down on.

Not that he cared. Not that he was concerned for her. She'd done far too much to kill any feelings he'd ever had for her.

The mess hall was by far the largest building on the compound. Light and the raucous sounds of the pride spilled out of it into the night through windows kept open, even in a snowstorm.

He knew Shana too well to expect she would betray any sign of hesitation. She didn't disappoint.

She strode up the steps and threw open the double doors, head held high, the queen returning.

The reaction to her entrance was instantaneous. Silence rippled out around her until the only sound was the scrape of chairs as those in the back of the hall stood, craning for a better look.

She slammed her hands onto her hips and scanned the room, aggression in every line of her body. Caleb tensed, ready to tackle her to the ground if she went for his sister's throat, but her eyes passed right over Ava, dismissing the Alpha's new mate.

Instead, her eyes locked on the more dominant females, who bristled under her challenging glare. One or two dropped their eyes in submission, but more than would have dared only months before met her eyes head-on.

"That's right," she snapped. "I'm back. Now, which one of you bitches stole my house?"

Shana kept her eyes locked in prepare-to-have-your-ass-kicked fashion on the three most likely bungalow thieves. She heard the door shut behind her and felt Caleb's heat as he crowded behind her—doubtless so he could take her down before she could rip out any throats—but she didn't blink.

Loralee finally dropped her eyes, but Shana made note of the fact that the uppity little bitch had dared question her dominance for as long as she had. Mara didn't last nearly as long, which left only Zoe.

Shana felt a growl start low in her throat. She should have known it would be Zoe who'd stolen her slot in pride dominance. The Alpha's bitch sister had been asking for an ass-kicking for too long.

Shana hadn't challenged Zoe when she and Landon first joined the pride, because she'd been trying to butter up the Alpha and snag the slot as his mate. But that didn't mean she couldn't take the Viking bitch down. The blonde may be just a fraction bigger and stronger than Shana in her lioness form, but Shana was fast and she fought dirty. As Zoe was about to learn.

Shana crouched forward slightly, letting the growl ripple out of her throat as her fingernails morphed sharply into claws. Zoe's eyes narrowed and Shana saw her muscles tense in anticipation of the fight, even though she made no move to step away from her table into the open center of the room.

"Enough!"

The bellow held an edge of authority Shana reacted to instinctively. Her claws retracted suddenly. The Alpha had spoken.

Landon stood, the scrape of his chair against the wooden floor loud in the echoing silence. He sat at a table among the lesser members of his pride, not bothering to separate himself according to rank as his predecessors had. Shana hadn't even noticed him sitting there. Until he stood.

When he rose, the mantle of the Alpha fell on his shoulders. He radiated dominance and authority. And disapproval.

"We do not fight for housing privileges anymore," he announced, his voice ringing out across the room.

Shana fought the urge to cower. And won. She was not so easily cowed. She met the Alpha's eyes across the room and did not blink.

"She doesn't have to fight me. She just has to give it back."

23

The Alpha growled, the low sound traveling the room to grip her spine, urging her to bend in submission. Shana stood straight.

"That isn't how we do things anymore," Landon rumbled.

"Our instincts don't change, no matter how *human* you might try to make us." Shana spat the word "human" in the direction of the Alpha's spineless mate.

When little Ava flinched, Shana wanted to crow her victory. The Alpha's weakling mate would never be strong enough to keep him. Only Shana had the strength to rule beside him. Her rightful place in the pride was so close she could taste it, sweet and bright on her tongue.

"You are *welcome* to return to the pride, Shana," Landon said, the welcome sounding forced and borderline violent. "But the same rules still apply. We are not a pride of animals."

The abrupt laugh burst out of Shana's mouth before she could stop it. "We aren't? What are we then?"

"Civilized," Landon snarled, sounding anything but.

"Yes," Shana purred, laughter rolling around in her voice. "I can see that. Just look how *civilized* I make you feel."

She wallowed in his anger. Anger was a kind of passion. There was power in it.

The Alpha's mate did nothing to defend her claim, tiny Ava shivering in her chair. But Zoe's lips drew back from her teeth and her body tensed. Shana's claws snapped out, eager and ready.

An arm locked around her stomach, hard and unmoving.

Caleb.

She hadn't for a second forgotten his presence at her back, but she never would have suspected he would interfere with a challenge. It simply was not done in the pride. Here, honor was found only in a fight, with fur and claws flying. No one stood in the way of that.

"I know an empty bungalow," he said to the Alpha, speaking past her shoulder. "She can sleep there, until she decides if she is willing to obey the new rules."

Shana hissed, so low only Caleb would be able to hear her, at the word *obey*. "I would rather sleep in a scorpion nest than lower myself to sleep in your sister's hovel," she whispered.

He ignored her, listening *obediently* as the Alpha gave his verdict.

"Fine. Just keep her out of trouble."

Shana snorted. "I'd like to see him try," she said, loud enough for the Alpha, and Zoe, and Ava, and anyone else who might be stupid enough to think she was cowed, to hear.

Caleb's arm tightened minutely around her waist. She knew he was stronger than she was, knew he could force the issue if he chose, and, for a moment, she almost considered fighting him. The only thing that stopped her was the fact that the entire pride was watching. She did not want her triumphant return to claim her place as the Alpha's rightful mate to be sullied by a scuffle with Caleb. She had her image as the future ruler of the pride to think about.

But, she also couldn't afford to be seen as weak.

Shana's claws flashed out, fast and lethal. She slashed at Caleb's forearm and twisted out of his grip before the blood had time to splash out. She'd always been eerily fast. Her size was an advantage in fights, but her speed was what made her dangerous.

Blood dripped from the gashes on Caleb's arm as the big, slow ox reached for her. Instead of dodging back, she darted toward the double doors. "Come on," she snapped irritably over her shoulder. "Show me where this empty bungalow is. I don't have all night."

She didn't have to look over her shoulder to know every eye was on her as she swept out of the hall.

She didn't want to look over her shoulder to see the slow fire she knew would be in Caleb's eyes. She had a feeling he wasn't going to take her little scratches lightly.

And he didn't forgive easily. She knew that all too well.

Chapter Three

The sight of blood dripping onto the pristine white snow blanketing the ground was oddly beautiful. Or it would have been.

If it hadn't been his blood.

Caleb flexed his fingers, feeling the pull against the bloody gashes on his arm. Even healing as quickly as shifters did, Shana's little love scratches were going to leave a mark.

His own fault. He'd learned long ago that she wasn't afraid to use her claws, especially when she was trying her damnedest to prove she wasn't afraid of anything or anyone.

She started to turn up the narrow path leading to Ava's old cabin, but Caleb caught her eye and jutted his chin toward the main walkway. "This way."

Shana stopped at the T in the path. "Dream on." She planted one hand on her hip and flipped her long red hair, shaking off the snowflakes caught there. "I'd rather sleep with scorpions than in your sister's bed, but I'd rather sleep there than in yours."

Caleb told himself he didn't give a damn where she slept, ignoring the feral urging of his lion to prove her words a lie. He'd scented lust on her earlier. Even if she had just clawed him, Shana'd always liked it a little rough. Drawing blood was probably a goddamn turn-on.

"Not Ava's bed and not mine. This way."

Shana gave a little sniff and fell into step beside him. Her eyes flicked down to his bleeding arm. He knew she was going to say something about it before she spoke.

Shay'd always hated to be proven wrong. She couldn't tolerate any hint of weakness. Any time anyone bested her in any way, she had to remind everyone she was tough. Always.

"Gosh, Caleb, that looks like it smarts," she purred, right on cue. "You really should put something on it."

"It's fine." It was better than fine. It was a necessary reminder that Shana was walking, talking poison.

"Are you sure?" She shot him a rabid smile. "I haven't had my shots."

Caleb just kept walking, stalking silently through the snow.

Shana bounced on the balls of her feet at his side, the movement jostling loose a memory. *His Shay sprawled across his bare chest. His fingers tangled knuckle-deep in her red curls. She twisted and bounced the bed, still energized after he'd done everything humanly—and inhumanly—possible to wear her out. Her happiness spilled around them, sunny and easy. "I love that you're so silent, Cale," she announced out of the blue, fingers then claws lightly flexing into his pectoral muscles to test his strength. "There shouldn't be two talkers in a relationship. I can talk enough for the both of us."*

He hadn't said anything then. At the time, the only thing he could have said was that he loved her. What a nightmare that would have been. Thank God he'd kept his mouth shut.

"Are we going to that bitch Zoe's place?" she asked, jarring him out of the depths of his thoughts and back to the present. "I'll just bet it's empty if she's in mine."

"She isn't in yours."

"No? Mara, then."

Caleb said nothing, but she'd always been able to read his silences better than anyone else.

"Not Mara, either? Not Loralee. Pathetic little bitch. I've been kicking her ass since the fourth grade."

Caleb didn't call her on the lie. Loralee was the closest thing Shana had to a friend in the pride. For years, she'd followed Shana around like a duckling and Shana'd made sure no one laid a finger on her. Their friendship hadn't soured until Landon had called a moratorium on challenges and Loralee hadn't needed Shana's strength anymore. Loralee stealing her bungalow would be another painful betrayal.

Though, knowing Shana, she would never admit to feeling pain.

"Not Loralee."

"Good." Shana frowned and worked at her lower lip with her teeth. "Then who? One of the males? Doesn't matter. I can still take him. Whoever it is."

"Drop it, Shana."

"You sure it wasn't you?" she persisted, ignoring his demand. "I can just see you, moving into my old place because it *smells* like me. Mooning over what might have been. Jacking off into my underwear drawer. That's what happened, isn't it? And you're too much of a pussy to admit it. Don't worry, baby. I won't hold it against you." She gave a little snickering laugh. "Much."

"Not me. Shut it, Shay." She was trying to hurt him, but he told himself not to take it personally. Hurt them first before they hurt you. That was Shana's motto, pounded into her by a lifetime with her toxic mother.

"I'll figure it out eventually. It's not like you can keep me from wandering by the old stomping grounds to see who's taken up residence." Her face twisted like she'd tasted something sour. "It's not some little girl you've been fucking, is it? In my bed. Probably calling my name when you come. Ugh. That's disturbed, Caleb. There are counselors you can see about shit like that."

"Shay." Her name was a warning.

She ignored it. "I always felt bad about that," she chirped, her cheeriness making the words a lie. "Ruining you for all other women. And at such a young age. It's sad, really. Poor Caleb."

His tongue itched with the urge to say something about the way she'd ruined herself. There wasn't a bed Shana hadn't slept in, a lion she hadn't spread her legs for, and the nastiest part of his nature urged him to call her every kind of whore.

But they'd arrived at the empty bungalow, and part of him still believed there was a breakable little girl beneath her tough-as-nails front, so he said instead, "Here it is."

Shana looked at the medium-sized, decently appointed bungalow and tipped her head to the side. "Not bad. From the outside. What's wrong with it?"

"Nothing. Go on." He would have shoved her up the path, under the porch overhang and out of the snow, but knowing Shana, she probably would have bitten him for his efforts.

"Is it booby-trapped or something? Trip wire?"

"Shana, for God's sake, just go in the damn house. It's a fucking blizzard out here."

She glanced up, seeming startled anew by the falling snow. "It's barely snowing. Some Storm of the Century. Pathetic."

The devil of it was he couldn't even disagree with her. The blizzard the weathermen had been talking about for days was turning out to be nothing more than an inch or two of lightly falling snow. No wind, no whiteout conditions, nothing. But even extreme torture couldn't have made him agree with her at that moment.

"Go, Shana."

She turned the same look on him that she'd given the questionable bungalow only seconds before. Then, slowly, her eyes grew calculating. Her tongue snaked out to wet her lips. "And what if I don't?"

He'd forgotten how exhausting it could be to deal with her. How nothing was ever easy. Even when he was balls-deep inside her, she was always testing his limits. Always pushing harder. His cock stiffened at the memory.

The answer Caleb suddenly wanted to give her was rough and sexual and would take their relationship right back to a place he had sworn he would never go with her again.

Shana must have sensed some shift in his mood, because suddenly she was three steps up the path to the abandoned bungalow, tossing him a disdainful glance over her shoulder. "Relax, tough guy. I'm going like a good girl."

She waggled her ass at him in a way no good girl had ever dreamed and he growled. Then she disappeared into the house.

Caleb held himself still, fighting down the lingering urge to follow her into that house and show her what happened to little girls who teased men like him. The itch at the base of his spine

29

simultaneously urged him to fuck and to shift. He fought both urges.

Until he felt the slight air pressure *pop* from the house, indicating Shana had taken her lioness form inside.

Caleb shifted involuntarily, the animal rising up fast and hard to claim his body.

In this form, the urge to break down the door and fuck her into submission was a hundred times more intense, the animal in him pressing humanity to the periphery of his consciousness. His lion told him the female he'd once thought would be his mate needed to be mastered, that she would welcome his dominance, but the man was still present enough to keep his paws firmly planted on the snowy ground.

When his animal snarled and snapped at his self-imposed tether, Caleb began a slow, prowling circuit around the house. Every fourth paw print was bloody from the bite of sweet Shana's tender claws. He paced around the house until the track was a circle of red. Guarding. Whether he was keeping her in or keeping others out, he didn't know. The animal in him didn't see a difference. It just insisted that he keep prowling.

So he prowled.

Shana woke and stretched, reveling in the pleasure of being in her feline form.

During her months away from the pride, she'd never had the luxury of sleeping as a lion—or really of living as a cat for more than a few moments of each day, safely behind locked doors and careful not to make any non-human sounds.

Shana arched her back and rolled to all four paws, pushing up to stand. Just for the joy of it, she filled her lungs and roared, long and loud. She flicked her tail just to feel the air brush through the tuft.

Tempted though she was to remain feline all day, Shana reluctantly shifted back to human form.

She quickly pulled a fresh pair of panties out of her pack and pulled them on, along with yesterday's jeans, bra and tank top. She'd get someone to bring in the rest of her clothes from the jeep today.

Shana opened the door to her borrowed bungalow—it was only hers temporarily, until she got her own back—and stood looking out over the snowy morning.

The big storm had only dropped a couple inches of snow on the ranch. Pale morning sunlight was already at work melting it. All signs of the so-called Storm of the Century would be gone by noon. Not far from her—borrowed—front porch, a pair of cubs rolled around in the slushy snow.

Shana frowned at a rusty brown stain on the porch—matching a similar stain circling her bungalow. She sniffed. Blood.

Trust Caleb to bleed out on her damn front porch instead of taking five seconds to have someone put a damn bandage on his arm. Goddess forbid he should disobey the Alpha's command to keep her out of trouble even as long as it took to patch himself up.

Of course, he wasn't around *now* to keep her out of trouble. Shana craned her neck and scented the air just to be safe. But no. No Caleb. Either he was hiding downwind, or he'd run off after making himself sick lying there bleeding on her porch all night long in the cold.

She had no sympathy for him.

A sleek young woman appeared around the corner of a nearby bungalow, giving Shana a tentative smile and a sheepish little shrug of her shoulders as she headed in her direction. Shana gritted her teeth. Loralee. She had no sympathy for her either.

"It's good to have you back, Shana," Loralee called, even her voice sounding pathetically subservient.

Did the girl have no self-respect? Shana appreciated Loralee's respect for power and dominance, but even doormats like pathetic little Ava demonstrated some spine *once* in a while.

"Is it?" Shana asked. Her voice was harsh and she did nothing to moderate the icy thrust of the words.

Loralee's wary smile faded a few degrees. "Yes. I missed you."

"Sure you did." Loralee'd missed having someone to fight

31

her battles for her is what Loralee had missed. "Who's in my bungalow?"

Loralee's face froze. She was never much of a quick-thinker and now she was trying desperately to figure out whether Shana was *allowed* to know the answer to her question. Which meant she acknowledged an authority higher than Shana. Unacceptable.

"Who, Loralee?" she demanded.

"Tyler!" Loralee bleated.

"Shit."

Tyler. Caleb's older brother. Not quite as big, not quite as rough, but not someone Shana could tangle with and win.

"You could have just told me," Shana snapped.

"Alpha said we couldn't. He said it didn't matter who it was. It was the principle of the thing."

Of course. The principle. Trust the demented Alpha to make a big damned deal about principles when he could have just told her she didn't have a snowball's chance in hell of winning it back.

Shana turned and looked at the borrowed bungalow. It actually wasn't that bad. As a starting point. A few challenges and she could trade up—principles be damned. Even if she couldn't get her own place back, that didn't mean she couldn't get some nicer digs. And when she was the Alpha's mate, even Tyler wouldn't deny her. She'd have her place back. And her rightful place in the pride.

Goddesses and queens did not beg. Or fight. People *gave* them things.

"Your mother's asking for you."

Shana flinched at Loralee's softly uttered words. Her mother. Living proof that queens did beg. Pathetic, deposed, drunkard queens who had lost all claims on self-respect. "What does she want?"

"She wants to see you," Loralee said gently. "She's missed you too."

Shana knew what Loralee had missed. It was a little harder to pin down what her mother might have missed in her absence. A handy chauffeur to the nearest liquor store?

Someone to look down on when she'd sunk so low it was hard to imagine anyone lower?

"She can go screw herself," Shana whispered, barely mouthing the words.

"What was that?" Loralee asked, sweetness and innocence and weakness personified. Pathetic.

"I'll go see her myself," Shana said louder, brushing past the smaller female.

She sloshed through the melting snow, her mind closed to the pleasures of the winter sun and the playfulness of a snowy morning. She was going to see her mother. Firing squads were more congenial.

Chapter Four

Brenna Delray's bungalow stood on the outermost edges of the residential compound, secluded and dark. There were no lights on inside, but Shana knew better than to think that had anything to do with whether anyone was home.

She knocked on the door sharply. A small, cowardly part of herself she hated to admit even existed hoped Brenna wouldn't be awake. Or had already passed out for the day, even though it was only mid-morning. Anything to keep her from having to walk through that door.

"Shana, honey? Is that you?" A thin, reedy voice floated through the door.

Shana closed her eyes for a second, slumping in on herself. She only allowed herself a heartbeat. *Goddesses don't wallow.* Then she snapped her spine straight and pushed open the door. "Hello, Mother."

All the shades were drawn, but Shana saw her mother clearly enough in the dim light.

Brenna never left the house, unless alcohol was being served in the dining hall. She hid behind her former position, using it as an excuse to ignore the unwritten rule that *everyone* contributed in the pride. The pride had its own doctor, carpenter, schoolteacher and mechanic, making it as self-sufficient as possible. Those who chose to worked in the nearby town or found opportunities to work online, like Shana did, to bring money into the pride. They weren't work-obsessed—Shana had never met a lion who defined himself by his day job or cared more about fancy cars than his afternoon siesta—but everyone pitched in.

Except Brenna.

She sat in a threadbare armchair, curled in a ratty knit shawl, with both hands curled protectively around a tumbler glass filled with amber liquid.

If it's Tuesday, it must be Scotch.

The air was musty and thick in Brenna's bungalow, or Shana's lungs were closing off, she never could quite determine which. She shoved a stack of *Star* magazines off a chair and perched on the edge. She was always on edge here. Her mother might be cheerfully buzzed now, sweet and docile as a lamb, but Shana knew better than to get comfortable. She knew what was coming at the bottom of bottle number two.

"How've you been, Mother?"

"Me?" Brenna batted her hand at Shana playfully. "Oh, you know me. Same old, same old. Did you hear about Brad and Jen? Breaking up like that? Isn't that sad?"

"That was years ago, Mom."

Brenna didn't respond to Shana's words. She just sipped her Scotch and sighed, shaking her head wistfully. "She was such a nice girl, that Jen. Not like that hussy, Angelina."

Shana braced herself for the inevitable comparison. She must've heard a thousand over the years. *"No one respects a trollop, no matter how many African babies she adopts." "You know better than anyone how a slut like that thinks." "A skank is as a skank does, wouldn't you agree, Shana?"*

But Brenna wasn't quite that drunk yet. Still in her friendly first bottle of the day. Instead of the biting words Shana was braced for, she just shook her head and gave a misty smile. "So sad."

"Yeah. Sad." Shana said nothing more. Words weren't power with her mother. They always seemed to become weapons that would boomerang back to her, slicing her open. So she said as little as possible as her mother finished her drink and poured herself another with hands that were surprisingly steady.

"You went away, Shana-bay," her mother cooed. "You left me."

Shana swallowed back the guilt that rose like bile, involuntary and unwelcome. "I thought you'd understand why. You were always talking about the proud tradition of the lions. You said without tradition we were nothing. That we had to honor Leonus as the Alpha, even though he killed..." She paused and cleared her throat. She knew better than to say her father's name. She'd already said too many words. Too many weapons getting ready to spiral back on her. "I thought you'd hate the direction the new Alpha is taking the pride."

"Of course I hate it," Brenna said with a vacant smile. "That's why you needed to stay. A strong mate can turn the Alpha's head whichever way it needs to go. Why, when your father was Alpha, I don't think he ever made a single decision without consulting me first."

Except the decision to accept a younger, stronger lion's challenge and get himself killed. He did that all on his own. And then the pride belonged to that bastard Leonus. The words itched to jump out of Shana's mouth, but she kept them tight to her chest.

Now was not the time to speak out. Her mother's nostalgic drunkenness came right after friendly drunkenness. And right before the worst part. At the rate her mother's glass was emptying and refilling, the worst part wasn't far away.

"You have the blood of kings in your veins, Shana," her mother mumbled dreamily, downing the Scotch like it was apple juice. "You were born to be the Alpha's mate."

"Yes, Mother."

"You're the strongest, Shana-bay. No one can take anything from you that you don't let them take. That's the beauty of the pride."

Shana studied the worn shag rug to keep from responding.

Strength was the curse of the pride. Nothing was sure unless you were the strongest. And not even then. Her mother had been the strongest and look what had become of her. She'd won the Alpha as her mate and fought hard to keep him, but it hadn't lasted. Nothing did.

Lions rarely mated for life. The strong fought for the right to the best mates. In the pride, mating wasn't just about procreation. It was about politics and dominance. Brenna's position hadn't been based on the Alpha's love or devotion, but on her ability to dominate the other females.

In her prime, Brenna had proven over and over again that she deserved to be queen. She'd ruled. And she had wanted nothing less for her daughter. Glory. Power.

Choosing a mate wasn't about love. It wasn't marriage. It was survival of the species. The pride's version of a divorce was more often than not a brutal brawl that left the unworthy without mating rights. The birth control shots the pride doctor provided could be a punishment for the weak just as easily as they could be prevention for lionesses like Shana.

For the first time in years, Shana found herself wondering whether her parents had loved one another. She could barely remember them together. And from the way Brenna spoke of the old days, love didn't matter. Tradition mattered.

The same tradition that demanded Shana honor the man who had killed her father to become the new Alpha.

She'd been spoon-fed tradition from the cradle, but it seemed only recently she'd begun to hate the word.

"Why would you leave, Shana? Why would you walk away from the pride?" Brenna's eyes locked on hers, the sudden eerie clarity in them warning Shana to brace herself. "How *dare* you run away?" The words lashed out like a whip, cracking in the air. "This is a proud family. We *rule* this pride. We. Do. Not. Run. How could you sully your father's name that way?"

Shana locked down, pulling tight into herself. As a teenager, sometimes she would shout back. Scream that her mother had destroyed their father's legacy more surely than she ever could, but the shouting only seemed to make Brenna's rages that much worse.

She'd been young when Leonus killed her father and assumed control of the pride. Only seven. She barely remembered the proud legacy her mother had dangled over her head for decades. She barely remembered a mother who hadn't crawled into a bottle each morning.

The drinking hadn't been so bad at first. *"Just something to take the edge off, Shana-bay."* But during Shana's teen years, Brenna had fallen to the bottom of a well of booze and never found her way out again.

"Are you listening to me, Shana? Listen to me!"

The scream was close to her ear. Brenna had launched herself out of the armchair and stood, weaving, beside Shana's chair.

"I'm listening, Mother."

She always listened. The words pounded like spikes into her brain, bloodily embedded there forever, but she'd never been able to stop listening. No matter how hard she tried.

"You are the Alpha's rightful mate. You are the queen of this pride. You should be *ruling* and what do you do? You run away!"

"I know, Mama. I'm sorry."

"Apologies are for the weak! Lionesses do not apologize. *Queens* do not apologize. But you aren't a queen, are you? You're nothing more than a coward and a *slut*."

Shana flinched. That word again, slashing at her viciously.

"Oh? It bothers you to be told the truth of what you are? *Slut.* Did you think I didn't know you lifted your tail for every lion in the goddamn pride and half the nomads to pass through?"

No. She'd never thought her mother didn't know. They'd had this conversation a thousand times, but she didn't expect her mother's alcohol-sodden brain to remember that. Any more than she expected her to remember that it was Brenna herself who had urged Shana to go after most of those men. *"That one looks strong, Shana. He'll be a good Alpha. He could challenge Leonus. He just needs a little push. The right kind of push."*

"Did it make you happy to shame your father and me with your promiscuity?"

A sarcastic smile curved Shana's mouth. "Cats are promiscuous, Mother."

Brenna's hand snaked out, slapping her hard across the cheek. Her head turned with the blow.

Shana pulled deeper into herself, feeling the ties to her childhood mother, that sober memory from her early years, snapping painfully tight around her. Her mother had never hit her before. She loved her. That was why she pushed so hard.

"*Queens* are not promiscuous, Shana. Queens are virginal

and pure."

Queens were sluts who knew better than to get caught or had the power to behead the ones who spoke against them, but Shana kept her lips closed tight over that thought. She'd learned her lesson about disagreeing.

"Are you a queen, Shana?" Brenna hissed. "Because all I see is a pathetic little slut who couldn't get a single lion to fight for her. Did they all see what I see? Did all those men you screwed, hoping to screw them right into the Alpha position, did they all see how pathetic you are? Did they all see a little slut who wasn't worth fighting for? They did, didn't they?"

Enough. Shana launched herself off the edge of the chair—*don't get too comfortable, Shay*—and shoved past her mother.

"You made me spill!" Brenna wailed. "Shana, get back here!"

Shana blocked out the words, wishing she could wipe her memory of every word her mother had ever said to her. She ran blindly out of Brenna's bungalow, down the muddy path, away from the rest of the residential compound. She ran until her legs ached and the icy air burned in her lungs. And then she kept running.

Her confrontations with her mother had been bad before, but this had been worse. So much worse. Evidently, Brenna had been saving up her acid for all the months Shana had been gone, building up her vitriol into a seething mass. Shana was a disappointment, Shana was a whore—she'd heard it all before, but this time had been so much worse. No dancing around the subject, just a swift verbal knife to the stomach and a vicious twist.

Why did it still hurt? Why hadn't she learned not to hurt like she had with all the other things that used to pain her? Why couldn't she be immune?

Only her mother and Caleb had ever been able to make her burn like this, acid eating at her from the inside out. But with Caleb, at least it was fair. At least she knew she could hurt him back.

Shana spun, breathing hard and running harder. But now, instead of away, she was running toward something. Someone.

She felt wild and unpredictable, a loose electrical cable whipping in the wind, ready to electrocute anyone who stumbled too close. If she couldn't contain it, at least she could control who she zapped.

He was strong. He could take it.

He was the only one who'd ever been strong enough to take her.

Chapter Five

Caleb shucked off sweaty clothes and stepped into the shower. Maybe the heat of the water could burn away the lingering scent of Shana in his nostrils. Nothing else seemed to.

He'd woken that morning on Shana's deck with dried blood matted into his fur, but the cuts she'd given him had already closed up. He'd run back to his own place to shift back to human form and grab a change of clothes, not bothering to do more than wash the blood off.

As strong as the urge had been to return to Shana and force her to be good—whatever that meant for someone like her—Caleb busied himself instead with towing the broken-down jeep off the ranch road. When he'd checked back on her at mid-morning, she'd taken off. He could tell the bungalow was empty by the lack of her scent alone.

He'd dumped the contents of the jeep into her room, marveling at how much crap the woman traveled with. When he was done, she still hadn't returned, so he found Michael, the youngest and most impulsive of his brothers, who was always up for a sparring match.

Caleb turned, letting the hard, hot spray of the water pound into the sore muscles of his shoulder. Michael was actually growing up enough to make besting him more of a challenge than it used to be. The cub had managed to get in a few good licks.

But even worn out and sweaty from wrestling with his brother, Caleb's mind was saturated with Shana. And he was half-hard from thinking of her. And smelling her goddamn stuff as he put it inside her room.

Caleb considered taking his cock in his fist and getting what satisfaction he could, but he didn't have any illusions that it would ease the bite of his lust for her. Lions were capable of sexual marathons that could last for days. His body had been designed by nature to take her over and over again. He wouldn't find relief so easily.

Shutting off the water, he stepped out of the shower and quickly toweled himself dry. He whipped on a pair of jeans, leaving them half buttoned, and stalked barefoot out of the bathroom.

Landon had asked him to keep her out of trouble. Caleb snorted as he crossed the room and yanked open a drawer. He'd have as much luck domesticating a rabid tabby.

Landon couldn't know about their history. Caleb wasn't sure even Ava knew how much Shana had once meant to him. There weren't very many members of the pride who remembered the way Caleb used to pant after Shana. Before she ripped out his heart and cut off his balls.

She'd been different then. Before she started sleeping with everyone and anyone who had a shot at the Alpha. Still crazy as a wildcat, but she'd laughed back then. Really laughed. Without the bitterness and ice that always tainted her voice now.

And he'd laughed too. God, he'd been gone for her. All she'd had to do was crook her little finger at him and he'd come running. But she hadn't been a tease. Not Shana. She'd delivered on every fantasy his teenage mind could conjure and some he hadn't even thought of yet.

He would have done anything for her. He would have died for her.

And nearly did. He'd nearly challenged Leonus. Nearly gotten his fool ass killed in his attempt to make Shana the Alpha's mate she always talked about being. If Tyler hadn't stopped him, Leonus would have easily defeated him and strung his internal organs up like party decorations. He'd been too young and too green for there to have been any other outcome.

But Shana hadn't seen it that way. All she had heard was him saying no to her. And so she'd run straight from his bed into the bed of a man who wouldn't say no. A series of beds, a series of men. Always trying to fuck her way to the top, but always picking the wrong pony. She'd gotten her lovers run off, maimed, and even killed in their attempts to please her.

Caleb was lucky he'd escaped with no visible scars. He'd just had to watch.

Over a decade of Shana screwing everyone in her path who might have a prayer of challenging Leonus. And then Landon had arrived. He'd arrived, challenged for, and won control of Three Rocks—doing what none of Shana's fucktoys had been able to do.

And she hadn't been able to get into his bed fast enough.

Landon hadn't been monogamous—or even picky—before he met Ava. Caleb knew he'd slept with Shana, and half a dozen other lionesses, before he claimed Ava as his mate.

But somehow, even knowing Shana was as dirty and used as used goods could get, Caleb couldn't make himself stop wanting her. Remembering her low laugh and the stroke of her body against his. The memories were burned into his brain like a brand.

The creaky second step to his porch complained loudly and Caleb's attention snapped toward the door. That familiar scent hit his brain, clouding it with want.

She didn't bother knocking.

Shana was the star attraction in so many of his fantasies, Caleb wondered if his imagination was playing games with him when she closed the door behind her and leaned against it with that familiar, hungry look in her eyes. Her gaze raked his bare chest and she licked her lips.

"Hello, Caleb." Her voice was raw sex, breathless and rough.

She was panting for breath and a sheen of sweat coated her skin, in spite of the cold of the morning. She'd tried to outrun herself, but she never could. He recognized the signs. And the wildness in her eyes.

"How's your mother?" he asked, knowing the words would be a slap in the face, but wanting her out and gone before his animal took over and he pinned her to the door and fucked her senseless.

Her eyes flashed as she pushed away from the door, stalking toward him. "Fuck you, too, sugarbear."

"No thanks," he growled, circling away from her. "I've lived this long without herpes and I'd just as soon keep it that way." Shifters couldn't transmit human diseases, but he needed to piss her off, get her the fuck out of his house.

"Ha-ha, look who's funny." Her fingers closed around the hem of her tank top and yanked it off over her head. The black bra contrasted against the pale silk of her skin, drawing his eyes. Her breasts rose and fell in their black-lace prison with the rapid tempo of her breath.

"What—" He didn't know what he was going to ask. What was she doing? What did she want? He already knew the answer to both questions. He'd known since she walked in the door and he recognized the wildness in her eyes. Just as he'd known he wasn't going to fight her, didn't have a prayer of resisting.

He wanted her just as badly as she wanted him. More.

Moving inhumanly fast, she closed the distance between them and cut off the question with her mouth, slamming it hard against his, her fingers grabbing fistfuls of his hair to hold him tight. Her body pressed fully against him and Caleb lost himself inside the warm, sucking, eager heat of her mouth. The drugging suction of it as she worked her tongue against his, feeding the flame that never died between them into a flash fire of lust.

She released her vise-grip on his hair and went to work on the fastenings of his jeans. In her eagerness, her claws flexed in and out. When one vicious tip nicked the skin of his abdomen, the small, surprising flicker of pain brought him a brief moment of clarity.

He shoved her away so suddenly she stumbled backward until she hit the bed, falling back into the unmade mess of sheets.

"If you wanted me in bed, Cale, all you had to do was ask." She gave a low laugh, her hands already unfastening the clasp on her bra and tossing it aside.

She quickly unzipped her jeans and began wriggling the tight denim over the smooth expanse of her hips. Caleb stepped forward and grabbed her wrists to stop her.

He knew he was squeezing too hard, but finesse was a thing of the past. Shana always burned straight through the reins he kept on his control. "What the fuck are you doing?"

She arched one auburn brow. "Undressing. It facilitates the fucking. Take off your pants."

"I wouldn't touch you with a ten-foot pole," he snarled, wishing he knew how to make the words true.

His mind might resist, knowing the hell Shana could put him through, but his body was more than willing. Inside his jeans, he was already hard beyond the point of pain.

Shana's eyes dropped to his erection and she slowly wet her lips. "Ten feet? That's a bit of an exaggeration, isn't it, big boy?"

"Stop it."

Far from obeying, she seemed urged to action by his demand. He still held her wrists, but she writhed on the bed, the movement of her full breasts hypnotizing. His vision was so fogged by want, it took her kicking the jeans off her ankles before he realized she'd been wriggling out of them.

She lay pinned to the bed by his hands on her wrists, in nothing but a sheer, purple thong. She hooked her ankles behind his knees and tried to pull him down onto her. Caleb stumbled, but kept his feet—and his distance.

"Come on, Cale," she purred, trying again to twine her legs around his. "You know what I need."

"You need a straitjacket," he growled. But then he met her eyes. Those wild, feverish eyes.

He'd seen her like this before, in a frenzy of need. She would run to him from her mother. Her face would be twisted as if she was crying, but her eyes would be dry. He'd never seen Shana shed a single tear, no matter how wretchedly she sobbed. He would try to hold her, but gentleness never soothed her. She needed the push and the heat. The frantic strain of her body against his.

And he always gave her what she needed, fucking her high

and hard until she screamed in release, trying to absorb all that panic and frenzy into his body.

Looking into those wild eyes, he knew he would never be able to walk away from her.

When Caleb suddenly went still, looming above her, Shana squirmed under the intensity of his gaze. "Cale? Come on, baby."

She was mostly naked on his bed with her blood boiling. Now was not the fucking time for soulful gazes.

She dropped her eyes to the ridge his cock made in his jeans. *Oh, yeah.* Caleb was ready to play, all right. So what the fuck was he waiting for?

She tried again to kick out his knees and force the weight of his body down on hers, but he just staggered and righted himself again, planting his feet. The rigid muscles across his chest and shoulders made her mouth water, her teeth aching to take a bite, but when she tried to push her shoulders up off the bed, he shoved her back down with her own wrists pressed against her collarbone. "Dammit, Caleb," she snapped, squirming against his iron grip. The bastard was so damn *strong.* She couldn't even seduce him properly if he wouldn't let her touch him.

And she *needed* to seduce him. She needed the hard, fast slap of his body against hers. She needed it hot and wet and so damn good it hurt. She needed to feel like her brain was melting into a mass of instinct and need.

Then Caleb growled, "I must be out of my fucking mind," a fraction of a second before his mouth hit hers and his weight landed hard against her, pressing her down into the mattress.

Yes. Goddess, it was perfection. Sensation swamped her. She moaned into his mouth as his tongue probed hers. She locked her legs around his waist. He was all muscle, everything firm and hot.

Caleb ground the rough denim covering his erection against her clit. Need spiked down Shana's spine, dragging a small scream from her as it burst into wet heat, drenching her thong. Caleb tore his mouth away from hers and finally released her wrists, but only so he could rip her sheer thong into postage-stamp-size scraps.

He shoved himself off her to attack his jeans. Shana's wildness was tempered by his sudden frenzy. She felt like the eye of a hurricane, an illusion of calm just waiting to explode into violent chaos. She squeezed her thighs together as Caleb ripped and swore at his jeans.

Her wrists held the imprint of his every finger. The bruises were going to be spectacular. He'd *marked* her.

Shana licked her lips, her canines sharpening to lethal points at the thought of marking her mate right back. And, that quickly, the eye passed and she was back in the hurricane.

He turned back toward her, shreds of denim hitting the floor. Naked, his body was glorious, a tapestry of strength. Muscle flowed into muscle. His erection stood out high and hard and straight. Maybe not ten feet, but just as thick as she remembered. Thick enough to stretch her just barely to the point of pain. Shana licked her lips. *Come to mama.*

She came up on her knees on the mattress and reached for him. He didn't catch her hands or push her away this time. Shana wrapped both hands around his cock as she sank her teeth into the skin beneath his left nipple. Caleb hissed, and she didn't particularly care whether it was from the bite of pleasure or pain. She worked her hands slowly up and down his shaft, simultaneously nibbling her way down, taking little bites across his flat stomach.

Then she was right where she wanted to be.

When she scraped her tongue across the head of his cock, he growled. Rolling it into her mouth elicited a hiss. She slid it deeper into her mouth, using her hands to slowly feed him to herself until his thickness threatened to choke her, knocking against the back of her throat.

"*Fuck*, Shay."

She chuckled, letting him feel the vibration of her laugh, and slowly withdrew, only to slide him deeper again.

His fingers tangled in her hair, but he didn't push her, just laced his fingers into the red mass, rubbing the heavy strands between his fingers. His head fell back on a groan as she found a rhythm she liked.

Shana felt like a goddess, luxuriating in her power over him. But it wasn't enough.

She released him from her mouth with a little *pop*. Licking her lips to catch every lingering taste of his skin, she stretched up onto her knees again, running her hands up across his pecs and shoulders to twine around his neck. "C'mere," she purred, hauling his head down to hers to slide her tongue into his mouth.

His hands gripped her ass. He lifted her as if she weighed nothing and she wrapped her legs around his waist. His erection bumped against her pussy, but the angle was wrong for anything more than a tease. But even the tease was enough to make her squirm.

Caleb turned and sat on the bed, keeping her thighs spread across his lap. His large hands petted her, gliding over the curves of her ass, over her hips, the curve of her waist, the planes of her back, across her shoulders, her collarbones, skating around her breasts without touching them to graze her ribs and the bones at the front of her hips. He teased the crease of her thighs, the backs of her knees, and along the outside of her thighs back up to her ass again, until she was ready to scream at him to get to the goddamn good stuff.

As he touched her, Shana's hands weren't still. She wrapped them around his cock and guided him to her entrance. She rose up on her knees and angled herself to take the thick head into her pussy. He notched into her and just that much sent shockwaves of pleasure rippling across her nerve endings.

And they were just getting started.

She pressed down, taking another inch before the edge of pain stopped her. She waited for her body to stretch, to adjust, holding onto every drop of feeling.

Caleb chose that moment to flick her taut nipples with his fingers. Shana cried out and sank another inch. He flattened his large hands on her back, holding her steady as he bent and drew his teeth across her breast, missing the nipple this time.

Shana arched her back and sank deeper still onto his shaft as Caleb followed the scrape of his teeth with a soothing swipe of his tongue. When he suddenly sucked one rigid nipple hard into his mouth, the accompanying flood of heat through Shana's body seated her fully.

She felt his primal growl through every inch of her skin.

Bracing her fingers on his shoulders, claws recklessly out, she raised herself slowly. The wet drag of flesh fired a delicious friction. She dropped herself back down, hard. He released her breast on a rough expulsion of air that teased her sensitized skin. Shana drew up and slammed down again. His big hands tightened roughly on her back. He bent his head and sank his teeth into the flesh at the juncture of her neck and shoulder.

The soft bite of pain merged seamlessly with the tide of pleasure rippling up her spine. His strong arms wrapped all the way around her, holding her a little too tight. Shana reveled in the surety of his strength as she quickened her pace, lost in the wet, sucking draw and wild, slamming return.

Pleasure built, coiling deep inside her and yet just out of reach. A chaotic explosion that would be so good, *so good*, if she could just get there, reach it, find it, claim it. Every sense tightened—*so close.* Shana's claws snapped out to full feline length and blooded themselves on Caleb's shoulders. A predator's teeth ripped like daggers through her gums as she threw back her head. Pleasure ripped through her body, her orgasm crashing through her in a destructive wave that was so damn *good*, wiping away every thought, every fear, every bit of her that was Shana and replacing it with bliss.

Caleb roared, his body pouring his need into hers in a bone-crushing rush. Shana felt her soul lock around his, holding on tight to this moment. She *needed* this moment. This goodness. He was the only thing in her life that had ever made her feel so *good*. She rode the wave of it, clinging hard.

Then she blacked out.

Chapter Six

The bed was cold when she woke up. She'd been alone for a while.

Shana rolled to a sitting position in the tangled sheets, grimacing at the sticky wetness on her thighs. What a gentleman. Let the lady sleep in the wet spot. He'd probably walked out the door as soon as he'd yanked on a pair of pants. If he'd even bothered. Shifting was faster than clothes any day when it came to immediate escape.

And he had escaped her. Abandoned her.

Bastard.

You give a man an earth-shattering fuck and he can't even be bothered to stick around until you regain consciousness. That's gratitude for you.

Shana kicked off the sheets, gathered her clothes, and padded to the bathroom. She quickly cleaned herself up and then took stock of what was left of her clothes. With the exception of her thong, everything she'd walked in with was in working order.

Pulling her jeans on commando, Shana winced a little at the tenderness between her legs. She hadn't had sex in months—humans just didn't have the same appeal—and she hadn't had sex with someone hung like Caleb since...well, Caleb. And they hadn't exactly eased back into the saddle. She'd been out for a rough ride and that's exactly what she'd gotten—and the soreness to go with it.

The bra and tank top quickly followed. Shana started out of the bathroom, only to pause as her reflection caught her eye.

"Damn."

Caleb had marked her all right. And not just with the purple bruises on her wrists. The skin where her shoulder met her neck was already turning a stunning shade of violet in the exact shape of Caleb's teeth.

Of course, judging by the little flecks of blood on the sheets, she'd given at least as good as she got. She hoped any little lionesses who might be tempted to poach got a good look at the claw marks she'd left on Caleb's shoulders.

Shana froze, frowning at the thought.

She was naturally possessive. Violently so. But Caleb wasn't hers anymore. She didn't want him. She wanted the Alpha. What's-his-name. Landon. She wanted Landon.

Caleb was just a pit stop on the way to her destiny as the Alpha's mate..

She was focused. She had goals. And they did not include mooning after a man she'd once been stupidly in love with just because he was strong and sexy and knew her inside and out.

Goddesses did not moon. Neither did queens. Queens kicked ass.

Shana kicked the door open and stepped out onto the porch. Dusk had fallen while she and Caleb were battling for supremacy in the Fuck-Olympics. The snow had long since melted, but the temperature had dropped again, leaving an icy chill in the air.

Shana sucked in the cold air, letting it cool any lingering heat Caleb had left in her. It was time to make herself a queen.

Caleb ran the outer perimeter, along the edge of the ranch property, but he didn't fool himself that he was doing any good as a guard. A soldier's best tool was his mind and Caleb's was poisoned by the viper who was likely still sleeping off their excesses in his bed.

His animal scratched against the inside of his skull, but he kept his human form. A neighbor or a passing car could see him this far out, though hopefully no one would. He ran too fast to be strictly human, infected by Shana's wildness. She had passed it to him and he couldn't outrun it.

He knew what would happen now. She'd come to him before over the years, when her latest boy toy failed to defeat the Alpha and her mother lashed out at her. Shana always came running to him, wild and hungry. And he still hadn't learned how to say no. Every time he tried. And every time he failed.

And every time, she sank her claws into another forgotten chamber of his heart and ripped it open. He was a goddamn medical miracle—his heart still beating after she'd demolished it piece by piece.

He didn't fool himself that this time would be any different.

She hadn't come back for him. She'd come back for fucking Landon. The fucking *Alpha*.

Caleb's mouth pulled into a snarl as he ran.

She wouldn't get him. Landon looked at Ava like the secrets of the universe could be found in her eyes. He wasn't going to give that up, no matter what tricks the redheaded minx might try to pull.

Images of her tricks flashed through his mind in living color, a lurid montage.

Caleb staggered to a stop. He propped his hands on his knees and gulped down air, ignoring the stitch digging a knife into his side. How far had he run? Five miles? Ten? However many, it hadn't been far enough. He could still taste Shana on his tongue. Feel her on his skin.

She was a virus he'd been infected with. Shouldn't his body have built up the antibodies to fight her hold on him by now? How many times would he have to go through this? Why couldn't he get her out of his blood?

He turned back to the ranch. Running wasn't helping.

It was time—past time—for him to face the feral lioness he'd been running from for the last decade. Time for them to fight it out.

He wanted her—not wanting her never seemed to be an option—and this time he was going to fight for her. Even if she was the one he had to fight.

Shana found the Alpha and his miniature mateling in the dining hall. The hall was beginning to fill as the dinner hour approached, but they acted as if they were alone, billing and cooing at one another, wrapped in their own lovey-dovey world.

Shana folded her arms across her chest and tapped her foot, waiting to be acknowledged. She had no intention of waiting long.

Around them, the rest of the pride trickled in. Seeing Shana standing there, her posture issuing the challenge she hadn't yet voiced, several of her pridemates hesitated, watching her cautiously, curious to see whatever spectacle she'd prepared for them tonight.

Impatient with the turtledoves cooing privately to one another, Shana cleared her throat. Loudly.

Ava looked up and arched her brows questioningly. The look Landon shot her was far from questioning. Irritated, yes. Questioning, no.

Shana didn't care if he was annoyed. She was annoyed too.

"I won't allow you to issue a challenge just so you can get a nicer house, Shana," Landon said, his clear, strong voice calling the attention of anyone who might have missed their little standoff.

Shana wasn't intimidated. She did her best work in front of an audience. "I'm not here for a house, Landon," she corrected. "I'm here for you."

The Alpha frowned. "Me?"

Shana smiled, oh-so-sweetly, and flicked her eyes to the mini-mate. "Or don't you think your little Ava is strong enough to keep you? Maybe she'd rather just forfeit her claim on you now and save us all the five seconds it would take me to wipe the floor with her ass."

The challenge filled the air with a subtle pressure, like a coming storm.

Landon rose slowly from his chair, drawing Shana's gaze away from his wide-eyed mateling. He was a behemoth of a man and his aura of power made him seem larger still. Shana tried to remember what he'd been like in bed—size and strength were

definitely among her turn-ons—but all she could recall was that
he had fallen somewhere in the Not Bad category, though a
little too vanilla for her tastes.

"If you think to touch my wife, you'll have to go through
me," the Alpha growled.

Shana managed not to roll her eyes. Barely. Landon's
chest-banging might have been impressive, if he weren't
negating his own mate's power with every overprotective word.

He'd better not try to fight her battles for her when *she* was
his mate.

Landon looked serious. And pissed. Shana didn't doubt
that he meant every word. And even though she was the
strongest, fastest female lion in the pride, the Alpha could still
kick her ass. Probably. Shana almost felt reckless enough to try
her luck. There hadn't ever been a female Alpha in a lion pride
before, but Landon was all about humanizing them. How about
a little equality of the sexes?

Shana prowled slowly toward the Alpha. He held his
position. She could practically see his mind racing as he tried to
figure out if she was coming closer to attack him or to bow in
submission. She made sure her eyes gave nothing away.

When she was less than a foot from him, she looked up
into his angry green-gold eyes and slowly licked her lips. "Are
you so eager to get your paws on me again, lover? That you'll
use any flimsy excuse?"

A low growl rumbled through his chest. A wild, suicidal
impulse made Shana want to laugh. She didn't know why she
provoked him. Her fight was with Ava. Landon was going to rule
at her side. But the delicious idea of fighting for the pride
herself made her feel rash and imprudent. She could be a
queen. On her own terms. No man needed. She'd been bred for
it. She was strong and fast and fierce. This was *her pride*.

"Obey our rules or leave our land," the Alpha growled,
taking a threatening step forward.

Shana's hands flexed, her claws snapping out. "Make me."

The roar that met her words was so loud, it took her a
heartbeat to realize it wasn't coming from the lion in front of
her. It rolled like thunder through the room. Before the echoes

had died, Caleb's body was between hers and Landon's. He shoved her away from the Alpha so roughly she was thrown to the ground.

Caleb's back bowed. He was still in human form, but just barely, and battling for every shred of humanity. "Don't. You. Touch. Her." The words were snarled out, guttural and low, more animal than man.

Shana's breath left her in a rush as lust poured through her body, inappropriate and so damn hot. *He's fighting for me.* From her position sprawled on the floor, she could see the muscles across his back tense and ready to kill for her. Delicious shivers rolled across her skin.

Landon didn't step back in the face of the threat Caleb presented—every lion in the room would have recognized the act as ceding to Caleb's dominance. Instead, the Alpha met his lieutenant's gaze steadily, holding his body perfectly still.

"Think about what you're doing, Caleb," Landon urged in a low, uncompromising voice. "Are you sure you want this fight? There's no going back if you challenge me."

Yes, Shana silently urged, *challenge him.* This was it. What she had always wanted, the man she loved, willing to fight for her, strong enough to win. She was so damn close. *Do it, Caleb. Do it.*

Caleb's shoulders relaxed, easing just a fraction, but that little change was enough for disappointment to spike sharply through Shana. "No," she whispered.

Caleb took a slow step back, away from his Alpha. "I'm sorry," he said, bowing his head to Landon.

"No," Shana wailed, louder this time. "Don't be sorry. Challenge him!"

Caleb continued his retreat, not so much as glancing in Shana's direction.

"Caleb!" Shana scrambled to her feet. "Come on. This is our chance! Challenge him. Caleb, *please.*"

He didn't pause, didn't hesitate. Caleb walked right out the door without looking back.

A tight heat pressed against the back of Shana's eyes and her throat felt swollen and thick. She wouldn't cry. She never cried. Goddesses didn't cry.

But goddesses also didn't beg, and they didn't lose.

"Obey our rules or leave our land," Landon said again, his voice ominous and dark.

Shana looked up at the Alpha, hating him with every fiber of her being. "Fuck you and your fucking rules," she snarled.

She stalked toward the exit, head held high, defiant and fierce. She half-expected not to make it to the door. The old Alphas—Leonus, her own father—would never have allowed her rebellion to go unchecked. She would have been forcibly put back in her place, but Landon's precious humanity made him weak in front of his entire pride. He just watched as she stormed out.

Outside, the wind wailed, a new storm rising. Matching the storm inside her mind.

Her emotions tangled, a savage knot swelling inside her throat until she choked on a sob. Why did it hurt so much? She'd been disappointed in her bids to become the Alpha's mate before. She'd always just shrugged off defeat—occasionally mourning the poor bastards who were the casualties of her personal war—but it never felt like this. Why did this one eat away at her soul, tearing out chunks of her heart?

Because it's Caleb.

The thought called the tears, hot and uncontrollable. It was different because of Caleb. Because he had always been the one she wanted. The One. Always the one she loved—in her way, no matter how twisted. She'd always clung to the promise that he would be the one to save her. If the others failed, what did it matter? Only Caleb mattered. He would fight for her. He would prove he loved her too.

And he'd come so close. He had almost loved her enough.

Shana choked back the tears, forcing them to stop out of sheer will.

He hadn't loved her enough, but she would love him. She knew she didn't deserve him. He was steady and honorable where she was deceitful and manipulative. She didn't know what she deserved, but it wasn't anything good. And Caleb was good. He was everything good to her.

But luckily, Shana didn't believe in getting what she deserved.

Goddesses didn't get what they deserved. They got what they wanted. And she wanted Caleb.

Chapter Seven

Shana was not the moony-eyed, heart-on-her-sleeve, Dr. Phil-confession-of-love type. Sex was her currency. She would win Caleb back, but she would do it her way.

With that in mind, she went back to her borrowed bungalow, took a quick shower, put on her skimpiest, sexiest scraps of lingerie lace, and began digging through her bags for the naughtiest invitation-to-sex outfit she could find.

She was debating between a schoolgirl outfit that no self-respecting schoolgirl would be caught dead in and the slightly less subtle black vinyl catsuit when she heard a footstep on her front porch.

Her heart quickened. Had Caleb had a change of heart?

Shana threw open the door before rational thought had time to weigh in on the decision, still wearing only a few scraps of see-through black lace and a garter belt.

If little Ava was shocked to see her dressed so provocatively, nothing in her face gave her away. The five-foot mateling craned her neck up at Shana and squared her tiny little shoulders, flipping her long white-blonde hair away from her face.

"I'm here to accept your challenge," she rasped, her throaty sex-kitten voice an odd contrast to her Mini-Me persona.

Shana groaned and rolled her eyes. "Oh, please. Does your keeper know you're here?"

Ava tipped her chin back even farther. "This is between you and me."

"Uh-huh. So I kick your ass. Landon hears about it.

Landon kicks my ass and throws me out of the pride. As fun as that sounds, I think I'll pass."

Shana flipped the door closed, but Ava caught it before it could latch and flung it open again, stepping into the room. Tenacious little midget.

"I can't let your challenge to my authority as Landon's mate stand," Ava declared. Her voice was sure and calm, nearly masking the fact that she was terrified out of her wits. Only the scent of fear coming off her in waves gave her away.

Shana crossed back to the bed and picked up her wardrobe options. The catsuit perhaps?

"Shana! I demand you acknowledge me!"

Shana waved the catsuit in Ava's direction. "Yeah, yeah, you're the Alpha's mate. Whoop-de-do."

"Landon is mine. You'll never change that."

Shana tossed aside the catsuit. Too obvious. Naughtiness was an art form. She picked up the three-inch-wide strip of plaid that would barely cover her ass. If she stretched the definition, it could almost be called a skirt. Subtle.

"I'm not interested in Landon," she said, shimmying into the skirt. "I never really was."

Ava planted her hands on her hips, her nearly colorless gray eyes narrowing. "You expect me to buy that? After you threw yourself at him? You warned me off!"

"I only chased him because he was the Alpha and the Alpha deserves to be with the best." She buttoned the single button of a stomach-baring, snug white blouse over her breasts and tied the ends in a slip knot. "You were easy to warn off. You really should grow a spine one of these days, Ava."

"I thought you had accepted me," Ava said, flicking her eyes downward in an automatic gesture of submission. The soft vulnerability in her voice made Shana's flesh crawl. She was so damn *weak*, so docile. "I thought you respected Landon's decision. Respected me."

Shana snorted. "Why would you think an idiotic thing like that?"

"The necklace," Ava said. "The one you took from me. You gave it back. I thought you were sorry you'd always bullied me.

It was a gesture."

Shana rolled her eyes and dug her white thigh-highs out of her bag. "You thought that meant I liked you? It was a *message*. If strength wasn't valued anymore, then nothing this pride had was of value to me. I was renouncing the pride. Goddess, you're thick, aren't you?"

"If you renounced the pride, why did you come back?"

"Golly, I must have missed your shining face, sunshine," she said acidly, clipping the first stocking to her garter belt.

"Landon will never want you," Ava snapped, the little mateling making a show of spunkiness.

Stocking number two snapped into place. "Don't worry, honey. You can keep your Alpha. I have bigger game in mind." She stepped into her stiletto Mary Janes and did a turn in front of the mirror. "How do I look?"

"Like a cheap hooker."

A short laugh burst out of Shana's mouth. "Careful, sugar, you keep talking like that and I might have to start liking you." She opened her makeup case and went to work on her face. Bright red lips, kohl-lined eyes.

"Caleb will never want you either. My brother would never fall for someone as trashy as you," Ava declared as she watched Shana vamp herself up.

"Sweetheart, I'm not surprised you don't know this about your brother, but, trust me, he likes it trashy. That is one dirty, dirty boy."

Shana caught a glimpse of Ava's slackened jaw in the mirror and laughed. "Goddess, your face. From the look of you, your Alpha doesn't even know the meaning of kink."

Ava snapped her mouth shut. "I'll thank you not to infer things about my sex life."

"You're welcome, but I'm gonna infer all I want, poppet. Goddess, am I ever lucky the Alpha picked you. I'd have been bored to tears inside a week. Of course, nothing says I couldn't have still fucked Caleb on the side."

"He would never betray Landon."

Shana just smiled. The little mateling had a lot to learn about men.

"You're wrong," Ava insisted. "You don't know him."

"I know him a helluva lot better than you do, sweet cheeks."

And she knew exactly what to do to him to make him forget his own name, let alone any loyalties he might have once had. Not that that would be an issue this time. No more betrayals and power plays. That was the plan. Just pure, unadulterated and unadulterous sex.

Shana added a pair of dangling earrings and blotted her lips, turning back to Ava. "Now, how do I look?"

The little blonde grimaced. "Like an expensive call girl."

Shana grinned. "Perfect."

She strutted toward the door, but the mateling suddenly barred her way. "Where are you going?"

Shana arched an eyebrow and waved a hand at her outfit. "Did you think all of this was for your benefit? I'm gonna go give your brother the night of his life. By the time I'm done, he'll be singing my name to the tune of the Hallelujah Chorus."

"He'll throw you out on your skanky ass."

Shana snorted. "Honey, have you looked at me lately? Men don't throw me out of their beds until I've wrung them dry."

Ava shook her head, her expression fierce and protective. A kitten testing out her claws. "You don't deserve him."

"Nope. You're absolutely right about that. But it doesn't change the fact that I'm gonna get him. You can have your precious Alpha, but Caleb's *mine*. Now why don't you get out of my way, half-pint, or would you really like to see how long it takes me to kick your ass?"

The blizzard promised for the night before had arrived in force. Caleb listened to the wind howl and felt like howling himself.

He'd nearly challenged the Alpha.

He couldn't even remember what had provoked it. Memory had been washed away on a tide of animal instinct. All he remembered was Shana and an icy cold rage that Landon would *dare* touch her.

How had he let himself get so tangled up in her again? Hadn't he learned his goddamn lesson by now?

Caleb sat on his bed with his head in his hands. Her scent still clung to the sheets. There was no way he would be getting any sleep tonight.

The door banged open. His head snapped up.

His brain shut off.

What the *fuck* was she wearing?

"Hello, Caleb." Shana kicked the door closed against the wind. She snicked the lock into place.

"Get out."

Her lower lip poofed out in a patently false pout. "Are you mad at me?" she asked, the baby-sweetness in her voice a lollipop complement to the fuck-me-suck-me outfit.

"Yes," he growled, even as his cock stood up for duty, and added, *but not mad enough to pass up what you're offering.*

The fake pout vanished and her emerald eyes flashed irritably. He wasn't playing her game the way she wanted it played. "Fine. You're mad. I get it." Then a feline gleam flickered to life in her eyes and a sensual smile curled her lips. "You wanna punish me? I've been a bad, bad girl."

"Get out, Shana."

She smoothed her hands down her thighs and bent so her ass flared out beneath the miniscule skirt. "I think I need a spanking."

His balls tightened as if she'd squeezed them in a goddamn vise. "Very funny. Get out."

Shana ignored his words, focusing on the flare of heated interest she'd seen in his eyes. He'd always had a thing for her ass. They'd never tried spanking before, but she had a feeling it was exactly Caleb's brand of kink. From the look in his eyes, she was right.

And from the way she was drenching her thong, it was her kind of kink too.

"I know I've been a bad girl. You have every right to be mad at me." She walked toward him slowly, twirling one red curl around her forefinger. "Won't you punish me, Caleb?"

She stopped in front of him and bent over just enough to tease, cleavage on full display. Caleb's hands gripped the sheets beside him. He didn't move to touch her.

"I'm in no mood for games, Shana."

Shana caught her lower lip between her teeth. What was she doing wrong? Why wasn't he taking what she was so obviously offering? Caleb never said no. Or if he did, he never actually *meant* it.

She straightened out of her pose and looked into his eyes. There was undeniable lust there. He wanted her, no question about that. But there was also a rawness, a wariness behind the heat that had more to do with hearts and flowers than the sweaty slap of skin on skin.

Shana resisted the urge to make a very unsexy face. She'd really hoped the mushy love stuff could wait until she had him doped up on afterglow, but it looked like he wasn't going to touch her until they had their girly talk about *feelings*.

"I love you."

Caleb frowned. Okay, her confession had been a lot grouchier than she planned, and accompanied by an irritable glare, but did he have to look so damned pissed off by her girly emotional moment?

"No, you don't."

Shana gritted her teeth. "Yes, I do. Honest."

He arched an eyebrow skeptically. "You love me."

Shana tossed her head, feeling the tips of her hair catch on the bottom of her skirt. "I might not do it the way other people do it, but I do love you. And I wanna be with you." She waved her hands in a vague gesture. "Like, forever."

Caleb snorted and Shana leveled a glare in his direction.

"I can be faithful," she snapped defensively.

"The only person you're faithful to is yourself."

"I was always faithful to you," she insisted. "Technically. I didn't sleep with anyone else when I was with you. And when I wasn't technically with you, I only cheated on the others with you. So in my way, I was always faithful to you. Even when I was with them."

He frowned. "That makes no sense at all."

"I only ever loved you." His eyes softened a bit and Shana quickly pressed her advantage. "And I promise you right now that I'll only sleep with you. Until you're dead. I'm not gonna be a celibate widow. That's just cruel and unusual. If you die young, I want lots of hot widow sex." The softness in his eyes hardened again and Shana internally cursed. She sucked at the mushy girl stuff. Sex she was good at. Love was trickier. "But I promise not to cheat on you until you're dead. You have my word."

"You break your word every day."

"Yes, but only when it doesn't matter. This matters. You matter. So I won't."

He closed his eyes and slowly shook his head. "Shana, I don't think—"

She cut him off before he could tell her no. No was not an acceptable answer. "Don't you want to spank me? It'll make you feel better, put us back on even footing. You can spank me once for every guy I was with when I should have been with you."

He snorted. "That would take weeks. My hand would fall off before I finished."

"Ha-ha."

She saw a flicker of a smile around his mouth and her heart jumped. Shana reached out and tentatively brushed his hair back from his forehead. He never used to let it grow so long. "Caleb?"

"You're trouble, Shay," he said without opening his eyes.

"You like trouble," she reminded him. She bent to brush her lips softly across his.

She kept the kiss no more than a seductive tease. When she pulled back, he leaned forward, chasing her mouth. She let him catch her lips, enjoying the slow, drugging pull of his mouth. He deepened the kiss, his tongue sneaking into her mouth. The man sure knew what he was doing. She could kiss him for days.

But she wasn't that patient.

Shana straddled his legs and began to lower herself down, sliding down his chest, but Caleb caught her waist and held her still. He pulled back from the kiss, opening golden eyes gone dark and intent.

"Caleb?" she asked, hating the shiver of uncertainty in her voice. Had he changed his mind?

"You've been a bad girl, Shana."

She licked her lips, a spike of nervousness threading deliciously through the sensual anticipation heating her blood. She nodded slowly. "Very bad."

He spun her abruptly away from him. She was still stumbling on her four-inch heels when he hauled her back and yanked her facedown across his knees. Her breath left her on a gasp. Caleb's hand hovered just over the skin on the backs of her thighs, so close she could feel his heat, but not quite touching. The teasing not-quite-touch moved up to the curve of her ass, left exposed by the thong and the too-short skirt. Shana squirmed, cream drenching her thong. He was really going to do it.

"Do you need to be punished?"

Her breath came in little pants now, her body tight with anticipation. *"Yes." Oh Goddess, did she ever.*

The first smack was more startling than painful. A sensual wake-up call. Caleb's hand landed and stayed, massaging her ass, soothing any trace of hurt.

"How naughty have you been?" he asked, his voice gravel rough, the erection riding her hip letting her know she wasn't alone in her need.

"Very."

Another slap, another slow caress. Shana hissed and squirmed, pressing up into his hand. This was nice, but it had better be just the appetizer. She wanted the main course. She wanted to lose control.

"Are you sorry?"

This time he didn't wait for her to answer before bringing his palm down on her ass. Her response was lost in the cry that ripped from her throat. He picked up the rhythm, a series of quick smacks, wringing a series of sharp, yearning cries from her throat. The feeling was perfection. Her ass grew hot from the blows that he kept just the right side of pain. Shana spread and braced her legs, raising her ass higher.

They were both breathing roughly when he paused, his palm flat on the curve of her ass. Caleb slid his hand down, his fingers sliding beneath her thong. He speared one long finger inside her and swore.

"Fuck, you're dripping."

Shana barely heard the words. She tightened her inner muscles around his finger, writhing helplessly on his lap. Enough spanking. They'd try more later. Right now, she just needed him inside her. Now. "Fuck me, Caleb," she urged. "Do it now."

He cursed jaggedly and flipped her off his lap onto the bed beside him. Shana watched him yank off his clothes as she sprawled seductively on her back. His body was a feast for the eyes, muscles gleaming deliciously in the low light.

She licked her lips. "God, you're gorgeous."

Caleb just grunted, kicking off the last of his clothes. Naked, he turned back to the bed.

Shana reached for the fastening to her miniskirt, but Caleb gave a single sharp shake of his head. "Leave it on."

His strong hands closed on her waist, flipping her and drawing her up onto all fours. He nudged her knees wider apart and pressed her shoulders down until he had her just the way he wanted her, with her ass raised up to him like an offering, her legs spread wide.

A single quick tug ripped the thong away from her body, but Caleb left the schoolgirl outfit intact, from garter belt to heels. His fingers slid into the wet folds of her pussy, probing. "You ready for me, Shay?"

Shana didn't think she could get any wetter. Moisture dripped down her thighs. "Yeah, Caleb, do me now," she urged, giving him a teasing little waggle of her ass.

"Don't move," he ordered, gripping her hips hard enough to bruise. The thick head of his cock pushed into her heat.

Shana grabbed fistfuls of bedding, needing to sink her claws into something. His hips shoved forward and his name ripped out of her throat like a curse. His fingers squeezed her hips and he rocked deeper, but it wasn't deep enough. She needed more. She needed all of him, pounding into her. This was taking too fucking long. She needed to come.

"Come *on*, Cale." She shoved her hips back roughly against his unyielding hold.

Caleb drew back and slapped her ass hard a fraction of a second before he pistoned his hips forward.

"Jesus, *yes!*" Shana screamed. Her inner muscles clenched tight around the invasion of his cock. He drew back and rammed home again. She bit her lip hard to hold in her cries. Her head thrashed back and forth, whipping her hair across his stomach. Caleb fisted one hand in the thick red mass at the base of her skull, holding her steady with his other hand at her hip as he drove into her.

Shana dug her nails into the mattress, her entire being focused on his cock sliding into her, his body slapping rhythmically against hers. Short, keening cries burst from her throat in time to his movements. He ruled her, body and soul. Untamable Shana was a puppet to his will, drawing her pleasure—so tight and sweet and hot and hard—only as he allowed her.

The sharp sting of one last rough smack on her ass sent her careening into her release. She erupted into contractions of pleasure. Caleb's body covered hers, slamming deep and high one last time. He sank his teeth into her shoulder and she came again with him. The lioness rippled under her skin, clawing to get out, and Shana didn't have the will to hold it back. Her spine arched on another sharp wave of bliss as, together, they shifted form, the animal wildness claiming their joined bodies as the lion claimed his mate.

Chapter Eight

Caleb was really going to miss that little schoolgirl outfit. It was a real shame it had been demolished when they shifted. Shana had looked like a thousand kinds of sin in that getup.

She shifted restlessly in her sleep at his side before settling again. She'd always been an uneasy sleeper. Caleb stroked her hair, remembering the way it had flowed down her back, loose and wild and longer than that postage stamp of a skirt.

He'd buy her a new one.

Provided she stuck around long enough to try it on for him.

Caleb winced. Dawn was breaking through the storm after a night of the best sex of his life and he was already waiting for her to renege on her promise to stick with him this time.

So much for trust.

Shana stretched against him and gave a low purr. In the dim light, he saw her emerald eyes open and blink at him sleepily.

"Good morning, lover." She kicked free of the sheets tangled around her ankles and flung one leg over his, draping herself across his chest, a blanket of warm, willing flesh.

Caleb combed his fingers through the disorderly mass of her hair. He longed to stay like this forever, in this quiet pocket of peace, but he knew it wouldn't be long before the devil inside her spurred her to something they would both regret. A part of him was already braced for it. Waiting for the ax to fall.

Shana stacked her hands on his chest and propped her chin on them. "So, do you forgive me? I forgive you."

Caleb frowned. So much for peace. "Forgive me for what?

You *told* me to spank you."

Shana rolled her eyes. "I *liked* the spanking. Obviously. I meant for before." She gestured off into the distance, letting him know she didn't mean the recent past.

"What before?" he asked warily, unsure what he was being forgiven for.

"For not challenging the Alpha. For not fighting for me."

"Fighting for you would have gotten me killed. I was a kid."

"You were strong enough," Shana insisted. For a moment she fell silent, and he thought he might be able to drag her kicking and screaming back to that peaceful place. But then she spoke, her voice soft and sly. "You aren't a kid now. You almost challenged Landon today. You could defeat him, Caleb. You could be Alpha."

A veil of red fell over his vision as anger coursed through his veins. She was still trying to manipulate him. Still trying to turn him into her own personal mercenary. *Will fight for sex.*

Disappointment and frustration warred with anger, but it was the anger that won, tightening every muscle in his body.

She would never change. No matter what sweet words she gave him, no matter how many different ways she found to tell him she loved him, he would never be more than a tool to her. A means to an end. Her *love* would always be a lie.

Caleb felt like a thousand kinds of fool. He had almost believed her this time. She'd almost had him.

"Is that what this is about?" The words felt like jagged shards of glass leaving bloody tracks as they dragged themselves out of his throat. "You thought you could fuck me into challenging Landon?"

"What?" Shana blinked at him, wide-eyed and innocent. "No."

He didn't buy her act for a second. He shoved her off him and quickly stood, grabbing his discarded jeans and yanking them on. "I'm never gonna be Alpha, Shana," he growled roughly. "I don't want to be. I may be stronger than Landon, but we'll never find out, because I'm never going to challenge him. *Never.* I'm not a leader. I never have been. You've always known that, but you could never get it through your thick head that

I'm not going to change. I'm not going to become the perfect Alpha just because you have some twisted need to be the Alpha's mate."

Shana pulled the sheet up in front of her, the move modest and distinctly out of character. "I didn't mean it like that."

"How did you mean it?" He held up his hand to stop her before she could reply. "Don't answer that. I don't want to hear whatever lies you dig up."

"I'm not lying!" She threw down the sheet, kneeling on his bed, wearing only her hair and her indignation.

"No? Then tell me you don't want me to challenge Landon."

Shana hesitated, her eyes flicking down to the mattress.

"You can't say it, can you?" Caleb shook his head. "I should have known. It was always about finding someone strong enough to best the Alpha. You never wanted to be with me. And, you know what, Shay? The feeling's mutual. I don't want to be with you anymore. I've had enough."

"Caleb, I did want you! I do!" she shouted, but the door had already slammed behind him.

Snow and ice covered every surface after the night's storm, but Caleb didn't feel the cold. He shifted into his lion form and ran, trying to outrun Shana's hold on him. Fearing he never would.

Shana took her lioness form, needing the comfort of her fur wrapping around her.

He'd left her. Again.

She'd confessed her feelings, did the whole mushy Dr. Phil crap, and he'd fucked her brains out. But, at dawn, he'd still run out on her so fast, he'd practically left skid marks. What did a girl have to do to get a man to stick around past breakfast? One lousy little comment—one extremely *true* comment—about the fact that he could be Alpha any time he wanted to be and he completely lost his shit.

Shana slashed her claws through his sheets, but the tantrum did nothing for her mood. She still wanted to claw and bite and savage something until it was unrecognizable. Preferably something live and twitching.

He hadn't really meant that. About being done with her. About having had enough. He couldn't have meant it.

Her throat and eyes felt tight. *Goddesses don't cry.*

Shana ran out of Caleb's bungalow before the growing urge to destroy something overpowered her and she demolished his furniture. She ran across the compound on four paws, through the heavy snow that had fallen the night before. The Storm of the Century had finally hit.

She leapt onto the snowdrift-covered porch of her borrowed bungalow, freezing in her tracks when she scented a male lion waiting for her inside.

Not Caleb.

She hoped whoever it was wanted a fight, because her claws were itching to oblige.

Shana shouldered open the door and stalked in, belly low and hackles high. Landon, in human form, rose from the chair he'd been waiting in. The Alpha stared her down. From the look in his eye, he was all too willing to give her the fight she wanted.

For a brief, reckless moment, Shana wondered what it would feel like to go for his throat. She wondered if he would be able to shift before her teeth closed around his throat, their sharp points easily piercing the vulnerable human softness of his skin. How would he fight back? Would he try to overpower her with his size and strength, giving her the advantage of speed and flexibility? Could she defeat him?

The thought swirled in her brain like alcohol fumes, teasingly toxic.

Shana shook it away and shifted form. Landon averted his eyes as she went to grab a pair of jeans and a sweater.

"It's not like you haven't seen it all before," she drawled as she yanked on the tight denim.

"And every time you remind me of that, I wonder why I haven't already thrown you out of this pride."

Shana snorted, unimpressed by the threat. "You can't do that. It would ruin your whole I-accept-you-you-accept-me bullshit plan for us."

The Alpha's jaw locked. "It isn't bullshit."

She turned back to face him, shoving her sweater sleeves up as she folded her arms beneath her breasts. "You're asking us to ignore hundreds of years of tradition and a hierarchy of strength that is as natural to us as breathing. It's bullshit."

"Equality is natural too."

Shana laughed out loud at that little gem. "Are you freaking kidding me? Equality isn't even *natural* to the humans. The drive to dominate, to *win*, is natural. This whole kumbaya crap is an attempt to overcome our natural urges. Not an extension of them."

Landon was silent for a long moment, studying her. There was an oddly speculative gleam in his eyes. And something else. Something soft. Mushy. Like the way he looked at Ava. The way Caleb used to look at her.

"What?" she snarled.

He shook his head. "I was just thinking how lucky I am not to have chosen you as my mate."

"Yeah, well, the feeling's mutual, asshole."

Landon sighed. "You can't call the Alpha an asshole, Shana."

"Oh, yeah? You're not a big fan of freedom of speech, then? Just equality. No freedom. I get it."

He wiped a hand across his eyes, groaning. "I didn't come here to argue with you. Ava told me about you and Caleb."

Shana's eyebrows flew up. "Your wife told you about my sex life? That must have been a real bonding moment for you two. Was it good for you?"

Landon ignored her snide remark. "He won't fight me for you," he said. "No matter what you do to him. Caleb's loyal and he doesn't want to be Alpha."

Shana's temper spiked. "God, what is it with you guys? That isn't what I want anymore, get it? How long are you going to punish me for the actions of the past?"

"The past?" Landon asked in disbelief. "We're talking about *yesterday*. You told him to challenge me in front of the whole pride."

"Yeah, but that was *yesterday*. Past. I've got a new game plan now."

"That's exactly what I'm afraid of. You and your game plans."

"I don't care about being the Alpha's mate anymore," Shana insisted, wondering as she said it if the words were actually true. They didn't feel true, but she wanted them to be. She wanted to just want Caleb. She wanted to not be twisted and power hungry.

"Look, Ava tells me your mom is no picnic—"

"*Don't you talk about her,*" Shana snarled, her claws flashing out as anger boiled hot in her veins.

Landon raised his hands in surrender, but his words continued, relentlessly. "Ava's worried about Caleb. She doesn't want you hurting him. And as long as you're tangled up in your mother's power plays, someone's going to get hurt."

"You're asking me to choose between Caleb and my mother."

"I'm asking you to think about what you're doing and who it's benefiting—if anyone—before you go starting any more fights."

Shana's blood cooled as the logic of what he was saying slowly penetrated her anger. "My mother would never do anything to hurt me," she said, even though the words felt like sawdust on her tongue.

Landon didn't call her a liar. Her estimation of him rose a few notches.

"Look, I believe in second chances," he said. "This is my second chance at a healthy pride and I'm going to make it work. But the thing about second chances is they don't work if you're carrying a grudge. Forgetting is a bitch, but you've got to at least try the forgiveness part or you'll never get away from your past." He moved past her to the door, pausing at the threshold. "If you want to get away from it."

After the Alpha disappeared out the door, Shana dropped down onto her bed, drawing her knees up to her chest.

She'd asked Caleb to forgive her that morning and he'd thrown it back in her face. What the hell else was she supposed to do? She couldn't *make* him forgive her. It wasn't like she could fight him for his forgiveness.

She'd offered to let him spank her—which had actually been damn hot—but that hadn't earned her any brownie points on the forgiveness scale. What did he want from her?

Anger boiled up again, hot and thick in her veins.

No one was satisfied. Caleb, the Alpha, her mother. Shana wasn't good enough for any of them.

The anger swirled around, seeking a target, finally settling on her mother.

It was *her* fault. If she hadn't filled Shana's head with tradition and her *rightful role*, none of this would have happened. Shana would have stuck with Caleb, happily paired off with him at the age of sixteen. She wouldn't be the wretched mess she was today, alone and likely to remain that way.

The anger burned, its acid turning in on her. Shana fisted her hands, her claws digging bloody gouges into her palms. The pain was welcome, the scent of blood hot and thick in her nostrils. Brenna had done this. She'd *ruined* her.

Then, suddenly, Shana realized what the Alpha had meant. Caleb wasn't the problem. He wasn't the one who needed to forgive. *She* was.

Chapter Nine

Shana crunched through the snow on her way to a reckoning that was long overdue.

She stopped in front of the all-too-familiar bungalow and braced herself for the confrontation to come. Backing out now wasn't an option.

She was going to lose Caleb—if she hadn't already lost him—all because of some stupid slip of the tongue. All because she couldn't seem to stop being her mama's girl. It was past time that changed. It was time *she* changed.

The house looked like something out of a goddamn painting, snowy and homey and sweet. Shana kicked a snowdrift off the porch to wreck the postcard perfection of the scene. She pounded her fist on the door, loud enough to be heard through an early morning hangover stupor. At the vaguely human groan of "Come in," she stomped in and kicked the door shut behind her.

Shana planted her feet and crossed her arms, hoping she looked like walking, talking menace, but feeling nervous and tremblingly small, as only her mother could ever make her feel.

Brenna pushed herself up to a sitting position on the messy daybed where she often passed out. She blinked at Shana blearily. "Shana-bay? When did you get back?"

"I've been back," Shana snapped. "I was here yesterday."

Brenna frowned in confusion. "Was that yesterday?"

"Memory a little foggy, Mother?" Shana kept her voice rough and merciless, letting all the anger of the last two decades bleed acid into her words. She was hurting and not caring who she hurt. "Why don't you have another drink?"

She crossed to the crates her mother had set up as an impromptu bar. Grabbing the first bottle that came to her hand, Shana held it up, angling the label toward the morning light seeping in through a crack in the blinds. "Ketel?" She grabbed a glass and splashed vodka up to the rim. She carried the glass and bottle over to where her mother huddled, watching her warily.

"Have a drink." She waved the glass toward her mother, careless of the alcohol that splashed out on the floor.

Brenna didn't reach for the glass. Her expression was cautious, but her eyes were locked on the glass. She licked her lips.

Shana's hand tightened spasmodically on the glass, shattering it. Shards bit into her palm, sterilized by the alcohol dripping from her hand. She threw away the remnants of the glass, not caring where they fell.

Her mother's nostrils flared as the alcohol fumes hit them.

"Not in the mood for vodka?"

Shana didn't have any conscious intention of throwing the bottle. One second it was in her hand. The next it exploded against the door in a shower of glass. Her brain didn't even seem engaged in the action. She didn't have any conscious thoughts right now, just an anger that had waited too long to be released.

Brenna flinched and cowered. "Shana-bay?"

"I'm angry with you, Mother," Shana said, the words distant and foreign on her tongue. "I've never said that before, have I? I think I've been angry with you my entire life."

Her mother's eyes grew wounded and misty. "Shana. Why?"

"*Why?* Are you fucking kidding me?" Shana's hands curled into fists. She needed something else to throw. Something else to break.

She stormed over to the crates, inspecting the inventory of bottles. Brenna could have thrown a party for a rock band without needing to visit a liquor store. Shana grabbed gin with one hand and vermouth with the other, ignoring the way the glass shards dug deeper into her palm. She didn't throw them, just gripped them by the necks.

"Do you remember what you said to me when Landon took over the pride?"

Brenna's eyes flickered nervously. "He seemed a good catch."

"'Fuck him.' That's what you said. 'If you're going to be a slut, Shana, at least fuck someone worthwhile. It's your time. Be his consort. Do whatever it takes.'"

"I'm sure I didn't say—"

"Oh, no. Of course not. You're the mother of the fucking year. You would never tell me to whore myself out to any man who might have half a prayer of being Alpha. You would never dream of telling me to leave the only man who ever made me happy because he was never going to amount to anything."

"You deserve to be with the best."

"I deserve to be happy!"

The vermouth bottle shattered against the door.

Shana tried to take a breath, tried to find a place of calm, but all she could feel was the bottle she held. "He made me happy, Mother. I *loved* him and he loved me. But all you could see was that he would never be more than a lieutenant, a good soldier."

Brenna's face screwed up with distaste. "Is this about that Caleb?"

"Yes!" The gin erupted, a fountain of pale green glass.

Her mother flinched at the violence, but her expression had turned mulish. "You were too young to understand what you were giving up by being with him. I only wanted what was best for you. You were bred to rule, Shana."

"I don't give a shit what I was bred to do! That's no excuse for turning me into the camp slut."

Disdain flooded Brenna's face. "You did that all on your own."

"Did I?" Shana hefted an oversized bottle of Scotch. "I suppose I told myself how easy men were to manipulate in bed. I suppose I decided all on my own to leave Caleb and sleep with a series of men you so kindly picked out for me. Richard..." the Scotch crashed against the door, "...Daniel and Dillon..."

Chopin and Tanqueray joined the destruction, "...Ari and Corin and Jato." Three more bottles exploded into hundred-proof debris.

Shana's throwing arm was starting to ache, but in terms of the men whose lives she'd destroyed to become the Alpha's mate, men hand-picked by her mother, she was just getting started. Names and bottles flew across the room, until she was panting and sweaty. Her face was hot and wet, but she didn't remember crying.

She looked down at the crates. There was only one bottle left. An industrial-sized plastic jug of cheap tequila. She picked it up and unscrewed the top. The mixed-drink puddle at the door crept across the room, soaking into the rugs. Shana splashed through it and kicked open the door. She upended the tequila over the snow on the porch, melting the pristine sweetness of it.

After the last drop had fallen, she dropped the jug beside the wreckage at the door, crunching through the glass. She didn't bother to close the door. She wouldn't be staying much longer.

"I'm done, Mother. I'm going to be with Caleb now, if he'll have me. No more machinations. No more plots. Just me and my good-for-nothing soldier."

"You deserve—"

"Shut up! Just shut up about what I deserve!" The words were a rabid scream that sucked the last of her energy. Shana felt battered and defeated, exhausted to her core. "I have to forgive you," she said softly. "I have to forgive you or I can never expect Caleb to forgive me, but every time you talk about what I *deserve* and my goddamn *legacy*, you make it so damn hard. I need you to stop, Mother." She took a deep, ragged breath, trying to get air back into lungs that had gone unbearably tight. "Just stop for me."

"Shana..."

"Stop." Shana turned and walked through the lake of poison and out the door. She didn't look back.

Chapter Ten

From the liquid still dripping down the front door and the shell-shocked expression on Brenna's face, Caleb had just missed Shana.

As soon as he'd run off his anger, guilt had caught up with him. He had realized that he'd never answered her question about whether or not he forgave her. Because he hadn't. He had been looking for a reason not to trust her. Looking for a way to pick a fight. He hadn't forgiven her at all. Not even close.

Shana wasn't the only villain in their relationship.

He'd been hurting her, shoving her away as hard as he could, ever since the first time she hurt him. Smacking her back every time she tried to get close again. But he'd never been able to forget her. Never been able to just walk away. Shana was in his blood. In his soul. He couldn't be happy without her. No matter how he tried to pretend.

And he was never going to be happy *with* her until he stopped clinging to past hurt. It was a choice. Forgive, move on, love her as hard as he could and hold on for dear life. Or live alone and miserable, clinging to his righteous anger.

As choices went, it wasn't difficult.

Caleb turned back to the ranch, intent on starting the rest of his life with Shana.

Provided he could find her.

Her mother's bungalow wasn't the first place he looked, but the chaos there was the first actual sign of Shana he'd found.

Caleb thought of tracking her immediately—her scent would be fresh—but some instinct stopped him. He stepped over the puddle of booze, drawing Brenna's dazed gaze. He crossed to crouch in front of her, sympathy warring with anger on Shana's behalf. The battered shell of a woman huddled in front of him had put the woman he loved through a lot of shit, but she was still Shana's mother and, in her own way, she loved Shana just as fiercely as he did.

Brenna's bewildered eyes met his. "She yelled at me," she said, visibly confused. Caleb didn't know what Shana'd yelled about, and he doubted Brenna did either. Only the volume seemed to have penetrated.

"You deserved it," Caleb said, but he kept his tone soft. He wanted her to hear every word. "This is a conversation we should have had a long time ago," he said. "You've been tying Shana up into knots for over a decade."

"I didn't mean to," Brenna whimpered.

"I don't care what you meant to do. I couldn't care less about your intentions. I don't give a shit if you blame the booze or blame Shana or blame me. I'm not going to let you hurt her anymore. She's mine now and I'm going to take care of her. That means no one is allowed to hurt her. Not you, not even Shana herself. No one."

"I would never—"

"You have and you will try to again," he cut her off brutally, though he kept his tone soft and smooth. "You need to stop drinking. I'm going to give you a chance to do it on your own, but if I see you with so much as a drop of alcohol, I'm going to have the Alpha put you into rehab so fast your damn head will spin. And I'll have him keep putting you there until you learn. You may not respect my authority, but you'll respect his. And he listens to me."

A sly gleam entered Brenna's watery eyes. "He does?"

"Yes, and you'd better be grateful he does. Because of you, Shana's done everything she can think of to piss off Landon. I am the only thing standing between you and your daughter being kicked out of this pride. So you're going to do as I ask. You're going to sober up and you are going to be a paragon of motherly love. Or I will make damn sure you never come within three miles of your grandchildren."

"Grandchildren?"

80

Caleb ignored the hopeful light in her eyes. He and Shana'd never talked about cubs, and she wasn't exactly the maternal sort, but he was willing to pull out any manipulation tactics necessary to get Brenna to toe the line.

"This is your one chance to shape up, Brenna," he said sternly. "I don't give second chances. Just ask Shana."

The three rocks for which the Three Rocks Pride was named formed a little cluster, marking the southernmost border of their land. They were the only landmark on the stretch of quiet plain.

Shana scrambled up onto the largest of the rocks, slipping and sliding a bit on the snow-slick surface. She perched at the top and hugged her knees to her chest, looking back over her solitary tracks through the snow.

She'd left her mother with the noble intention of finding Caleb and proving her love to him, but she'd quickly realized she didn't have the first idea how to do that. Seduction was so much easier than sincerity. How could she possibly convince him that this time, unlike all the others, she really meant to stay for good? It seemed a hopeless task.

Shana dropped her forehead onto her knees, hoping for divine intervention. Now was definitely the time for some help from a goddess.

The winter wind buffeted her back, carrying on it the possibility of yet another storm. Shana usually loved wild weather, but she wasn't sure she could take another blizzard right now. There was only so much chaos a soul could take.

"You're a hard woman to track down."

Her head snapped up at the sound of his voice. He'd come from downwind, the sound of his steps vanishing under the cloak of the wind. He looked amazing, so tall and strong, with bits of snow clinging to his hair. Shana's heart gave a little jump, but she didn't let herself hope yet. Just because he'd sought her out didn't mean he would take her back.

Caleb walked forward slowly, as if afraid he'd spook her. He leaned against the massive rock on which she perched, his

81

head a couple of inches below hers.

"I have an answer to your question," he said.

"My question?" She didn't remember asking a question. Had she asked a question?

"If I forgive you."

Shana's stomach did a slow somersault. "Oh. That question." She didn't want an answer. Really she didn't. She just couldn't handle another heartbreak right now.

"I've been thinking about it. About all the things I've been mad at you for over the years. It's quite a list."

Oh, Goddess. Please stop him from giving her a list. She couldn't handle a list.

"But I've done some pretty shitty things too."

Shana felt her body tighten and still as her awareness sharpened.

"It won't be easy for me to trust you again." He gave a small grimace. "Any more than it will be easy for you to trust me. Trust that I'm not going to go off like I did this morning and run out on you."

Her entire life dangled precariously from his words. Was he saying what she thought he was saying?

"But my answer is yes. I do forgive you." His shoulders tensed like he was bracing to take a hit. "I love you, Shay."

She didn't move a muscle, but her heart took off like a racehorse out of the gates. "Seriously?" she whispered.

He met her eyes, his own open and resolute. "You think I'm messing with you? I'm sorry about this morning. I just..." He shook his head sharply. "No excuses. If it happens again, you have my permission to kick my ass. I'm always going to be there for you, Shay. Always."

Shana eyed him warily. If something seemed to good to be true, it always was. "I'm not going to get nicer. Just because you love me, I'm not going to turn into some sweet young thing. I come as a package. Bitchiness included."

"I know. Believe me, I know."

She slugged him lightly on the shoulder, relief and something warmer flowing through her. He did know her. And he loved her anyway. Shana gently pushed his hair back away from his face. "You need a haircut."

He arched a brow, incredulous. "I tell you I love you. I tell you I will stand by you forever and that's what I get? 'You need a haircut'?"

She made a face. "I did the confession thing last night."

"You can say it more than once, you know." Doubt suddenly darkened his eyes. "Or was that a limited-time offer?"

She bit her lip and slowly shook her head, threading her fingers through his hair. "No time limit."

"Shay?"

"I love you, okay? You're a piece of me. And if you mean it, about giving us a shot again, I promise I won't fuck it up this time."

His eyes lit, filling with that adoring look she'd been missing for years. The one she thought she'd killed. It was like sunshine, and her heart soaked up the rays.

"I mean it. And I won't fuck it up either."

"Good." Better than good. Caleb loved her. Life didn't get much better than that. She shot him an impish smile. "So now that we're done with the mushy love crap, can we get on with the hot make-up sex?"

Caleb gave a short bark of laughter. He yanked her ankle and she slid down the rock and straight into his arms. Her arms wound around his neck and she smiled against his skin, breathing in the scent of her mate. *Hers.* And this one was forever. She was strong enough to keep him. And he was strong enough to keep her in line.

"If you're a good boy, I might even let you tie me up," she whispered darkly into his ear.

Epilogue

"I was thinking I might challenge Ava for mating rights to Landon. What do you think, hon?"

Caleb looked up from his sprawl on the rug and growled at her. The pair of cubs crawling all over their father quickly mimicked his growl with little mewling snarls of their own, prowling toward her on furry feet, with their tiny teeth bared.

Shana held up her hands in mock surrender. "A joke! Come on. At some point it has to become funny."

He couldn't have honestly thought she was serious. She was so pregnant with their second set of multiples—why couldn't the man just impregnate her with a single child for a change?—she made Shamu look dainty.

Caleb rolled to his feet, his liquid grace making her mouth water. He lifted her out of the chair—Shamu belly and all—and sat, settling her back down in his lap. "The idea of you with someone else will never be funny," he rumbled in her ear.

The twins attacked his ankles, but when he didn't react, they quickly lost interest and went tumbling together across the floor.

"It's ridiculous. By this point, we all know that the idea of me with anyone else is ridiculous, so it can be funny. Ha-ha. Get it?"

"You're mine. End of story. Get it?"

Shana burrowed into his embrace, but still quietly grumbled, "At some point it will become funny."

"Never."

She tucked her face against his chest to hide her smile at

his possessiveness. She wouldn't want him to know how much she liked the way he owned her, heart, body and soul. No one owned goddesses.

But she didn't need to be a goddess for Caleb to make her feel like one.

Serengeti Lightning

Dedication

Sitting at a computer to write a book is a solitary venture, but lots of people help these stories get from my brain to the shelves. I can't say enough of my at-home support team of fabulous friends and family, nor of all the wonderful people at Samhain who've been nothing but amazing to me. Many thanks to all the unsung heroes of publishing—from Samhain's uber-boss to the author liaison, from our marketing guru to the (invaluable) folks who send us royalty statements and checks, create the beautiful covers, format ebooks, take them to print, update the website, and generally keep things moving along. And, of course, to our editors from whom I continue to learn with each new book.

Chapter One

Mara Leonard tipped the tumbler, watching the whiskey slide thickly over the ice in the glass as she contemplated her new addiction. She'd never done anything even remotely risky before, but Michael Minor was a drug. He'd infiltrated her system and unlocked a wildness inside her she hadn't even known was there.

She was under the influence. Habit-forming lust. What other explanation could there be for the fact that practical, logical Mara was tarted up in a black minidress that showed off every inch of her legs, waiting for a man in a musty honky-tonk at one thirty in the morning?

She needed a twelve-step plan.

Mara liked plans. She adored steps and lists and clear, concise rules. She was born for organizations with anonymous in the title, except for the fact that she'd never let her hair down enough to even consider indulging in addictive behavior until *him*.

With one long fingernail she drew a swirling pattern through the ring of condensation her glass left on the bar. The Bar Nothing was all but deserted at this time of night. Only a few die-hard drinkers still hunkered over their glasses, wallowing in their addiction of choice as she waited for hers.

He was late.

She didn't wear a watch and she refused to twist around to check out the clock on the wall behind her again. She'd give him until she finished her drink and then she was leaving.

Mara took a small sip of the whiskey, rolling it over her

tongue.

Where the hell was he?

Chair legs squealed out a nails-on-chalkboard melody and her gaze flicked over to track the sound. A couple of the local lushes had apparently decided they were daring enough to stumble hopefully in her direction. She pinned them with an icy stare, the same gimlet gaze that never failed to cow rowdy second graders and smartass middle schoolers alike. Her overly optimistic Don Juans immediately retreated for a round of eighty-proof reinforcements.

Mara smiled to herself, turning back to her drink.

They wouldn't be back. There wasn't enough liquid courage in all of Texas to give those boys the balls for another go.

On an instinctive level, they recognized her true nature. She may look like just another piece of ass, flashing enough leg to be an open invitation in a place like this, but the acres of golden skin and long fall of sun-streaked dark blonde hair couldn't completely disguise the predator beneath.

Mara was a shape-shifter. A lioness. And no matter how fanatic her pride was about keeping the secret of their true natures, humans sensed, if only in the deepest, darkest corner of their psyches, that something wasn't entirely *safe* about the residents of the Three Rock Ranch. The local cowboys would give her a wide berth.

Now if only Michael would get his ass in here.

The idea of going on a *date* had been his, after all. The least he could do was show up.

Mara should have vetoed his night-on-the-town idea the second he mentioned it. Their relationship to this point had been based on sex, only sex, and lots of it. They didn't need dates.

Michael wasn't Mr. Forever. He was the guy who made your eyes roll back in your head with ecstasy while you were waiting for Mr. Forever to come along.

The man was a drug, all right. A familiar tingling sizzled along her nerves at just the thought of him. He was creative in the bedroom, with the stamina of a teenager—unfortunately, that was disturbingly close to his actual age. He was so damn *young*—a twenty-something boy toy—which was just one of many reasons Mara needed to end it now. Before she got any more addicted to him.

Better to go cold turkey before she lost sight of what she really wanted. A partner. A mate. A lion who would be steady and stable. Father to her children. A reliable, faithful, *mature* man to grow old with.

None of which described Michael Minor.

He could make her pulse rate skyrocket with just a look, but stable was about the last word she would think to call him. And mature? Not in this lifetime. He brought out a passionate streak she hadn't known she had, but that didn't mean she wanted to grow old with him.

He was a fling and Mara wasn't so young that she could afford to waste time with a dead-end relationship. She'd long since tipped onto the unfortunate side of thirty. She wanted that life—the kids, the mate, the happily ever after—and she would never get it unless she stopped playing games with little boys like Michael Minor and focused on grown men.

She had a plan designed to find her Mr. Forever, and she'd already set it into motion. Now all she had to do was break things off with Michael.

Her stomach clenched at the thought, and Mara swallowed some more whiskey to ease it.

She'd been dragging her feet, waiting for a good time to tell him, but she realized now there wasn't going to be a good time. The sex wasn't suddenly going to stop being mind-blowing. Her playful, passionate lover wasn't suddenly going to morph into an asshole just to make this easier on her. Michael wasn't going to give her an excuse to walk away. She was going to have to be a big girl and do it herself.

Tonight. This had to be their last night together.

Just one last time. They'd have their date, and she'd take him back to the ranch and screw his brains into putty as a farewell present.

Then she'd tell him. She'd already mentally rehearsed how she would do it. Quicker would be better. Like ripping off a Band-Aid. He probably wouldn't even flinch. Michael knew as well as she did that their relationship couldn't go anywhere. He might be disappointed for a second or two, but a man with washboard abs and a lazy, toe-curling smile wasn't going to have any trouble replacing her in his bed.

Mara ignored the spark of irritation that thought inspired—surely that couldn't be jealousy? This was better for everyone involved. Maybe he would even find someone to fall in love with.

The spark flared into a full-grown fire, but Mara smothered it with logic. She wanted Michael to be in love. To be happy. She had every intention of being deliriously happy with her Mr. Forever. Just as soon as she found him. Breaking up with Michael was necessary, for the best.

Maybe she'd ease him into it. They could discuss the logic of her decision and part as friends. Provided he ever deigned to show up for their fricking date.

On cue, the door squeaked open behind her and her breath caught. The hairs on the back of Mara's neck stood to attention. She didn't need to look to know who had just walked in. The temperature of the room escalated until Mara was tempted to press the ice-cold glass against her temple. She swirled the amber liquid in the tumbler, her eyes locked on the glass. She refused to look at him, but her breathing quickened as her sharp ears picked out the sound of him prowling up behind her. All thought of lists, plans and break-up speeches flew from her mind.

"Mara."

His voice was a delicious rumble. She felt it like a hand, stroking from her nape to the base of her spine. Mara tightened her fingers on the cool glass, focusing on the tactile sensation to keep from melting into a puddle of hormones at his feet. "You're late."

Muscular arms appeared on either side of her, caging her between the heat of his body at her back and the unyielding wood of the bar at her front. "Sorry, gorgeous. Unavoidable. I got held up."

He was so close. The warmth of his breath carried the words to caress the skin of her neck. Mara couldn't have suppressed her reaction even if she wanted to. A shiver snaked down her spine. Goose bumps leapt up on her forearms. She set the whiskey glass back on the bar before she dropped it—or crushed it in her grip, no longer sure of her ability to control her leonine strength.

She braced her hands on the chipped wood of the bar. Her fingers flexed and gripped the wood as she fought against the instinctive urge to press back against the firm wall of his chest. She so rarely resisted anything where Michael was concerned, throwing herself into each moment. Coyness and playful obstinacy provided a delicious novelty.

"You know I would never keep you waiting if I could help it," he continued, the words stroking against her skin.

Her eyes fell closed at the slumberous intent in his voice. Heat pooled low in her belly. God, to think he hadn't even touched her yet.

Just the thought of his touch was enough. Her mind provided a thousand vivid images of his hands on her, half memory, half fantasy. She knew his touch, inside and out. She could almost feel his fingers probing her slick folds. Her thighs clenched on another rush of wet heat.

He inhaled sharply and she knew he'd scented her reaction. "Am I forgiven?" he asked against her neck. The whisper-soft brush of his mouth was the only point of contact between their bodies, but she felt him on every inch of her skin.

Mara's breath shuddered out. "Just this once," she whispered, too hungry for him to be mortified that he'd reduced her to panting need in the span of a minute and a half.

"Good." His mouth curved in a smile against her throat. He pressed a quick kiss to her pulse point. Then his heat shifted, drawing away from her abruptly as his arms released her from the cage of his body. Mara bit her lip to keep from moaning at the loss.

Michael snagged the barstool next to hers and dragged it closer. He didn't so much sit on it as lean against it, keeping his body angled toward hers. His eyes dropped to her legs and his lips quirked in a little smile to let her know he appreciated the view.

She kept still, turning only her head to meet the wicked sparkle in his bright blue eyes. Landon, the pride's Alpha, looked like a lion even in human form—all tawny golds and browns. Not Michael. His hair was nearly black, his eyes a striking pale blue.

Mara's own feline pelt was the exact shade of her not-quite-dark-enough-to-be-brown hair, her eyes a greeny-brown that would have looked at home on any feline. When Michael walked as a lion, his mane was nearly as dark as his hair, which was unusual but not unheard of among lions.

It was his eyes that stood out. The pale, crisp blue looked unnervingly human in his leonine face.

At one time, Mara had wondered whether the oddly human appearance of his lion form was part of why he had such difficulty drawing a line between the human and feline aspects of himself. The animal was so much stronger in Michael than in any other shifter she'd ever met. At first, that animalism had unnerved her. Now she found herself drawn to his wildness. Something she never would have expected, given her own rigid control.

He propped one muscled forearm on the bar in front of her and Mara's eyes locked on it. She'd been surrounded by strong men her entire life. She didn't know why the play of muscle beneath his sun-bronzed skin should be so hypnotically fascinating, but she couldn't tear her eyes away from the visible evidence of his strength.

He scanned their less-than-impressive surrounds. "So this is your idea of a romantic night out, eh, gorgeous? You never cease to surprise me."

Mara forced herself to focus on the playful words, rather than the heavy pulse of lust still throbbing in her veins. "You said you wanted a date. No one said anything about romance."

He shrugged and her attention snagged on the play of muscles across his shoulders. Had he been working out? He'd always been strong, but now he was almost as heavily muscled as his brothers. The youngest Minor brother had finally grown into those divine shoulders. Mara licked her lips. *Hallelujah.*

"I thought the romance angle was implied. This is...rustic." He coughed.

Mara followed his gaze. Rustic. That was putting it nicely. The Bar Nothing was a seedy meat-market on a good day. Wednesday was apparently not a good day.

The gloomy dive was populated by morose drunks at scarred tables, a chipped, almost-sanitary bar, and a battered jukebox which had been stuck on moaning country ballads ever since she walked in the door. He was right. It was a far cry from romantic.

Michael grimaced as he took in the pair of hard-drinking cowboys at a nearby table. "I feel like I'm on suicide watch."

Mara couldn't even contradict him. This place was damned depressing. And it was definitely killing the mood. The buzz of sexual friction faded as the miserable reality around them sank into her skin.

She felt like she was counting down the seconds to the death of their relationship. This was supposed to be their last hurrah. It couldn't end like this.

Mara polished off the last mouthful of whiskey and set the empty glass on the bar. "Let's go home. I don't know why we're here in the first place."

Michael caught her barstool when she tried to spin away, spinning her back. "Hey, I'm taking my girl out for a good time. That's why we're here. And we're going to have a good time." He flashed her a grin, slathered in charm, and laid his hand, palm up, on the bar in front of her. "Come dance with me. We'll make our own ambience."

"Michael..."

"One dance. Then I promise to take you straight back to the ranch and do unwholesome things to you all night long."

A smile tugged at her mouth. "Promise?"

He grinned. "Scout's honor, gorgeous. C'mon."

Mara couldn't work up much enthusiasm for swaying back and forth to the world's most depressing country song in the world's most depressing honky-tonk, but she took his hand anyway. She trailed her lover onto the uneven slab of floor in front of the jukebox that doubled as a dance floor and slipped naturally into his arms.

Two minutes ago she'd been ready to jump his bones and now she just felt tired. Michael was so damned charming. So determined to make their date a success.

He had no idea she was going to break up with him tonight.

Guilt sliced through her, further souring her mood.

Not that he'd probably give a rat's ass. But the thought of having that conversation—the one where she told him there would be no more sexual marathons and mind-blowing orgasms—weighed heavily in her stomach, like she'd swallowed a boulder of doubt.

She kept her distance, leaning back in the circle of his arms. No sense getting comfortable there. Those arms wouldn't be wrapped around her for much longer.

But Michael didn't know that.

"What're you doing way over there?" he grumbled, hauling her closer. He tucked her tight against him, her breasts pressed against his chest, her thighs rubbing his firmly muscled legs as he swayed. The heat of his body enveloped her, his strength a warm contrast to her softness, and the boulder of doubt melted away.

She couldn't think about tomorrow, or even later tonight. All she could do was feel him.

The man was sin incarnate. His strong arms wrapped around her, keeping her snug to his body as they rocked in time with the lazy drawling rhythm of the song. The music was more heartache than sex, but somehow in Michael's arms it sounded like *Let's Get It On* and *Sexual Healing* all rolled into one. Her body felt thick and warm, as if every molecule were heating and expanding, but at the same time lighter than air. If she weren't holding onto his rock-hard biceps with both hands, she could have floated away.

The hand he curved into the small of her back began a slow, deliberate circle, teasing the upper flare of her ass, then retreating again. His erection rubbed her stomach, a promise of the night to come.

The last night.

Mara dropped her head onto his shoulder. He really was the perfect height. She pressed her face to his throat, breathing in the rich masculine scent of him. Engine oil, aftershave and the dark musk of the lion. Ambrosia.

"Michael…"

That hand continued to work in lazy circles over the base of her spine, until she felt like all her nerve endings spiraled out from that spot. "Hmm?"

"Why did we think it was a good idea to go out?" If they were home, at least one of them would be naked right now. Just the thought of repeating this dance with bare flesh against her skin had another spike of pure, hot need shooting down to her core. She bit back a moan.

"Aren't you having a good time?" His voice rumbled through his chest. Her nipples peaked instantly, pressing against the fabric of her dress.

If she were having any better a time, she'd orgasm right there on the dance floor.

He didn't wait for an answer. Which was good, because coherency wasn't a strong suit at the moment. How was it this man could take her perfect control and melt it with one searing touch? And why did she love it so much when he did?

"I asked you for a date," he said for her ears alone, "because I thought it would be novel if we had an excuse to keep our clothes *on* for a change." The hand at the back was killing her. Who knew there was a direct line from the small of her back to her G-spot? "I knock on your door and two minutes later I have you naked beneath me." *Or on top of him. Or in front of him. Or...* The boy was nothing if not adventurous. "I thought, for a change of pace, we could try a little delayed gratification."

Delayed gratification was great, in theory, but Mara'd had about as much slow simmer as she could stand tonight. She lifted her head from his shoulder to meet his eyes. "Exactly how long are we delaying this gratification?"

She leaned into him, canting her pelvis to rub against the base of his cock. Michael hissed, his eyelids flickering. His hands tightened on her. She reveled in his response...until she felt the telltale scratch of claws through her clothes.

Oh shit.

She'd forgotten, for a minute, why Michael so rarely left pride land, why she'd never suggested they go out before, why she'd chosen someplace she'd hoped would be abandoned at one a.m. on a Wednesday night.

Mara jerked back, even as a forbidden thrill curled in her

stomach at the thought that she'd unleashed that wildness in him.

Michael Minor was never fully in control of his lion. Whenever his emotions ran high, it sprang out, forcing a shift, no matter how hard he fought against it. From the shallowness of his breath and the bite of claws against her back, he was fighting it right now.

Mara's eyes flicked nervously to the drunks scattered around the bar. Had they seen anything? Were they sober enough to remember if they had? How close was Michael to losing it completely? A few claws might go unnoticed, but a fully grown lion suddenly appearing in the middle of a Texas cantina was bound to be memorable.

And just how depraved was she that the idea of being discovered was turning her on in a big way?

"Michael?"

"Let's go." His voice didn't sound entirely human, like the lion was caught in his throat, trying to get out.

Mara's breath left her in a rush. She grabbed his hand, tucking it against her skirt to hide the wicked claws. As they passed the bar, Michael threw a bill down to cover her drink. Mara was grateful he, at least, had remembered. The last thing they needed right now was an angry bartender chasing them outside.

"Relax." Michael squeezed her hand and tried to smile reassuringly, but where his human teeth should be, there was a mouthful of wicked feline points.

"Shit. Michael," Mara whispered, pointing to her own mouth.

His smile vanished and he didn't say another word, hustling her toward the door and out into the warm spring night.

Haloed by the light of the neon Budweiser signs, Michael looked like a fallen angel, beautiful and untamed. Mara's breath caught in her throat. She knew the danger of exposure was real, but so was the excitement it sent rushing through her blood. Adrenaline mixed with lust and whiskey in her veins.

She was a planner by nature, contained and analytical.

Mara didn't do anything on impulse, but in that moment she wanted Michael in a way that had nothing to do with Mr. Forever checklists and viable fertility schedules.

He was on the edge of control and Mara wanted to tip him over into wildness, a headlong rush into risk and need. Just one last time.

Chapter Two

The need to shift pressed against the inside of his skin, a clawing animal compulsion that pushed into the base of his skull, making each rational thought a struggle. It took every ounce of his control to keep from bowing his spine and giving into the impulse to take his lion form.

Michael swore under his breath as he guided Mara across the parking lot toward the SUV.

He knew he had limitations. His lion was always too close to the surface, ready to break through his skin. He'd adjusted to the fact that he had to be extra cautious whenever he left ranch land. The other shifters could go into town whenever they pleased, but Michael was different. They had to be *careful* with him. He was *unpredictable.*

Which apparently meant he couldn't even take his girlfriend out for drinks and dancing without ruining it by almost going feline in a room full of humans. Dammit.

"Michael? Are you okay to drive?"

At least she wasn't using her teacher voice—smooth, a little stern, and unswervingly calm, as if he was a cub on the verge of a tantrum who needed to be talked down. There was a breathy quality to her words, but Michael still barely restrained the urge to snarl at her. He felt three-quarters feral.

"I'm fine," he bit out. "Did you bring a car?"

She shook her head. "No. I took a taxi. Do you want me to dri—?"

"No. Come on." He was being a Neanderthal, dragging her across the parking lot and grunting out monosyllabic commands, but he didn't have the control for manners right now. Thank God she didn't seem to mind.

He'd parked on the far edge of the lot, instinctively drawn to the cover of the shadows there. The other cars left in the lot all clustered under the single lamppost near the door.

Michael pulled Mara around to the passenger side so the bulk of the Cherokee blocked them from view. He dropped her hand and leaned against the rear passenger door, pressing his forehead to the warm metal. Silently, he reached for calm. It had to be in him somewhere.

"Michael?" A feather-light touch brushed across his tensed shoulders. "Is there anything I can do?"

He was on the edge of losing it, his lion riding him hard, but something in her voice, the low, suggestive throatiness, called him back from the brink. "I'm fine," he repeated, starting to believe the words. "Just give me a sec."

He could practically feel her restlessness pulsing off her in waves. She fidgeted at his side. Out of the corner of his eye, he saw her twisting her hands together, as if that was the only way she could keep herself from touching him.

Shifters were tactile creatures. Touch was traded casually. Michael could see it was driving Mara crazy not to touch him, to soothe him the only way she knew how. Without lifting his head, he snaked out one arm and wrapped it around her, crushing her against his side.

Her arms came around him instantly, her body curving to align with his. He felt her ribs expand beneath his arm as she took a deep, relieved breath and let it out slowly, burrowing closer.

She was one of the most dominant females in the pride, but asking for the reassurance of touch wasn't a sign of weakness among their kind. She rubbed her face back and forth on his shoulder and he wasn't sure which one of them she was trying to soothe.

"I'm sorry," she mumbled against his shirt. "I shouldn't have teased you. I forgot—"

A flash of irrational anger had the lion surging to the surface again. "Don't," Michael growled. "You didn't do anything."

He wouldn't let her apologize for something that was a failing in him. A woman should be able to flirt with her lover in public without worrying he was going to turn into an animal and expose all of their secrets to public scrutiny. If he let her apologize to him for his weakness, that came dangerously close to accepting her pity. The proud cat that was so much a part of him rebelled at the thought.

He ran a hand down the curve of her spine, the soft fabric of her dress catching on his calloused palm. "You look amazing tonight. I wanted to touch you the second I walked in the door." He buried his face in the loose, dark-gold mass of her hair. He breathed in her scent, the familiarity of his pride overlaid with the unique sweet tang of jasmine. He whispered the next words, more for himself than her. "I wanted you to wear my scent, so everyone would know you were mine."

Mara made him want to mark her on the most primitive level. Something about her cool, analytical reserve had always fascinated him. It seemed so foreign to shifters who often reacted quickly, instinctively. She stood apart.

Her low, controlled voice. The efficiency of her movements, each gesture deliberate, each shift perfectly contained. He'd been nothing more than a hormonal teenager when she completed her master's work and returned to the pride to take up the teacher position, but she'd called to him on an animalistic level even then.

He hadn't been stupid enough to make a pass back then. Cool, elegant Miss Mara was a million miles out of the league of a horny kid like him. It was almost a decade later, after he'd finally come to terms with the fact that he was never going to grow into his control the way all the other cubs did, that he finally made a play for the prim schoolteacher...and discovered she was just as wild beneath that restrained primness as he'd always fantasized.

Their relationship had started out as all sex and only sex, but Michael knew she wanted more than that. Mara wanted cubs. She wanted a family. And he wanted her. What had started off as a fling, pure chemistry, had subtly shifted until it was something more.

He loved kids, but he'd never really thought about being a father. Up until Landon took over the pride a year ago, a shifter who hadn't developed control by his twenty-fifth birthday would have been sterilized to prevent the spread of an unstable gene. A family hadn't really been an option. But now...

He knew Mara wanted kids like an ache in her gut. He saw the hunger on her face when she watched the little ones play. At first, he'd just wanted to do whatever he could to ease that ache, but lately he'd begun to entertain his own fantasies about tawny miniature Maras tripping around his feet.

His heart tightened. He'd never been in love before. For someone who felt every emotion as keenly as Michael did, to have skipped one felt significant. Like he'd been waiting for her.

He'd wanted tonight to be perfect. This date was his chance to prove he deserved her, to show they were more than just hot sex. He knew she didn't think he was steady enough to be her mate, but he'd hoped to prove her wrong tonight.

Instead, all he'd proven was that he hadn't changed at all.

His sister, Ava, would remind him it wasn't his fault. He couldn't help it. The pride doctor said Michael was missing a neural inhibitor that drew the line between animal and man.

The science was small comfort. He would never be worthy of the woman curled against his side. How long could he expect her to stay with someone who could never give her the stability she craved? One more month? Two? Then who would she run to?

Michael forced the thought of the man who would take his place out of his head. Jealousy was savage—more likely than any other emotion to bring on a shift. He needed to get her back to the ranch, back onto pride lands, where a loss of control wouldn't expose them all.

He started to set her away from him, preparing to load her into the front seat, but her scent curled around him. Michael froze in place, his hands tight on her. He barely managed to keep his claws from snapping out.

Intermingled with the sweet twist of jasmine was the sinuous spice of lust. He could taste her desire on the air. While he'd been contemplating his sabotage of their relationship, Mara had apparently been thinking more much luscious thoughts. *Naughty girl.*

"Michael?" She spoke softly, a whisper on the warm spring breeze, but he felt that sigh of sound like a fist around his cock.

She slipped between him and the SUV, rubbing her body against his front every inch of the way.

Over the last few months, they'd learned one another's wants and needs. At first, they'd both assumed they would eventually grow tired of each other, but familiarity had only intensified each experience. They'd learned to play to their personal vices. He knew exactly how to touch her to get her wet in a heartbeat. And she knew he went hard at just the idea of pinning her to things—walls, doors, slippery shower tiles. He couldn't seem to get enough of crowding her against firm surfaces until she had no choice but to yield her softness to him.

Michael leaned into her, looming over her and pressing her back against the door until he heard the telltale catch in her breath. She loved this too. Mara may be dominant, but she almost never wanted to be on top. She wanted the man who would push her until she gave in, trusting her pleasure to his strength. She wanted *him.*

Now if only he could convince her their compatibility didn't end at the bedroom door.

Heavy-lidded eyes beckoned him. "Your wildness makes me feel wild," she purred.

Michael hesitated. Mara was never reckless. She reasoned things out and made the good decision, every time. So there was absolutely no explanation for her current behavior.

He had calmed. He was ready to take her home. All she had to do was hop in the car and drive back to the safety of the ranch. So why was she inciting him?

She urged him forward and he followed her lead. He bore her back against the metal wall of the SUV until the vehicle rocked slightly. She seemed to bask in the warmth of his body, drawing him tighter against her, if that was even possible. A small, sinful curve of a smile flashed out around her mouth.

Was she thinking what he was thinking? If he took her here, against the Cherokee, would they tip it? He knew he shouldn't want to try, but was captivated by the image teasing his thoughts. When she bit her lip, he wanted to bite it for her then suck that plump curve into his mouth.

"We should go." His voice was as rough as the gravel beneath their feet, but he kept his hands gentle as they stroked down her sides, over the flare of her hips, pausing above the hem of her skirt.

They *should* go. He should back away. He could yank up that little skirt, wrap those long legs around his hips and fuck her senseless just as soon as they were back on pride land. A fucking parking lot, no matter how late it was, no matter how deep the shadows, was no place for this kind of game. He gripped her hips, fully intending to step away, but Mara—never, ever reckless Mara—forced his hand.

She wrapped her arms around his neck, pushed up onto her toes and captured his mouth in a ravenous, open-mouthed kiss. She begged him with her mouth, drawing him into her madness with each longing pull of her lips and strong sweep of her tongue. Or was it his madness she was surrendering to? Right now, he didn't know or care. Her willing heat fried his last working brain cells and he fell into instinct and need.

Michael took command of the kiss. He sucked that luscious lip and gently scraped his teeth across it. His hands fisted in her skirt, jerking the stretchy fabric up, and Mara sighed into his mouth. God, he loved the noises she made, the little murmurs and sighs, not quite caught in her throat. She was musical in her passion, an instrument his fingers loved to pluck and strum.

The skin of her thighs was satin beneath his fingers. He wrapped his hands around the backs of her thighs. His fingertips brushed against her heat and he hissed out a curse.

She wasn't wearing panties. And she was dripping already. His slightest touch called forth another rush of moisture. Her need hit his nostrils, fogging his already blurry thoughts.

With one swift pull, he lifted her. Her legs wrapped snuggly around his hips. He notched his denim-covered erection against her pussy, but he didn't push like he wanted to, concerned about the rough fabric against her sensitive flesh. He shouldn't have worried. Mara ground herself on him, tearing her lips away

105

from his to gasp out his name.

"Easy," he murmured into the hair at her temple, barely recognizing his own voice. He slid his hand between them and slicked a finger through her folds. The touch was designed to be more soothing than arousing. He wanted to wind her up a little tighter before he let her take off. Her hips shoved his hand restlessly, and he speared one finger high into her slick heat, then two, scissoring them apart as he ground her clit with the heel of his palm. Her moans spiked to a high note and a surge of satisfaction shot through him. *He* had done that, pulled that sound from her.

She rode his hand, her head thrown back, eyes half-closed. There was no moon tonight, but his feline eyes didn't need one to see the ecstasy carved into every gorgeous line of her face. She tossed her head impatiently and her long dark gold hair flicked along the roof of the SUV. He changed the angle of his thrusting fingers so they stroked against the front wall of her pussy. A choked gasp and a rush of moisture rewarded him as her inner muscles clenched tight around him.

Then he eased back, releasing the pressure on her clit and slowing the thrusts of his fingers until they were long, soothing strokes. She gave a short, frustrated keen and her fingers scrabbled at the fastenings of his jeans. She was too frantic to be firing him up on purpose, but every clumsy brush of her fingers over his cock, where it pressed hard and tight against the rigid denim, made his blood pump hotter. She was driving him mad, but she was no closer to getting his damn jeans off.

Michael withdrew his fingers from her wet heat and she moaned in protest. It couldn't be helped. He needed both hands and a shitload of good luck if he was going to get the zipper down over his rigid erection. As he worked slowly with the uncooperative zip, Mara's hands roved beneath his shirt, her claws softly drawing patterns in the muscles of his back.

Finally, the zipper yielded. Relief and impatience made his hands clumsy as he shoved his jeans to the base of his hipbones. Michael wasted no time taking himself in hand and fitting the head of his cock against Mara's entrance. She hissed out his name as he drove in the first inch, forcing himself to go slowly.

Shallow pulses, each a fraction deeper than the last, rocked him into her slick channel, until he hilted, high and deep. Their sighs whispered out together into the night. She tightened around him. Her pussy squeezed his cock, milking him hard, and his knees almost buckled. He gripped the frame of the door beside her hips and shook his head once to clear his vision.

Her eyes challenged him, filled with equal parts wicked delight and bone-deep pleasure. Michael grabbed the roof to brace himself. He drew back and thrust home, feeling his claws sinking into the metal roof like butter and not able to bring himself to care. They could be standing in the town square in broad daylight and he wouldn't have been able to retract his claws, not with Mara's slippery heat wrapped around him. He drove deep two more times, pleasure burning in a hard knot inside him.

Then the door to the Bar Nothing squeaked open.

Michael froze, his gaze locked on Mara's wide green-gold eyes.

His lion-keen hearing picked up the sound of several pairs of shuffling feet and a chorus of moans about closing time. The door squeaked again, this one changing pitch in the middle as if someone had caught the door and wrenched it open again. More footsteps followed the others into the night.

The SUV was on the opposite side of the parking lot, hidden in the shadows, but that was no guarantee no one would wander over to check out the seemingly abandoned Cherokee.

Michael stroked Mara's hair back away from her face, never taking his eyes off hers. Sweat had begun to curl the tendrils at her temple and the heady scent of their arousal still filled his nostrils. Her breath came in shallow little pants and he could tell her attention was locked on the crowd milling across the parking lot, but when he tried to ease back, her claws clenched in his back and her inner muscles tightened fast enough that for a fraction of a second his vision went black.

"Don't stop," she whispered, more mouthing the words than giving them voice.

The woman was trying to kill him.

He'd had good intentions. He really thought he was going to be able to pull out, tuck her in the car and get her home. But that whisper killed every noble inclination he'd ever possessed.

He couldn't have stopped now if his life depended on it.

Keeping his eyes locked on hers, Michael sank his claws back into the Jeep—as much to keep it from rocking as to keep himself steady—and pulsed his hips forward. Mara whimpered, catching the sound with her teeth snagging her plump lower lip. "Quiet," he reminded her, so low the words barely carried the two inches to her ear.

Another shallow thrust. Another not-quite-contained moan. He watched her eyes, drinking in every flicker of sensation.

A bark of laughter from the direction of the bar had her shuddering around him. His sweet little schoolteacher had discovery fantasies. Who knew?

As the sounds of lazy conversation floated across the parking lot, Michael took up a steady rhythm, his focus on Mara complete. Half a dozen men loitered twenty yards away, but only she existed. The tight, wet fist of her pussy, the dazed, wicked gleam of her eyes in the darkness. The need to come built, drawing up his balls, but he fought it back. She was close. It was there in the way she worked at her lower lip and the mindless flexing of her claws in his back.

Michael bent his knees, shifting his angle slightly, and drove up into her higher, dragging the head of his cock against the front wall of her pussy. She came with a silent jerk, clenching around him. Her eyes squeezed shut and a single drop of blood formed on her lip where her teeth cut into it to hold back her cries. He slammed deep and hard, one last time, before giving in to a savage, soundless orgasm that blew the top of his head clean off.

The only sound was the soft complaint of metal warping under his claws—too soft to carry to their unknowing audience.

When the world stopped exploding, Michael collapsed forward against the door, Mara's body still trapped between him and the vehicle.

Not exactly what he'd had planned for date night. But, damn, what a way to end the evening.

He stroked a hand down her side, drinking in every shivering aftershock that rippled through her body. If this wasn't love, he didn't know what was. She was perfection. Wild and uninhibited in bed—or up against a car—but poised and controlled in the pride. Michael caught his breath, drunk on the scent of her.

Their date may not have gone exactly as planned, but it had redoubled his determination to make Mara permanently his. Whatever it took.

Chapter Three

Mara had lost her mind. There was no other explanation. How did Michael always manage to fry her connection with the rational, thinking part of her brain? She'd just had sex in a *parking lot*, for crying out loud.

And it was the best goddamn sex of your life.

Mara ignored the smug, feline voice in her head. Bad enough she'd had sex in a public place, with people standing only twenty yards away. Add to her moral tally the fact she was supposed to be breaking up with Michael and finding her stable Mr. Forever...

Oh God, what would her Mr. Forever think if he found out she'd just come like a rocket while pinned to the side of a car in a dusty parking lot?

She shuddered at the thought and wrapped her arms tight around herself, staring out the window at the night-kissed scenery flying by. Michael, seeing her shiver, reached out and adjusted the air conditioner.

Did he have to do that? Did he have to be so damned considerate? She was trying to break up with him and here he was giving her rock-the-very-foundations-of-my-soul sex and making sure she didn't catch a chill afterward. How was she supposed to break up with that?

"I'm leaving the pride."

The words jumped out of her mouth, in direct defiance of all her carefully laid plans to ease him into the idea slowly.

The SUV swerved toward the double yellow line running down the middle of the country highway. "What did you say?"

She looked at him. His muscles were rigid, his hands locked so tight around the steering wheel it looked like the bones of his knuckles were about to bust right through the skin. He'd heard her. She was sure of it. But he was going to make her say it again.

Mara ignored the little voice inside her wailing in protest, and set her jaw. She wasn't going to back down. "I'm leaving the pride. It's already arranged."

Michael didn't move a muscle, but she heard a sound like joints popping. "No."

She gave a breathless laugh, any guilt she may have had startled out of her by his cheek. "I wasn't asking permission, Michael. This was my decision."

"Why?" he ground out through clenched teeth, apparently reduced to monosyllables.

"Why not?" she replied, keeping her tone light and easy. He didn't look like he was in danger of shifting, but he also wasn't responding to her announcement the way she'd anticipated. "I thought you'd be okay with this. Sure, we had fun, but that was all it was. You're a great lover. You'll have no trouble finding someone closer to your own age to keep you company while I'm gone." The words left a bitter aftertaste in her mouth.

"How long will that be?"

Mara shrugged, feigning a casual air she didn't feel. "Months, years. Who knows? Until I find what I'm looking for, I guess. And when I find it, I'll probably stay there...indefinitely."

The Jeep swerved toward the ditch. Michael corrected it quickly, clearing his throat with a rough cough. "What is it you're looking for?"

He wasn't taking this like she'd predicted. Why was he asking her all the wrong questions? This wasn't how she'd planned this conversation to go at all. Mara folded her hands in her lap, trying to project a calm she no longer felt.

"I need a mate."

The car didn't jerk this time. There was no reaction at all from the cat gone eerily still in the driver's seat. "You can't find one here?"

"It's not like I haven't looked," Mara said irritably. "Three

Rocks is my home. It's not like I want to leave the pride, or the cubs..." Her throat closed off and she had to pause.

For the last decade, the pride's one-room schoolhouse had been her world. She'd taught the little ones, practically raising them, until they were old enough and had enough control of their shifting to be sent to the high school in town. They were *hers*, and even knowing her teaching assistant was more than capable of taking over for her, she still felt like she was abandoning them by going to another pride.

But she didn't have a choice. Not if she ever wanted to have a family of her own. The desire for a mate and a family had grown in her until it was a constant ache, pressing harder against her heart every day.

"I want the kind of mating my parents have. I want someone who is going to be with me for the rest of my life, not just until someone with a tighter ass comes along. Lions don't normally mate for life, I know that, but my parents—hell, look at your sister and your brother. Landon didn't just mate with Ava, he married her. And Caleb and Shana—that woman is the biggest bitch in five counties, but Caleb would never think of leaving her."

"Not unless he wants his testicles removed with a melon baller."

"For whatever reason. They're together for *life*. That's what I want."

"A life sentence."

"Someone who doesn't think spending the rest of their life with me would be a life sentence," Mara snapped. "Someone who is steady and stable and grounded. A good father to our cubs, a partner through thick and thin—"

Michael shook his head stubbornly. "There are plenty of men here—"

"Show me one who isn't rubbing up against a different lioness every night of the week—and don't say Tyler, because unless I grow four inches, bleach my hair and start calling myself Zoe, we both know your brother isn't going to even look in my direction."

"I wasn't going to suggest you hook up with my older

brother, Mara. For fuck's sake."

She cut him off as all of her frustration came pouring out, her anger fueled by a decade trapped in a pride where disloyalty was accepted as part of their *natures*. "One, Michael. One lion who isn't going to fuck around on me. One who is going to love me for me and not just want to screw me because I'm a handy piece of ass. I am so sick of—"

"What about me?"

"You?" The laugh ripped out of her throat, abrasive and disparaging. It was a terrible sound. Mara regretted it the instant it came out, but it was too late to take it back.

His rage filled the car like a physical presence, a fog of anger. She heard the bones in his back snapping against one another as they tried to force his body into a feline shape. His claws sliced out and a ragged growl ripped from his throat. As his body contorted, his foot must have punched down on the accelerator. The SUV shot forward, careening toward the midline.

"Michael!" Mara lunged across the middle and yanked the steering wheel. The SUV straightened with a jerk but was still racing down the highway at deadly speed. She grabbed his shoulder with her free hand. There was no way she could prevent him from completing the shift, but she dug her fingers into the muscle of his shoulder anyway, trying to hold onto something human in him.

She didn't know if it was her touch, her voice, or their impending death by fiery gasoline explosion in the ditch, but Michael caught the shift midway and jerked himself back to full human form. He panted like he'd just run a mile as the SUV dropped below death-and-dismemberment speed.

Mara kept her voice icy cool, the same tone she used in the classroom when the cubs were out of control and needed to be reined in. "Pull over, Michael. I'm driving the rest of the way."

He hissed at her, baring teeth that had suddenly gone feline. "The day I can't drive my own car—"

"You *can't*," she snarled, all traces of soothing calm drowning under the tide of her own anger.

She never lost her cool. Keep your head when all around

are losing theirs, that was her M.O., but Michael could get under her skin and bring out a violence in her she'd never known was there. She stopped thinking and reverted to just reacting, feeling. And what she felt was anger. Bright, vivid anger.

"Look at you. You can't even control the shift for five minutes. You nearly got us both killed!"

Michael slammed the brake and wrenched the steering wheel to the right. Mara gripped the doorframe, relieved he was obeying her demand, though a small, irrational part of her would have preferred he scream back at her. She didn't want him to give in. Some wild, foreign part of her wanted a fight.

Then Michael punched the accelerator. The SUV jumped forward along a rutted dirt road and Mara realized he hadn't pulled over. He'd just pulled off onto the ranch road. They were on pride land now. The wildness inside urged her to shift and run the rest of the way home on four feet—even if they were still too close to the outer perimeter, close enough to make being seen in feline form a danger.

She wanted the danger. "Stop the car."

"Shut up, Mara. I'm driving you home. Deal with it." Michael didn't even glance in her direction. His eyes stayed trained straight ahead, locked on the unlit dirt road.

"What is your problem?" The rational part of her brain was completely submerged in stupidity, apparently. She was goading a man on the verge of losing control. She actually hoped he would. What the hell was wrong with her?

"What's my *problem*?" he repeated incredulously, though he appeared no closer to shifting than he had five seconds earlier. "Half an hour ago I fuck my girlfriend's brains out and fifteen minutes later she tells me she's leaving me and never coming back. And why is she leaving me? Because she wants to find a *real* man who can give her what she really needs. What is my fucking *problem*? What the fuck do you think it is?"

"So my timing was bad. Sue me. You had to know this was coming."

"Did I? What was my first clue? The way you got wet for me the second I walked in the bar? Your scent was so damn strong I couldn't smell anything else. Or maybe I should have caught on when you were telling me not to stop and digging your claws into my back. That was a big fucking red flag right there."

"You can't honestly have expected us to live happily ever after. Our little fuckfest couldn't last forever. I'm going to be thirty-five next month, Michael. I can't waste my time fucking around—"

"With guys like me. Nice to know where I stand. Tell me, which was the bigger issue—the fact that I'm only twenty-four or the fact that I make you lose control?"

"I notice you don't mention the fact that you nearly killed us both a few miles back."

"You gonna answer me?"

Mara clenched her fists in her lap, trying to find some memory of calm. "This isn't about us."

"The fuck it isn't."

"It's about *me*. What I want. Everything is arranged. I've already talked to Landon about it."

Michael snarled. "My brother-in-law knew about this?"

"By this time next month, I'll be visiting a pride in Florida. I need to have time to meet the lions in the other pride and gauge our compatibility before I go into heat in six weeks. I'll need to be off the birth-control shots and on a prenatal vitamin regimen by then if I want to have any shot of conceiving. I only have a certain number of viable breeding years left."

The lion in the driver's seat hissed. "Nice to know it's all about practicality and your viable breeding years. God forbid *emotion* should get involved in anything as messy as who you choose to spend the rest of your life with."

"This is emotion," she said, practicality pushing down the tide of irrational feelings and putting her back in control. "I want a family and I need to know I can rely on the father of my children. This is the best way to go about finding the happiness I want. The stable, abiding relationship I've always wanted." She swallowed around a thickness in her throat, trying to think how she could make him understand. "You know my parents, Michael. You've seen how deep their love for one another runs. It's not a passionate flame that only burns on the surface and vanishes with time. It's built on companionship and friendship and compatibility. I won't settle for less than that."

He pulled the car to a stop in the middle of the ranch compound. Normally he would have driven her around to the front door of her bungalow, but Mara was glad he hadn't. She didn't want to have to tell him he couldn't come in. It was better to leave it like this. To leave *him* like this. On neutral territory.

He cut the engine and turned to her, resting his arm along the back of her seat but not touching her.

"What if there could be *more*?" he asked in a low rumble.

Mara shook her head. "For me, there isn't anything more important than that. I'm sorry, Michael."

He started to reach for her, as if he would touch her face. She ducked away from his hand. "I'm sorry," she whispered again. Mara jerked open the passenger door and jumped out.

She shifted immediately, not caring that the change would destroy her eye-candy dress. She could run faster on four feet than two and she needed to get away, as far and as fast as she could. Mara ran, ignoring the roar of a wounded lion behind her.

Chapter Four

Michael couldn't handle seeing anyone right now, least of all his brother Tyler, but life didn't seem to be in the mood to grant him any wishes tonight.

He felt like he'd just been smacked in the face with a crowbar. Repeatedly. The woman he'd been stupid enough to think might actually consider becoming his mate had planned to leave him from the start. Knowing he wasn't good enough for her wasn't the same as hearing her say it. Hearing her scream it in his face.

He needed to be alone, to lick his wounds in private. But as he pulled the slightly worse-for-wear Cherokee into its slot in the massive garage, he saw the lights in the mechanic shop were still on, even though it was coming up on three in the morning. If Tyler was still working, Michael could guarantee he'd be in a shitty mood.

For a second he was tempted to go into the shop, pick a fight and vent some of this rage. But the anger couldn't compete with the ache in his chest, like a piece had been carved out of him, leaving behind a gaping hole. He didn't want a fight. He was too drained to put up much resistance, and violence wouldn't touch the emptiness.

Michael hung the keys on their hook and crept toward the door. Maybe he'd hide out for a few days. Kane could handle the maintenance tasks around the ranch without him for a while. He could use a break. He didn't know what he'd do with his time, but maybe a day or two to himself would bring things into focus.

Michael shook his head, flinging away the thought. Crappy idea. He needed to work. Like Tyler. Twenty-four-seven. If he was busy, he wouldn't think about Mara and the way she'd ripped his still-beating heart from his chest and taken a bite.

"Hey, Mike."

Michael winced before turning to face his oldest brother. So much for solitude.

Tyler prowled out of the shop and past the pride vehicles lined up in the garage. He was taller than Michael, though not quite as heavily built as their other brother Caleb. He moved gracefully, like the cat he was. Tyler could take you down in a fight, and he wouldn't hesitate to do so, but he wasn't a bruiser by nature. Michael was more likely to get a disapproving frown than a smack upside the head, but tonight he would have preferred the smack.

"Where've you been?"

Tyler was as much a father to him as a brother, but the question still rankled. He wasn't a fucking child. He didn't owe anyone an explanation. "Out."

His unflappable brother didn't twitch an eyelash. As a kid, Michael had wondered if Tyler had used up more than his fair share of the control genes and there'd been none left over for him.

"Out," Tyler repeated. "At two a.m. The Cherokee's LoJack showed you took it off pride land. There a reason you went to see the humans in the middle of the night?"

"What? Do I have a fucking curfew now? Like a cub? I'm twenty-four fucking years old. If I want to take my girlfriend out for a drink, whatever the hour, there's no law against that." Michael's temper rose with every calm word his brother uttered.

Tyler held his gaze steadily, his voice low and unruffled. "It isn't about your age. You know that."

"What do you want to know? If I shifted? If I exposed us all? If the villagers are on their way out here with pitchforks? Well, rest easy, big brother. No one saw us."

Tyler's chin slowly lowered an inch. "No one saw you. So you did shift. Where?"

Inside Mara. Somehow Michael didn't think that answer

would go over well. "I didn't shift. Not all the way. We were at the Bar Nothing. Everyone there was falling-down drunk, so no one saw a thing. There wasn't even much to see."

Nothing to see. Right. As long as no one saw him pin Mara to the side of the Cherokee. Michael tried to hold his brother's gaze without flinching, but his eyes flicked over to the Jeep, returning to the scene of the crime.

Tyler frowned, more a tightening around his eyes than a full facial expression, but it was ominous all the same. He glanced over his shoulder, following Michael's gaze to the claw marks he'd gouged in the metal frame. Tyler turned, walking slowly over to the Jeep and running a finger along one particularly deep divot.

"Subtle."

Shit. Michael grimaced. Now he was in for it.

Why did he have to be such a terrible liar? His sister liked to tell him it was one of his best features, but he'd never had her appreciation for the lack. And now it looked like Tyler was gearing up to rip him a new one.

"I don't suppose you'd like to tell me why you thought the Cherokee would make a good scratching post?"

Michael locked his jaw, sticking to his original defense. "No one saw us."

"Ah." Tyler still didn't look at him, continuing to study the damage to the SUV. "So you lost it, in a public place, and went feral enough to leave your ride looking like it's been attacked by a bear, but that's okay because no one saw you. Is that it?"

He was twenty-four freaking years old, but Tyler could still make him feel like a cub who'd just been caught clawing the furniture. One silky-smooth question was all it took to send shame and embarrassment spearing into his stomach.

Michael didn't remember their father. The bastard had left the pride when Michael was three and Ava two, leaving his mate and all five of his kids behind. Tyler had become the man of the family. Their mother wasn't dominant. She protected her cubs, but Tyler was the head of the household from the time he was fourteen. He had been mentor and disciplinarian. When he was little, Michael had wanted nothing as badly as he wanted to

119

make Tyler proud.

Now that ingrained urge dug its claws into him again, bringing with it a surge of angry bitterness that he would never be good enough, controlled enough. Tyler would never consider him an adult because until he could control his shifting, his brother would see him as nothing more than an oversized cub.

His animal ran close to the surface, but in all other ways he was a man. He couldn't go away to college, but he read everything he could get his hands on to ensure he was just as educated as anyone else in the pride. He couldn't hold a job outside the pride, but he worked twice as hard as anyone else at the work he took on at the ranch. He may be emotional, but that didn't mean his brain didn't work. That didn't mean he wasn't a thinking, productive, *adult* member of the pride who deserved to be treated as such.

He wasn't a fucking cub to be taken to task for staying out too late at night. He was a man. Why couldn't anyone else see that? Not Tyler, not Mara. None of them.

Michael's breath came in short pants, the urge to shift a tight fist in his gut.

"Mike? Take a deep breath. Let it out slow."

"Fuck off, Tyler. I've heard all the Zen bullshit before and not a fucking bit of it helps."

Tyler was as unfazed as ever by his explosive temper. "What would help?"

"Respect," Michael snarled. "I *know* my control is bad. I know better than anyone what a threat it is to our security to shift in public. I've had it drilled into me. I may be trapped on pride land for ninety-nine percent of my life because no one trusts me enough to leave for even an hour—in the middle of the night, when no one saw me—but that doesn't mean that during the time when I am here, on the pride, not threatening exposure to anyone, that I deserve to be treated like a fucking *child*. I'm not four anymore, Tyler, and you aren't my father. So back. The fuck. Off." His claws were out, his teeth sharp, and his shoulders hunched under the urge to shift, but he fought it back and managed to stay in mostly human form.

Tyler watched him with expressionless passivity. At least he stopped petting the damn claw marks on the Jeep.

"Respect is earned, Michael," he said in a quiet rumble, the growl in his voice the only indication that his animal was up too.

"I've earned it," Michael snapped. "The only thing I haven't done is what I'm not *able* to do. In every other way, I've been a full, adult member of this pride for six years. All I'm asking is to be treated like one."

Michael didn't give his brother a chance to get in the last word. He was done listening. He slammed out of the garage and ran across the ranch compound to his bungalow. He forced himself to stay in human form, if only to prove that he could. He focused on the heat and the feel of sweat against his furless skin, the beat of his soft-soled shoes against the dirt path. It was pure ornery stubbornness, but he refused to let the lion out. Denying the shift was like ignoring a piece of his soul. He wanted to punish it, even if it was punishing himself. The lion was destroying his life, taking Mara away from him, stealing the respect he deserved.

Michael ran into his bungalow. He kicked off his shoes and stripped off his shirt, but still he didn't shift. Instead, he pressed his hands against the door, concentrated on the wood grain beneath his palms, and forced the animal back.

Chapter Five

"Momma!"

Mara's heart lurched as the pigtailed girl streaked across the schoolyard. She flung herself into the air with a blind certainty that her momma would never let her fall. Instinctively, the muscles in Mara's arms contracted, preparing to catch that squirming bundle of eager young shape-shifter.

But she wasn't that momma. She wasn't anybody's momma.

The momma in question looked more like an escapee from cheer practice than anyone's mother, complete with pink streamers in her high ponytail. She tossed her little girl, Sanka, high into the air and caught her giggling, squirming form.

A savage pang of jealousy squeezed Mara's heart. *This* was why she was leaving the pride, why she'd put Michael through that awful fight last night. So she could be someone's momma and cuddle that precious baby against her heart whenever she wanted. So she would never again have to experience the jabs of bright green envy when her charges' mommas and daddies came to fetch them at the end of the school day.

It wasn't fair. Tria could skip a birth-control shot at seventeen, get knocked up at the first dirty look from a randy lion, and name her child after a crappy decaf coffee, while Mara devoted her life to teaching and nurturing other shifter's children, was the prototype for a responsible, stable parent, would *never* name her child after food or drink, and yet she didn't have a child of her own. How was that for justice?

Tria bounded over to her, a puppy in a Playmate's body.

She bounced her daughter on her hip and flashed Mara a sparkling smile—equal parts eager and vacant. Whatever Tria's failings—and Mara was petty enough to mentally list them whenever the opportunity presented itself—the girl really did love her daughter and was fiendishly invested in her education.

"How'd she do today? Did she, like, get that L, M, N and O are all separate letters? We've totally been practicing," Tria vowed, as if Sanka's ABCs were right on par with World Hunger and Nuclear Proliferation in global importance. Which, to Tria, they *totally* were.

"She's doing great," Mara soothed the nervous mommy. "Sanka's developing right on schedule."

The four-year-old squirmed until Tria set her down, and then launched herself across the schoolyard to tackle a boy three years older and a solid thirty pounds heavier than her. Sanka may look like pigtailed innocence, but even though she'd only joined the preschool group last month, Mara had already learned that dimpled grin camouflaged one of the most devious minds in the pride. She must have gotten her conniving from her father, because Tria was an open book—probably a picture book, colorful and pretty and not too intellectually challenging.

Mara kicked herself for her nasty thoughts. *This* was why she had to leave the pride. Her petty jealousies were starting to interfere with her teaching and that was unacceptable. She would go off, find Mr. Forever, and Michael would get over it. Though why he had anything to get over in the first place was a mystery. They were just about sex. Weren't they?

"Miss Mara?" Tria bounced on the balls of her feet. "Did you hear me?"

Mara shook away her preoccupation. She had plenty of time to obsess over Michael later. "I'm sorry, Tria. What did you say?"

"I'm preggers!"

The words were like a mule kick to the stomach. "Congratulations," Mara gasped.

"I know! I'm, like, totes glowing, right? Duncan was all, it's official, Tria. And I was all, what? And he was all, you're my mate for, like, life."

Vivi Andrews

"What?" The question came out more sharply than Mara had planned. Duncan was the prototypical alley-cat lion. He'd sleep with anyone who waved her tail in his face and now he was settling down? With *Tria*?

"It's totes serious." Tria blinked her big green eyes solemnly. "At first I thought he was messing with me and I was all, seriously? And he was all, seriously. We're gonna be, like, a real family. How sweet is that?"

"Sweet," Mara repeated numbly.

She was going to be sick. How would Tria react if she regurgitated her PBJ sandwich all over those cute little sandals?

Duncan was older than Mara. She'd always known he was Sanka's father—secrets like that just didn't get kept in the pride—but she'd also seen him with a dozen different women in the four years since Sanka's birth. Sure, he spent a lot of time with Tria, but what guy wouldn't want to spend time with a sweet, bubbly, uncomplicated and notoriously flexible cheerleader?

Men wanted Tria for *fun*. That was all the single men in Mara's age bracket seemed to want. Fun. A good time. Nothing serious.

Mara was too serious. She'd never lied about the fact that she wanted a family. She wanted a partner. So those middle-aged children who had avoided mating into their bachelor thirties steered well clear of her and her serious-relationship vibes.

Then, while they were having fun with someone like *Tria—* frivolous, twenty-one year old Tria—they decided they really did want forever and happily ever after. With a pubescent bimbo.

It wasn't fair. Lions were promiscuous. Mara understood that. She accepted that. She just needed one—*one*—who was like her daddy. Steady and true.

Why was it they could only be faithful family men with stupid little cheerleader sluts like Tria? Did Mara really have to be a twenty-year-old trollop to land the man of her dreams? Was that how it worked? Because if it was, she was wasting her energy going to another pride. She was never going to be Tria. She didn't *want* to be Tria, adored by every man she met. She

124

just wanted to find *one man* who would love her for herself.

Michael's face flashed in her mind, as she had seen it last night, lined with anger, and a frisson of unease slithered along Mara's conscience. He had reacted so unexpectedly. Almost as if she were breaking his heart. Which was ridiculous.

Wasn't it?

The idea that young, impetuous and uncontrolled Michael might actually have had serious feelings for her...it was too ludicrous. But the memory of his rage brought her up short. Could that possibly be the explanation? Was Michael Minor in love with her?

The answer to the question leapt into her mind as another question, harsh but necessary. *Did it matter if he was?*

No. It couldn't.

He wasn't her Mr. Forever. Mara had criteria for the man she was going to spend the rest of her life with and Michael didn't qualify. She crushed the little voice in her head that wondered if she was doing the right thing by leaving.

There was no guarantee that she would find her Mr. Forever at the first pride she visited, or in any other pride, but she had to try. She couldn't stay here, knowing she would never find what she needed. She needed the possibility. The hope.

Without it, before long there would be nothing left of her but bitterness and might-have-beens. Even if she failed, she had to go out into the world and open her heart. She couldn't live the rest of her life closed off from the possibility of love.

Mara forced herself to smile at Tria as the girl gushed about morning sickness with unnatural enthusiasm. She refused to turn into a bitter old maid. If that meant leaving Three Rocks to give herself the opportunity for the life she wanted, so be it.

She was doing the right thing. The intelligent thing. She *was*.

Chapter Six

Michael couldn't sleep. Restlessness clawed at him.

He still hadn't taken his lion form since last night and he refused to. Instead, he prowled on two feet, walking the familiar paths of the ranch compound until his legs ached.

His thoughts were unsettled, out of balance. He saw the logic of Mara's decision—he wasn't exactly prime genetic stock—but his heart still couldn't makes sense of it, and the clashing of emotion and logic refused to give him any peace.

"Michael?" The raspy, feminine voice was nothing more than a whisper on the breeze, but his lion-keen hearing picked it out easily.

Michael paused, waiting for the quiet footsteps to catch up to him. "Ava."

He didn't want company, but his little sister was the one person he couldn't brush off. She'd had all four of the Minor brothers wrapped around her finger from the day she was born.

"I thought I heard you out here."

Michael glanced around, taking in his surroundings, and realized he'd just passed Ava and Landon's bungalow. For the third time. "Always the diplomat. Did Landon send you after me?"

"My husband doesn't *send* me anywhere." Ava tossed her head, her white blonde hair catching what limited moonlight there was. "I heard you walk past, *again*, and came to walk with my brother. You got a problem with that?" She tipped her chin back aggressively, staring him down even though she had to crane her neck back to do it.

He snorted softly. "Not at all. Let's walk."

She fell into step beside him. Michael measured his pace, reining in the ground-eating prowl into something his petite sister could match.

"You wanna talk about it?"

"No."

"Tough."

Michael choked out a laugh. Landon had been good for his baby sister. The flashes of spunkiness that had always been part of her personality were now matched by a steady confidence she never used to have. He would have sworn allegiance to the Alpha for no other reason, but the man had turned out to actually be damn good for the pride.

When he wasn't arranging to have Mara deported.

Michael lurched to a stop as if his feet had taken root. He fixed Ava with an angry glower. "You knew," he snarled.

"I knew what?"

"You knew Landon was transferring Mara to another pride. He would have discussed it with you. He discusses everything with you."

Her eyebrows flew up. "Yes, I knew Mara was leaving, but I had no idea you would care."

Anger bubbled up, but Michael pushed it back down. He couldn't shift now. If he shifted, he wouldn't be able to vent his anger. "You knew we were together. It's not like it was a fucking secret."

"Yeah, but no one thought you were a good match."

Michael snarled at her, baring sharp teeth.

"Michael!" Ava cried, shocked.

He hastily reined in his anger. He'd just sniped at *Ava* of all people. He didn't think he'd ever been angry with her before. Now he could barely see through the rage. "Not a good match," he forced the words out through a throat that felt bumpy and rough. "Meaning I'm not good enough for her."

"Meaning you're a flirt and she's desperate for kids. Everyone thought you just wanted to get laid, but the entire pride knows that isn't all Mara wants."

"That isn't all I want either," he growled. "Just because I'm young and emotional, I can't want kids? I can't want a family?" A bitter laugh ripped out of his throat. "Oh, that's right. I *can't* want children. I can't be allowed to pass on an unstable gene. I'm a threat to our entire species. I could expose us to the entire world. God forbid I be allowed to *breed.*"

"Michael. That isn't how it is anymore and you know it. The Alpha doesn't control who is and isn't allowed to breed anymore. Landon picked me as a mate, didn't he?"

She was right. Landon was changing things, but accepting the runt of the litter as his mate wasn't the same as allowing a threat to the pride to expand into a second generation. He'd said he would allow Michael to mate, but he was sending away the only woman Michael wanted in that role.

Michael met Ava's pale grey eyes, holding them steadily, forcing her to see the agitation eating at him. "You could have convinced him to make her stay."

Ava looked away, her fingers absently plucking at the fabric of her pants. "Why are you doing this? Do you really love Mara or is this just wounded pride talking?"

Michael didn't need to ask which she thought it was. Ava wouldn't have asked the question if she thought he loved Mara.

Puppy love. That's what everyone thought it was. It probably didn't help that he'd had a crush on Mara in school. But this was not a crush. Not anymore. He was not a teenager and this wasn't a fling.

Even Ava, his baby sister, didn't treat him like a grownup. By human standards, Michael had been an adult for years. In his lion form, his mane had fully grown in. He wasn't an adolescent by any definition of the word, but they wouldn't stop treating him that way.

Just a crush. Nothing serious. Because Michael wasn't *capable* of being serious. He was just a kid. A flirt.

"No."

"Michael?"

He rolled his shoulders, feeling the lion pressing against the inside of his skin, goading him. He'd been ignoring the beast riding him for too long. "I'm not a cub."

"I never said—"

"I'm sick of being treated like a child. None of you have any faith in me. That's fine. But you don't get to decide my life for me."

He would prove he was man enough. Prove he deserved Mara. Show her she didn't need to go anywhere else to find a mate. The right mate for her was right here.

The lion inside him roared in agreement.

Michael bolted down the path as fast as his human legs would carry him, ignoring Ava shouting his name. Rational thought had been burned away by instinct and need. He would go to his mate, prove himself to her, convince her to stay. The beast urged him on, hungry for dominance and the scent of her skin.

Mara was his. They both knew it. Tonight, he would hear her admit it.

Chapter Seven

Mara couldn't sleep. She should have been resting easy, secure in the knowledge that she'd made the right decision, put herself on the right path, but she couldn't seem to stop thinking of Michael.

She couldn't stand the way they'd left things. Of course their relationship had to end, but she didn't want his memory of her last words to him to be whatever she'd said. She couldn't even remember now what she'd thrown at him before running away. All she could remember was her frustration.

She had to talk to him. They could part as friends, at least. And he was her friend, as unlikely as that seemed. Over the course of the last few months, Michael had become one of her best friends. She would miss the way he could make her crazed with lust, but she would also miss the lazy conversation in the quiet hours before morning. They would talk about everything and nothing. Nonsense conversations that hadn't really meant anything, until she realized how much they meant to her.

He listened to her. He didn't always understand her—they came at life from such different angles—but he always listened, with such intense concentration, bringing everything he had to puzzling her out.

Through the stillness of the spring night, she heard footsteps rushing up the path to her house. A fist pounded on her door and Mara hesitated for a moment before going to open it.

She was safe, protected here in her pride. But would she have that same confidence in another pride? Or would she have reason to fear an unexpected knock in the small hours of the morning? Doubt seemed to be wrapping around every aspect of her plan.

She knew who would be waiting on her front porch before she opened the door, but she made herself walk slowly. Michael often surprised her. They'd played out this moment dozens of times before and the thought that this would be the last shortened her breath. Mara wanted to drag out the feeling of nervous anticipation, to live in it forever.

As soon as she turned the knob, the door sprang open. He stalked through, grabbing the door from her hands and flipping it closed behind him. The sheer size of him made her breath catch. He exuded strength, his blue eyes lit from within by the force of his determination.

"We aren't done yet," he growled. Michael caught her around the waist, jerking her forward, and she fell eagerly into his arms. His body slammed hard into hers. His mouth was rough and demanding, dragging against hers hungrily. He closed one hand around the back of her neck, kneading her nape with firm pressure as his kiss turned the world inside out. Everything was pressure and heat, every touch a push, as if he could press his will into her until she was nothing but his.

She tugged at his shirt and he ripped it in two, flinging aside the pieces. Mara gasped, more turned on than she cared to admit by the sight of the animal driving him so hard. He was out of control and her only thought was *bring me with you*. She wanted that wildness. If this was going to be her last time, she wanted everything. She wanted all the insanity in his blood to be rushing through hers too. Only if she got it all would it be the closure she needed.

Their clothing only lasted a matter of seconds, and then they were flesh to flesh. He was so hot his skin seemed to burn right through hers, branding her with his scent, his need. He pivoted, pinning her between his body and the wall. Mara cried out, surprise and arousal blending in the sound. He was so strong. For a man with no control of himself, he was in perfect control of her.

Michael caught her wrists, trapping both of them above her head with one hand. "Admit it," his dark voice rumbled into her

131

ear before his mouth slid down the side of her neck. His sharp teeth nipped at the sensitive point where her neck met her shoulder and Mara moaned.

"Admit...what?" she panted, arching into his touch as his free hand cupped her breast, plumping it then sharply tweaking her nipple. Sensation shot straight to her pussy. She pressed her thighs together, wet and wanting.

"You need me," he growled against her skin, licking his way down to her breasts, teasing flicks that made her writhe. He shifted his hand to torment her other breast and sucked the nipple he'd released into his mouth.

"Michael."

"Admit you love me." He took her other nipple into his mouth, catching it gently between his teeth. His fingers speared between her folds, sliding to either side of her clit and curling just barely inside her. Mara gave a ragged gasp. She was tuned to his touch, primed to do nothing but feel, all thought long since abandoned. Her only coherency was the need for *more.* Michael released her breast and lowered himself to his knees. A devilish smile quirked his sexy-as-sin mouth and her heart stuttered. *More.*

Michael pressed her back against the wall and hooked one of her knees over his shoulder, so she was completely open to him. His hand held her pussy, inches from his face, though his fingers stayed still and he made no move to bring her over the edge. Mara squirmed in his hold, urging him to give her the rhythm she needed.

"Michael," she murmured breathily, his name both praise and plea.

He leaned forward and flicked his tongue across her clit. Mara gave a short, sharp shriek and her hands locked on his shoulders for balance. He was the only steady point in her world. He lapped against her again and she nearly saw heaven. Need built underneath her, coiling like a spring.

"Admit it, Mara."

What was she supposed to be admitting? She could barely remember her own name. Right now she'd admit to being the Queen of Sheba, as long as he didn't stop what he was doing.

"Yes," she moaned, the only word she knew.

He set his mouth against her, sucking her bud into his mouth. The delicious pressure popped inside her and she came in a rush, sobbing his name. Pleasure rippled through her limbs, making them feel heavy, but Michael wasn't done. He kept sucking and teasing her clit until she was back on the edge of need before she had time to come down.

He brought her again, a fast, hard, shuddering orgasm that wrenched through her, bone-deep.

In a moment of pleasure-induced clarity, Mara remembered why they were here. Their last time. She wanted it to be good for him. He'd already made it beyond good for her.

She threaded her fingers through his hair, palming his scalp and pulling him back. He put his thumb on her clit, as if marking his place, rubbing it in a slow circle.

"Come up here," she pleaded. "I need you inside me."

He shrugged her knee off his shoulder, rising so quickly he had her leg wrapped around his hip before she had a chance to lower it. He caught her other leg and lifted her, settling both her legs circling his waist. Mara wrapped her arms around his neck, expecting to feel him pressing into her, but Michael surprised her. Always surprising her...

He spun them away from the wall, crossing to the bed and lowering her gently onto her back on the mattress.

Something in his care, his tenderness, brought tears to her eyes, but Mara blinked them away. Michael was wonderful, but even if this was their farewell, she refused to cry. He pressed a kiss onto her lips, so soft and sweet it was more the promise of a kiss than a kiss itself.

She wanted more than promises she would never be able to redeem. Mara sank her hands into his hair again and pulled his head down to hers. She feasted on his lips, drawing on them and rolling her body in a sinuous wave beneath his until they were both back on the sharp edge of need.

He notched himself against her entrance and Mara released his mouth on a moan. "Last time..." she panted. "Make it good."

An odd flicker passed through Michael's eyes, but then he pressed inside her in a slow, luscious stroke and Mara couldn't think to wonder about it. She couldn't think of anything but the thick, hard feel of him stretching her tight.

He brushed her hair away from her face, framing it with his hands and dropping a kiss on her cheeks, her temples, and beneath the curve of her jaw. His eyes were an intense, burning blue and she couldn't look away. Holding her gaze, he drew back and thrust slowly back again. Mara angled her hips to take him a fraction deeper. He thrust again and she released a ragged sigh. Before it had been a thundering rollercoaster of lust, but this was a sultry, sensual vise of passion, tightening slowly around them.

Michael took up a measured, punishing rhythm. Each stroke dragged along every nerve inside her. She gripped his buttocks, trying to urge him higher and harder, but Michael kept his brutal, deliberate pace. Her breathing matched his, their groans catching together at the end of each thrust. Mara felt like she was being held at the edge of madness.

Then, finally, he began to increase his tempo bit by bit. His eyes still bore into hers like blue lightning, branding her to her soul. His speed picked up, his thrusts growing rougher, and Mara reveled in the animal behind each fierce lunge. She needed all of him, every bit, even the wildest parts. Only then would she be free of him. She couldn't find closure without a complete surrender.

She threw herself into this moment with all the passion he poured into his life. He pistoned into her, growling words that might have been her name or something more tender. They raced for completion together, a wild, bruising sprint. Mara flew over the edge first, with Michael a heartbeat behind. She burst into a thousand points of light as his hips jerked between her thighs.

He collapsed against her, his weight pressing her down into the mattress. Mara closed her eyes, drinking in that delicious heaviness for the last time, trying to imprint this moment into her memory so she would have it forever.

No wonder people always talked about break-up sex. It was incredible. Transcendent. Mara couldn't think of better words to describe it, at least not until her brain came back online. She wanted to hold onto this moment, make it last, but exhaustion stole over her. Wrapped securely in her lover's arms, Mara slept, resting easy.

Chapter Eight

Mara leaned against the schoolhouse window, watching the kids tumbling over one another in the schoolyard. It was a gorgeous day. Probably one of the last perfect days of spring. The sun shone warm and pleasant, gearing up for the ungodly hot summer days to come.

Mara glanced around the schoolroom, looking for distraction. She'd already cleaned up the spilled glue, straightened the desks and put the stray articles of clothing back into the cubbies. Shifter kids went through clothing faster than their human counterparts, their outfits destroyed by the shift. She kept an extra set or two for each of her kids here at the school. Those extra outfits always managed to end up scattered around the room by the end of the day—even when none of the kids had shifted during class.

Normally, the kids would clean up after themselves, but Mara had released them early, wanting to do the task herself. Needing the busywork to occupy her hands. But now the schoolroom was spotless.

She had no more excuses.

Any other day, Mara would be outside with the cubs, watching over them or perhaps even joining in a game. Today, she pressed her forehead against the window, hiding behind that barrier of glass. She was being cowardly and she knew it, but she didn't want to go outside.

Michael was out there.

He'd still been in her bed when she woke up that morning. Until she'd seen him there, she hadn't realized how much she'd hoped he would make things easy on her and slink away into the night. When she'd thrown him out, he'd gone without a fight, thank God, but not before he dropped a few choice phrases into her ear.

I want a family too, Mara. One woman for the rest of my life, the kids, the house, all of it. Don't write me off just yet.

Mara had felt unsettled all day. She couldn't seem to get those words out of her thoughts. Had she been wrong about him? Her conviction to leave the pride was starting to feel forced and uncomfortably restrictive.

And then he'd shown up as school was letting out.

The kids had run to him, climbing all over him in an eager tumble. The pride was a tight-knit community, but this was more than just a standard reaction to any member of their pride. It was obvious the kids adored him.

He'd make a good dad. The thought crept up on her like a stealth attack. Mara shook it away, forcing herself to think rationally. "Of course the children love him," she said aloud to herself in the empty classroom, her voice making the words seem more real. "He's practically a child himself."

He would play with his kids and they would adore him, but who would discipline them? Who would have to be the bad guy every time? Not Michael. Mara wanted a man who would love their kids, but he had to be a partner and a father, not another child to look after.

Michael was smart, funny and generally amiable. Hard not to like. But he was also impetuous, young, foolish and uncontrolled. Not mate material.

She would not waver just because he'd figured out the children were the way to woo her. Mara was not influenced by sweet gestures and pretty words. She made her decisions with her head. Her heart would just have to fall in line.

Mara stepped away from the front window, taking another lap around the classroom but finding everything in its place.

She needed to remind herself why she was doing this. Why it was so important she not make the wrong decision when it came to picking her mate. Mara crept out the back door of the schoolhouse, grateful the wind was in her favor and Michael wouldn't immediately know she'd escaped.

She had to see her parents.

At the far edge of the ranch's residential compound, distant enough to be private but close enough to be sociable, a little house looked out over the southern pasturelands. Roger and Martina Leonard's house was different from most of the other bungalows on the ranch, in that it had its own kitchen, in addition to the separate bedrooms and sitting room. Most of the buildings in the pride took open-concept to a new level, but the cottage Mara had grown up in was unique.

The door swung open as she started up the path. A cuddly bear of a man with a bushy white beard stepped out onto the porch. "Mara!" he boomed, smiling broadly.

"Hi, Daddy."

He swung her up in an enthusiastic hug before ushering her inside. "Your mother's psychic," he stage whispered as soon as her mom was in earshot. "She knew you were coming."

Her mother flapped her hands at her father. "It's Friday, you old goof," she said affectionately.

Mara realized with a jolt that it was, in fact, Friday. The night of their weekly dinners together. Her father returned to the kitchen to finish preparing dinner and Mara set about helping her mother set the table, comforted by the rote ritual, the normalcy of it.

Her parents had been together for over forty years, but they had gotten a late start on their family, not having Mara until they were both in their thirties. That was part of why they'd both been so consistent in their support of her decision not to rush into marriage with the wrong man. *Wait, Mara, you have plenty of time.*

But somewhere between thirty and thirty-five, *you have plenty of time* had turned into *lots of people are perfectly happy never having children.* They still supported her, but now there was a tinge of pity tainting their support. They wanted so badly for her to be happy. It was hard not to feel like she'd failed them by not finding her Mr. Forever and living happily ever after. If she couldn't do it, even with their love as her guiding light, what did that say about her? How pathetic was she?

"Chicken marsala, just the way my girls like it." Her father shouldered open the kitchen door and strode out with a steaming platter that smelled like home.

They all took their seats around the table, the same chairs they'd sat in for every Friday dinner over the last three decades. Mara's heart gave a pang as she realized she'd be giving up these Fridays if she went in search of her Mr. Forever. And if she found him in another pride, would he want to return to hers with her? Or would Mara only see her parents on the occasional visit, showing off their grandchildren only on scheduled trips?

She'd tried to think all this through, but the little sacrifices kept surprising her. She'd known she would be leaving her pride and all the people she'd grown up with, but the fear of isolation from her family and the keen ache she felt when she thought of leaving her students startled her.

"Delicious as ever, Rog," her mother said.

Mara realized she'd been eating without tasting a bite. She looked up in time to see the small smile her parents shared, the same smile they'd been sharing for forty years. Her resolve firmed.

"I'm going to visit the pride in Florida next month," she announced.

Her father stilled with his fork in midair. "Florida?" he repeated, as if she'd just announced a trip to the moon.

Her mother covered her father's free hand where it rested on the table. "For how long, sweetheart?"

Mara squirmed in her chair, inexplicably unnerved by her mother's calm acceptance. "For a while. Until I see if...if there might be someone there...for me."

Her mother simply nodded, like she'd been expecting this for a while. Her father cleared his throat roughly. "Right..." he mumbled, then repeated the word with more conviction. "Right. You should go."

It was back, the pity in their eyes. It stung to see it there, but Mara couldn't say she was surprised. Now that she thought about it, she'd been seeing that expression on a lot of faces lately. Everyone knew how she'd failed. She was officially pathetic. The desperate spinster. A figure of ridicule.

Would people in her new pride look at her that way? Would they know she'd run away from Three Rocks as a failure?

"It's a good idea," her mother said with forced cheer. "A fresh start."

Mara's stomach churned and she set down her fork. Would it really be a fresh start or would she carry her shame with her, as obvious as a scarlet letter? Pathetic, unlovable Mara.

Her father reached across to pat her hand. "It'll work out, Mara. Don't you worry. Fate has wonderful things in store for you, baby."

Tears pricked her eyes, but she forced out a smile. "Thank you, Daddy." If only she had his faith. Fate didn't seem to be doing her any favors lately.

Chapter Nine

Michael was not above asking for directions and he'd never felt more lost in his life. And so he found himself on Ava's doorstep begging for advice.

When she opened the door, he scanned the room behind her, feeling a surge of relief when he saw that Landon wasn't home. He wanted Ava's guidance, but he'd rather get it in private, if possible.

"I need your help."

Ava didn't ask questions. She just waved him toward the round table and chairs she and Landon had recently added to their bungalow. Ava was a natural diplomat and she'd taken up the role of counselor in the months since her marriage to Landon. Michael grabbed one of the chairs as Ava curled into a ball in another one, always the cat.

"I take it this is about Mara?" she asked gently.

Michael raked a hand through his hair. "I've done everything I can think of. I've told her I want more than just a fling. I've shown her that I can be good to her, that I'm good with kids and I'm not going to give up, but nothing I do seems to change her view of me. In her eyes, I'm still just a kid with a crush." He leaned forward, bracing his forearms on the table. "What did you do? How did you persuade Landon to look at you in a different light?"

Ava shook her head regretfully. "Landon saw more in me from the beginning. I was the one who needed convincing."

"Shit." There went that plan.

"I wish I could tell you how to change her mind, but other

than appealing to her sense of logic, I don't think there's much chance of that. Mara's stubborn, and when she's decided something is the most sensible course, you need dynamite to shake her conviction."

"She wants to be with me," Michael insisted. "I know it. I just don't know how to get her to see that." He raked a hand through his hair. "I'm getting desperate."

Ava hesitated, taking a deep breath, and he knew he wasn't going to like what she said next. "Have you considered just letting her go? If she is right for you, maybe visiting another pride will convince her of that and she'll come back to you. If not...there are other women in the world."

Michael glared at his little sister. "If I told you to just let Landon walk out of your life, would you do it?"

Ava's pale grey eyes flicked down to lock on the table. "The difference is that no force on earth could get Landon to leave me, Michael. You yourself tested that when we first got together. You and Tyler and Caleb and Kane threw yourselves between us, but it didn't faze him. He kept coming for me. Would Mara do that for you?"

He didn't answer. He couldn't. For Ava, who hated confrontation, to be so blunt, she had to truly believe that Mara didn't love him. That she never had.

Could he have been wrong about her?

"No." He was sure of her. He'd never been more certain in his life. "She's my mate. She should be with me. I just need to make her see."

Ava opened her mouth to respond, but the door to the bungalow opening halted her words. Landon paused in the doorway, glancing between his wife and her brother. "Should I come back later?"

Michael shoved himself to his feet. "No, you stay. I'll go."

Ava rose too, putting her hand on his arm. "Michael, it's probably for the best."

Somehow he managed not to snarl at her. "Ava, I love you, but if you say that one more time, I might have to bite you."

"Don't threaten my mate," Landon said without heat, tossing the duffle he'd been holding next to the bed. "This about

Mara?"

Ava glanced at Michael. He shrugged. Ava was going to tell Landon everything as soon as he left anyway. Might as well get the indignity over with.

"Yeah, it's about Mara. She thinks I'm a kid and nothing I do can convince her I'd make a good mate."

Landon frowned. "You want me to give you more responsibility in the pride? Some really important position?"

Michael blinked, surprised by the offer. "You would do that?"

The Alpha shrugged. "I'd been planning to anyway. You're limited by the need to stay on pride land, but you're also just about the most honest person I know. I figure you can handle a little more weight on your shoulders."

Satisfaction and pride blossomed in his chest. "Yeah, I can handle whatever you throw at me," Michael vowed. "But I don't know if that's enough to change things with Mara. She'll be gone in a few weeks. Can't you do something to delay her? Keep her here a little longer?"

Landon shook his head. "Sorry, Michael. That isn't how I run things."

Michael scrubbed a hand over his face. "I know. I don't want to force her to stay if she really wants to leave. I just wish I could make her see she doesn't need to go halfway across the country to find what she already has right here."

Landon gripped his shoulder and squeezed. "You want a drink? We can get shitfaced and compare notes about all the ways we would tie our women up and make them see reason, if they'd only let us."

"Landon," Ava scolded, rolling her eyes.

Michael snorted. "Yeah, let's do that."

Mara left her parents' house no more confident than she'd been when she arrived. She'd hoped seeing them together would reinforce that she was making the right choice, but instead it had just made her wonder even more if she was being smart or running scared.

A figure stepped out of the shadows onto the path in front

143

of her. Mara almost turned back. She wasn't sure she wanted to see anyone. If there was even a trace of pity…

But as she grew closer, she recognized the Alpha's sister, Zoe, coming from the direction of the garage. Zoe was refreshing. She was also one of the only people at Three Rocks who had changed prides looking for a better life. If anyone would understand why Mara was doing what she was doing, it was her.

"Hey," Zoe called, closing the distance between them and falling into step beside her. "You look like shit."

A short laugh burst out of Mara's mouth. She shoved her hands into her pockets and kept walking. "Don't hold back, Zoe."

The tall blonde shrugged. "I call 'em like I see 'em. You okay?"

"Fine."

"Uh-huh. Fine isn't a way to be. Fine sucks." She cocked her head to the side. "Wanna talk about it?"

"Not really."

Zoe nodded sagely. "Me either." They walked in silence for about two steps before the restless energy in Zoe had to be verbally released. "Men, huh? Can't live with 'em, can't rip out their entrails to wear as a necklace."

Mara snorted. "Something like that."

Zoe swung her arms and bounced on the balls of her feet, bubbling over with kinetic energy. "You should talk about it. You'll feel better."

"Zoe." Mara used her teacher voice. The one guaranteed to snap recalcitrant pupils back in line. Unfortunately, Zoe appeared to be immune.

"You want kids, right? And none of the guys around here look like viable daddy material, yeah?"

Mara winced. Even Zoe, who'd been with the pride for less than a year, could tell she was desperate and pathetic. Great.

"I know how you feel," Zoe continued.

Mara stayed silent. She couldn't imagine Zoe's claim was true. She had a decade on the pretty blonde. It was a long way from twenty-five and annoyed to thirty-five and frustrated.

"I'm staying with Three Rocks to support Landon," Zoe confided. "I'd be long gone if he weren't so determined to make a go of it as the Alpha here. There aren't exactly a lot of hot prospects for a girl here, am I right? We both know what a pain in the ass the Minor brothers are, but they're the only quality lions in this damn pride."

"I don't—" Mara wasn't sure what she was going to protest, but it didn't matter because Zoe didn't give her a chance to finish.

"I know, I know. You aren't serious about Michael. A girl like you isn't gonna be dumb enough to get serious about a guy like that. But what are you gonna do? It sucks, but there aren't a lot of options. Sometimes you're just stuck. Sorry 'bout that."

"I'm not stuck," Mara snapped. She wasn't annoyed with Zoe so much as herself, but the frustration would take any outlet. And the idea that a woman would have to be stupid to want to be with Michael rankled on some level. He deserved a goddess. Just not her. "I'm not some pathetic little girl waiting for a man to sweep me off my feet."

Zoe's blonde eyebrows flew up. "Hey, *chica*, a dominant female is only pathetic when she lets herself be." She glared back over her shoulder in the general direction of the garage.

"Well, I'm not. I'm doing something about it. I'm going to Florida."

"I've been to Florida. The traffic sucks."

Mara walked faster, fueled by irritation. "I'm taking my fate into my own hands. I'm going out, actively looking for a mate. I'm not running away from my problems. I'm facing them head-on."

"Hey, no one said you were running away."

"Well, I'm not. It takes a lot of courage to do what I'm doing."

Zoe held out her hands in surrender. "No one's arguing with you, *chica*."

"I'm doing the right thing. I *know* it. There's nothing for me here."

"Uh-huh. You ever seen *Hamlet*?"

Mara stopped in her tracks, turning to frown at Zoe.

"*Hamlet*? What does *Hamlet* have to do with anything?"

"The lady protesteth too mucheth and all that. You sure you aren't running away from someone?"

"I said I wasn't—"

"Yeah, you said. You said nice and loud and emphatic, but the thing is, I never said anything about running. You came up with that one all on your own."

Mara's irritation spiked high, aimed straight at Zoe. "Are you always this annoying?"

"Mostly." She shrugged, utterly unoffended. "I'll leave you alone. I think I'm gonna go run off my troubles. Thanks for the chat though. A little girl talk is always good to take your mind off your own issues, yeah?"

Zoe gave a jaunty wave and took off at a lope, her long legs eating up the ground.

Mara stared after her, feeling like she'd just been run over by a steamroller. She'd never spent a huge amount of time with the Alpha's sister. The woman was a force of nature.

But was she right? Was there something Mara was fighting not to see? Maybe she should delay her trip. Not forever, just long enough to make sure she was doing the right thing. She was so confused right now. She could take a few more weeks, maybe even a month or two, and make sure she was making the right choice. She could make a list, weigh the pros and cons, clarify her thinking.

Maybe Michael would help her make a list...

Low voices penetrated her preoccupation and Mara looked up, taking in her surroundings. She'd stopped in front of Ava and Landon's bungalow. Conversation floated out the window, the low drawl of the Alpha, Ava's distinctive, raspy alto... Then a third voice raised above the other two.

"Hell, Landon, why don't you just give me permission to handcuff Mara to my bed until she sees reason."

Michael.

He was in there. Talking to the Alpha. Behind her back. The betrayal stole her breath.

How dare he meddle in her life? Trying to convince her to change her mind was one thing. Going to the Alpha was something else entirely.

She had trusted him. She hadn't realized how far she'd gone toward thinking of him as her partner, even possibly her future mate, until those arrogant words shattered everything. Handcuff her to the bed, would he? Mara ignored the flicker of interest that slithered beneath her anger. Instead, she nurtured the rage burning hot in her veins.

She stormed up the steps. Michael had no claim on her. She was her own woman, independent. She'd show him. She'd give him so much independence his head would spin.

Chapter Ten

Michael tipped back in his chair and studied the liquor in his glass. He wasn't much of a drinker, and he hadn't had much tonight, but commiserating with Landon, even with Ava there acting as referee and defender of the female gender, had loosened the tension in his shoulders considerably. He felt almost human again.

Until the door slammed open and Mara appeared on the threshold looking like the Queen of the Underworld ready to drag him back to Hell.

"How *dare* you," she shouted, her eyes locked on him as if there was no one else in the world. "I can't believe I was actually starting to trust you. Do you actually expect me to believe you would be a good mate, a partner, if you go behind my back to the Alpha at the first sign of dissent?"

Michael blinked at her, his ability to form words and arguments lost in the face of her stunning rage. He'd never seen Mara so out of control, outside of the bedroom. Part of him wondered if this was a good sign, even as the majority of him tried to play catch-up and figure out what the hell she was so angry about.

"How dare you presume you have some claim over me. I am not a *possession*. You don't own me."

"I never said I owned you." He surged up out of his chair.

Ava and Landon stood by, watching the show in silence.

"No? Then what are you doing here? Why did you come running to the Alpha when I wouldn't give you your way?"

Michael opened his mouth, but Mara didn't give him a

chance to speak.

"Don't bother explaining. Just listen up. This is my life and you are never, *never* going to have any part of it, is that clear?" She didn't wait to hear his answer, spinning on her heel and running out of the bungalow, the door slapping shut behind her.

Ava shifted from one foot to the other. "Michael, I'm so—"

"Don't." Whatever she had to say, he didn't want to hear it. He'd heard more than enough for one night.

What the fuck was that? She stormed in here like a Valkyrie, out for blood, and then ran out. Always running. Always pushing him away with one hand and stringing him along with the other.

She didn't get to do that anymore. He wasn't going to let her. Michael was sick of being teased and toyed with. She wanted it to be over between them? Fine. It was going to be over.

But not until he'd said his piece. She didn't get to blindside him and run away from him this time.

Michael roared, the shift taking his body to lion form with a sudden painful jerk. He lunged forward, his speed fueled by anger as he sprinted into the night. He caught the scent trail of the female and raced down the path after her. She was headed away from the residential compound, into the pasturelands beyond. He didn't care. Wherever she went, he would catch her.

He knew the moment she realized he was following her. He felt the soft *pop* of pressure as she took her own feline form. He poured on the speed, knowing she would be faster and more evasive as a lioness. That knowledge only reinforced his determination to catch her.

She was fast, but he was faster. He could see her ahead of him now, her sleek, sandy form little more than a shadow streaking across the dusty plain. The heady satisfaction of a successful hunt began to pulse through his blood as, with each leaping stride, he grew closer to his prey.

He closed the distance, gauging her speed, and leapt. His paws struck her shoulders. Her feet flew out from under her and they rolled in a flurry of snapping teeth and swiping paws.

149

She snarled and fought like a hellcat, but size and blind rage were both on his side.

He sank his teeth into her scruff, pinning her beneath his bulk. She hissed angrily but stopped struggling, her breath panting out onto the dirt raising puffing dust clouds.

He eased his teeth off her, making sure he kept his weight pressing her into the ground. He shifted back to human form, trusting she would follow suit. If she stayed in feline form, she could easily get away from him, but she must have known he would only shift again and come after her. Michael could keep this up all night.

Mara shifted beneath him. Both of their clothes had been destroyed in the change, so naked flesh pressed warm against naked flesh. Michael's body immediately took notice, but his thoughts were still fogged with anger, not lust. He flipped her onto her back so he could look into her eyes, then pressed his forearm across her shoulders and used his legs to pin hers. She would hear him out. He would make sure of it.

Mara swiped her tongue across her lower lip, her eyes wide but unafraid. "What do you want?" she asked defiantly.

Michael kept his voice low and controlled. He couldn't remember ever feeling so angry, but he didn't want to risk an involuntary shift. He would say his piece, tell her every thought burning through his mind, and then he would walk away.

"I've begged you to say," he said darkly. "I've done everything in my power to prove I deserve you, to be good enough for you. That changes now. I am sick of being treated like a child because I feel things strongly and my lion rides close to the surface. I am more than just my deficiencies. I deserve to be with someone who recognizes that. Someone who respects me in a way you never have."

The last *you* broke something open inside him. Michael growled, staring into the greenish-brown eyes he would have sold his soul to protect only twenty-four hours ago.

"Maybe it's you who doesn't deserve me," he snarled. "Maybe you aren't some poor lonely creature who hasn't been lucky enough to find love, but rather someone who refuses to give any piece of herself to anyone else. Maybe you are the reason you're alone. Incapable of accepting love into your heart.

Always in control. Always *thinking*. Maybe, just maybe, my passion isn't a curse, but something to be admired. Cherished. I would rather break my heart a thousand times than live in the cold, safe bubble you've built for yourself."

The smug hauteur in her eyes had chilled to something harder, but she made no move to push him off or speak.

Weariness weighed on him, that little speech more exhausting than running a marathon. But he wasn't quite done yet. There was one last thing he needed to say.

"Mara, I love you." There was no affection in the words. Just a flat, hard fact. "But if you can't see that I'm worth staying for, I hope you leave tonight. Right this minute. Pack your things and go." Michael swallowed, forcing himself to say the last words. "Do me a favor and never come back."

He rolled away from her, shifting form with the movement and coming to his feet on all fours. He didn't wait to see her reaction.

He'd clung to their relationship so hard for so long and now it was over. The finality of it felt strange, heavy and light at the same time. His chest was tight, his head floating.

Michael spun on his tail and ran. He didn't know where he was going. Anywhere. Away from Mara. Away from the permanence of that last moment. Away from the end of them.

Chapter Eleven

Mara lay on her back long after Michael had disappeared into the night. There were no stars above her, only clouds. That seemed fitting somehow.

She didn't know what had just happened. She'd shouted at Michael and run out on him. He'd chased after her and caught her. She'd been so certain he was going to offer some explanation, beg her to reconsider, do something to convince her to give him another chance, *something*. Instead...

Mara lay, stunned. The things he'd said...

Did she push men away? Hold them at a distance? No one had ever said it might be her fault before.

Why was that? Did they think she was breakable or something? A victim of her own romantic woes? She was an alpha female in a lion pride. She *defined* strength. So why did she have the feeling that the only person who'd ever seen that strength for what it was was Michael.

He had always treated her like an equal, but how had she treated him? Like shit. Like she was too good for him. Just toying with him, using him as a pretty plaything until someone better came along.

An image of Tria flashed in Mara's mind and her stomach rolled. She was worse than Duncan. At least that philanderer had some sort of noble intentions toward Tria. He'd become her mate, the father to her children. Mara had never had honorable intentions toward Michael. She had used him from day one.

He deserved so much better than that.

The clouds opened up above her, the sudden downpour

slicking her skin. Mara took her lioness form and rolled to her feet, shaking out her fur. She moved quickly in the direction Michael had gone, hurrying before the rain could wash away his trail.

He was a passionate lover, an intense listener, and a good friend. He could be so heart-wrenchingly gentle with the cubs, but he would be firm when called on to be. Michael was everything she'd always had on her list, but what's more, he was a thousand things she'd forgotten to put on her list, including the man she loved.

And she had treated him like a cabana boy because of his age.

Mara had to find him. She didn't know what she would say when she did. She wasn't sure there were enough apologies in the world to convince him to forgive her, but she couldn't let things stand the way they were. She had to at least *try* to win him back. For once in her life, she had to throw her heart wide open, expose herself to the possibility of heartbreak and just pray he still loved her enough to let her back in.

Mara tracked Michael's scent in a wide arc around the compound and back to his bungalow, but he wasn't inside. She didn't even need to go up on the porch to know he hadn't stayed there long. A fresh trail led away from the house. Mara chased his scent down another path until it dead ended at the garage.

The Cherokee's spot was empty and fresh tire tracks cut through the mud. Michael had left the ranch.

The Bar Nothing was packed on a Friday night. Mara had to circle the parking lot twice before she found a space to wedge the truck she'd borrowed. She spotted the Cherokee with its distinctive claw marks on her first pass.

Michael was here. Her heart picked up pace to thunder like a jackhammer in her chest.

She'd yanked on a pair of jeans and the first shirt to come to her hand, not caring what she looked like as long as she found him. She buttoned an extra button on the shirt and shoved open the door to the Bar Nothing. The last thing she needed was some overeager asshole with a practiced come-on.

Find Michael. Beg forgiveness. Get out. That was the plan.

She pressed through the mass of bodies crowding the seedy bar. It was apparently prime time to get drunk and rub up against strangers in the hope of getting lucky. She couldn't see three feet in front of her for all the people, but she shoved toward where she remembered the bar being, hoping Michael would be there.

If not for his height, she never would have found him. He had his back to her, those lovely shoulders encased in a tight black T-shirt. Those shoulders stiffened suddenly as she came up behind him. He must have scented her beneath the layers of beer fumes and cowboy sweat.

"Michael." His name was a plea, the opening gambit of her apology. "Michael, I'm so sorry. You were right. About me. I should never have treated you the way I did. You—" Her throat closed off and she cleared it roughly. Why wouldn't he turn around? She needed to see his face. "You deserve better."

He turned and Mara's heart sank. His blue eyes were cold, closed off and angry. "Go away, Mara."

"I'm not leaving," she insisted, standing her ground. She had to make this right. She *had* to. "I love you."

Michael shook his head sadly. "Mara..."

A heavy arm fell across her shoulders, accompanied by the smothering scent of stale beer and horses. "Hey, baby, he don't wanna love you, thas jes fine. You come on over here and love me all you want."

Michael surged up off his barstool faster than thought, snarling viciously in the drunken cowboy's face as his lethal claws snapped out. "Back off, asshole."

A pocket of silence instantly descended around them in the noisy bar. The cowboy staggered backwards, stumbling in his haste, and fell to the floor. More heads turned in their direction. More curious gazes morphing quickly into frozen shock.

"Michael." Adrenaline surged through Mara. There were so many people. *Witnesses.* "Michael, we have to go."

Even over the blaring jukebox, Mara could easily distinguish the much closer sound of a shotgun being primed under the bar. "I'd listen to the lady, if I were you, friend," the bartender said, with lethal calm.

Mara's heart drummed in her ears, unnaturally loud. *This is bad. This is so bad.*

Michael dragged himself under control, his claws snapping back in, but the damage had already been done. Even if no one knew quite *what* they'd seen, this crowd of people had all seen too much.

Mara grabbed his hand. As soon as they took a step toward the door, a path cleared for them, humans sideling out of the way. The Red Sea effect lasted halfway to the door. Far too long for Mara's comfort. She was unspeakably relieved when the people closest to the door—the ones who hadn't seen Michael's magic act—had to be shoved aside.

They burst out into the parking lot, but even there humans surrounded them. Smokers leaning against the building, flirting in the relative quiet.

"Can you drive?" Mara asked urgently. "I brought a truck."

Michael nodded sharply. "I'll walk you to the truck and you can follow me out."

She didn't argue. Part of her kept waiting for that shotgun to chase them into the night. Even in the cab of the truck, zooming down the highway tailing the Cherokee, Mara couldn't relax. She gripped the steering wheel tight to still her adrenaline-fueled shaking.

This was it. What they'd always been afraid of. The humans had *seen* them. Though Michael hadn't gone all the way through the shift. They were just claws. The humans would probably think he was packing weird switchblades or something. Wouldn't they? Special effects, maybe? Some *Wolverine* party trick.

Mara's eyes flicked to the rearview. No taillights in the mirror. No one chasing them.

The humans had all been drunk, right? They'd probably think Michael was on steroids, but that was no reason to call in the National Guard. It would be fine. They'd be fine.

Mara flexed her fingers around the wheel. She wanted Michael here with her so badly it hurt. He was just a few yards ahead in the Cherokee, but she needed his touch. Some instinctive part of her brain insisted everything would be okay as long as she could touch her mate. She *needed* him.

Michael took the turn onto the ranch road and Mara spun the wheel to follow. The rain continued to pour down, even harder than before. The dirt road was a mud pit, but the two vehicles surged through the muck in four-wheel drive.

They were a mile from the main road, but still two miles from the residential compound when the Cherokee suddenly swerved off the road. Mara swore, slamming on the brakes as she saw Michael jump out into the rain. She rammed the gearshift into park and leapt out of the truck, chasing him away from the drive.

"Michael! Michael, wait." He either didn't hear her or didn't care, continuing doggedly into the rain. Mara ran, slipping on the muddy terrain, closing the distance between them.

"I'm sorry!" she shouted. "I don't know what else you want me to say." Her foot slid to the side and she caught herself, slowing now that she was only a few feet from his back. "Michael, *please*. I love you."

He spun abruptly to face her. "After that, you love me?"

Mara stumbled to a stop. She wiped the rain out of her eyes, shoving back her sodden hair. Had he thought she would change her mind? "Yes. After that. After anything."

He nodded, but he didn't step toward her. He didn't yank her into his arms and make the world go away. She craved his touch, but he stood apart, ignoring the rain that drenched them.

"I'm sorry. What else do you want me to say?" There had to be words that would make it right. She couldn't have ruined her chance with her Mr. Forever. She needed him. Mara's tears mingled with the rain on her cheeks.

"Are you still going?" His voice was emotionless, so horribly controlled.

"What?" Mara's heart lurched. Did he want her to go? Was that what he was saying? She swallowed thickly, blinking away rain.

"I need more than *I love you*," he growled. "I can't settle for a stay of execution. You love me, *but*. You love me, but I'll never be good enough for you. You love me, but you're still leaving me, looking for someone better."

Mara rushed forward without conscious thought. "There is no one better than you." She threw herself against him, pressing her face to his chest and wrapping her arms tight around his waist. He didn't hold her, but she didn't let that stop her. Seconds ago, she hadn't been able to find the words, but now she couldn't get them out fast enough. They burst out of her on a tide of uncontrolled emotion. "I need you, Michael. You're my Mr. Forever. I need your passion. You're the only one who's ever made me lose control and we both know I could stand to let my hair down more often." She looked up into his eyes, cupping his jaw in her hand. "You're the bravest man I know. You're never afraid of what you feel or what you want. And the fact that what you feel is always so close to breaking through just makes you more beautiful to me." Her chin trembled, fear and hope and a thousand uncontained feelings making her feel more alive than she'd ever felt before. "I'm staying. Forever, if you'll have me. Will you love me, Michael?"

He searched her eyes and slowly raised one hand to rub his thumb across her jaw.

Was that a yes? *Please God, let it be a yes.*

He bent until his lips hovered right above hers. "I couldn't stop loving you if I tried. You're my heart, Mara. You're the reason I feel."

His mouth closed over hers, perfect, passionate and sweet, and the rest of the world fell away.

He always kissed her with his soul wide open, but her eyes had been closed to the beauty of it until now. He loved her and she loved him right back. That wasn't a new development. She'd been such a fool not to see it before. Love was there in the reverence of his touch. It added an extra light to the fire in his eyes.

But the love hadn't softened the lust. If anything, the bite of it was sharper than ever. His hands were everywhere, molding her damp shirt to her body, but it wasn't enough.

"Clothes..." She panted, tearing at his with eager claws.

"Fuck the clothes. Shift."

157

They both snapped to feline form and back a heartbeat later. They would be exhausted later from all the energy they'd expended jumping from form to form tonight, but in the moment neither of them cared. All that mattered was naked, rain-slicked skin to skin.

They tumbled to the muddy ground and Mara's animal side, so often restrained by logic, roared satisfaction at the primal, natural feel of the earth hard beneath her. Michael rolled onto his back, pulling Mara on top of him. She threw a leg over him and shoved herself up with her hands flat on his shoulders until she was straddling his stomach.

The rain drilled into her skin, chilling and cleansing, wild and fresh. Mara felt like a priestess in an ancient ritual. She'd never felt more powerful than she did in this moment, with her love's impossibly warm hands burning a path across her body, stroking away the rain.

She slid down, impaling herself on him then giving a sinuous roll of her hips. Michael groaned and his hands gripped her waist. She flexed her fingers against his pectoral muscles and executed another slow roll. It was sensual and delicious, but tonight she needed more. She needed what only Michael could give her. He was the love of her life. The only man she'd ever trusted to take her to the edge of control and beyond. She needed him to set her free.

Mara released her claws and lightly scored his chest. Michael growled, his own claws unsheathing in response. When she felt their bite against her skin, Mara smiled. When he tried to push up and roll her beneath him, Mara shoved back, pressing his shoulders down. This time it was her turn to pin him down and drive him wild. She was a priestess tonight and Aphrodite's handmaidens got to be on top.

Mara picked up her pace, taking her cue from the driving force of the rain. Her eyes locked on Michael's. His expression was naked and hungry, and completely open to her. She watched for the signs that he liked that swivel and she ought to repeat that grind just so.

Lightning flashed on the plain, illuminating the stark lines of Michael's face, straining and urgent. Thunder boomed, too close for caution, but Mara didn't care. Lightning couldn't hurt them. They were electricity. Pure, wild heat.

Michael thrust up into her as Mara drove down. Lightning cracked, near enough for Mara to feel the static in the air, its bright striations flashing across the sky. Michael arched beneath her, his muscles straining as he came. Mara watched him in the strobes of light, captivated by the primal beauty of her lover's pleasure, needing nothing more in that moment than his satisfaction.

Then he reached between them and flicked her clit. That was all it took to send her into an explosion of her own.

Michael groaned and made a halfhearted move to get up, but Mara's body draped over his torso kept him down. "We'd better go tell Landon about the shitstorm I've brought down on our heads."

"The humans?" Mara licked the rain off Michael's neck with a slow sweep of her tongue. The storm had passed, leaving only a lingering dampness in the air. "Do you think they know what they saw?"

"Whether they did or not, we have to be ready."

Michael rubbed his hand in a circle against the small of her back, and she closed her eyes to live in the touch. Even the sobering thought of exposure to the human world couldn't completely dampen Mara's spirits. "Will they come after us, do you think?"

Her head was pillowed on his shoulder and she felt him shrug. "I doubt it. It was a bar. People were drinking. By tomorrow they'll all be rationalizing away what they thought they saw."

Mara sat up so she could look into his eyes. The impossibly blue eyes. "How can you be sure?"

His lips curved in a familiar lazy grin, melting her from the inside out. "The Fates must love me," he said. "I've got you."

Epilogue

Dawn was breaking by the time the Three Rocks' Alpha and his mate crawled into bed, after the emergency meeting to discuss the night's developments.

Landon curled around his wife, breathing in her scent. "As glad as I am that your brother has landed his dream girl, it would have been nice if he could have managed it without the public display," he muttered against her skin.

Ava shifted restlessly in his arms. "You don't seem worried."

"No sense borrowing trouble. The humans will come or they won't. Only time will tell." Landon soothed his mate, stroking her hair. "We'll deal with the next crisis as it comes."

For several moments, only soft rustling sounds disturbed the quiet of the Alpha's bungalow. Then, "Do you think they'll be happy, Landon? Michael is so much younger than she is."

A soft growl rumbled in the Alpha's throat. "Is your brother older than you?"

"A year."

"Are you unhappy with your old mate?"

"You aren't old. And you know I couldn't be happier."

"Is your brother fickle?"

"Michael? God, no."

"Then stop worrying about him. If you want to worry about someone, try my sister."

"Zoe?" A soft laugh. "She can take care of herself."

"That's what I'm worried about," the Alpha grumbled.

Silence fell again, broken only by Ava's soft sigh, as both the Alpha of the Three Rocks pride and his mate took a moment to forget their worries. Until the next crisis arose.

Serengeti Sunrise

Dedication

For you, my lovely readers, who ~~nagged me~~ sweetly asked for Zoe's story from the moment she stepped onto the page in *Serengeti Heat*. Thank you for returning to the pride with me.

Chapter One

Zoe King was screwed—in the least fun interpretation of the word.

You break one little rule and it bites you on the ass. Every. Damn. Time.

She glared at the white smoke billowing out from under the jeep's hood. Lately, her luck sucked donkey balls.

So much for her secret, back-before-anyone-knew-she-was-gone trip into town. She hadn't even made it out to the main highway before the jeep decided it would rather be a fog machine.

Stranded on a dusty country road. Zoe King, kickass rockstar goddess of the lioness persuasion, had been reduced to a *Texas Chainsaw Massacre* cliché.

Pathetic.

She could've hoofed it back to the ranch, but she'd still have to explain how the jeep had come to be broken down on the side of the road, four miles outside the property boundaries. Confess later or confess now—at some point there would be shit hitting fans.

Zoe wasn't the kind of girl who put things off. She lived her life by the motto: now or never, preferably *now*.

So she called her brother and admitted she left the ranch without permission. *Permission.* As if she was an infant who couldn't take care of herself. She was a grown woman and a shape-shifter, for Christ's sake. A lioness lived inside her skin and on a good day she could even kick her big brother the almighty Alpha's ass. How much trouble could she possibly get into?

Of course, Landon didn't see it that way. She had to listen to a solid ten minutes of her brother playing Master of the Pride before he finally got tired of bitching her out—or decided he'd have more fun doing it in person—and told her he'd already sent out the cavalry.

And she knew just who he'd sent. Dammit.

Zoe propped a hip against the dented side of the old jeep, folded her arms and tipped her face back to soak in the sun, trying for a Zen state as she waited. The heat crawled over her skin, thick and heavy, but at least it hadn't reached the please-God-kill-me-now levels of midsummer yet. They were still a few months and a dozen degrees shy of that lovely experience.

And, if there was a God, she'd be long gone before the summer heat hit. Off to greener pastures. Independent again. Free.

Of course, she needed more than God. She needed a car that could make it more than four miles from the ranch before breaking down.

Goddamn useless mechanic.

Zoe shifted her weight against the jeep's dented door and closed her eyes. *Think Zen, dammit.*

The heat from the metal bled through her jeans. She didn't have a lot of experience with Zen states, and she had a feeling she was sucking at this one, but luckily she didn't have long to wait.

Zoe barely had time to perfect her I-don't-give-a-shit pose before she heard the distinctive coughing roar of a truck's engine speeding toward her, sounding eerily like the pissed-off lion she knew would be sitting behind the steering wheel. She didn't open her eyes to watch him approach. Her other senses were a fraction sharper with her eyes shut, and she wanted to focus on the little sensory details so she wouldn't think about the asshole bearing down on her in the tow truck.

He already got too many of her stray thoughts as it was.

Gravel scuttled beneath the truck's tires as it pulled off onto the shoulder behind the jeep. Zoe's nose twitched as a whisper of a breeze carried grainy dust particles to tease her nostrils and stick against the sweat-kissed skin of her temples.

The constant dust was just another of the joys of living in west Texas. She couldn't step two feet outside her bungalow without feeling like every inch of her exposed skin had been coated in a fine film of dirt. How Landon could actually like it here, she couldn't imagine.

Well, actually she could imagine. But Landon's affection for Bumfuck Nowhere, West Texas had more to do with his mate Ava's manifest charms than it did any driving need to be bathed in dust on a daily basis. If Zoe had gotten laid *once* over the last goddamn *year*, she might be in a slightly better frame of mind herself. But the pussified lions at the pride wouldn't lay a finger on the Alpha's baby sister. The cowards.

The truck's engine gave one last coughing roar before it cut off abruptly. Zoe held herself perfectly still. *Zen,* she reminded herself as she drank in her surroundings from behind closed eyes.

The groaning squeak of the truck's door opening. The soft scrape of footsteps on gravel. The teasing, musky scent of male lion mingling with engine oil and the dry dusty scent of earth on the breeze. The slam of the truck's door. Then the sound of his voice, the low, rumbling growl coming from deep inside that broad chest.

"What did you do to it?"

Zoe ground her molars. God, he was an ass. Why couldn't she just hate him? It would make things so much easier.

"I didn't *do* anything to it," she snapped, leaving the *asshole* implied. "Other than try to drive it. I had no idea that was such an unreasonable thing to demand from a car."

She tipped her chin down so the wide brim of her cowgirl hat hid her eyes before she opened them. The sight of him hit her in the gut like it always did. And *that* was why she still couldn't seem to hate him. *Goddamn chemistry.*

He strolled past her toward the smoking hood of the jeep with the rolling, liquid gait that would have been equally at home on a cowboy or a cat—which was only fair, since Tyler Minor was a little bit of both. He was tall, as all the Minor brothers were tall. Corded with muscle, as all the Minor men were strapped. But he was the only one of the Big Bad Minor

167

Foursome who'd ever made her heart gallop just by walking into a room.

Tyler had presence, that indefinable awareness of a man who knew he was the ruler of all he saw. It was the unmistakable aura of an Alpha—but Tyler had never been, nor did he appear to ever want to be, the Alpha of the pride. Instead her lummox of a big brother got to boss everyone around while Tyler watched it all with stoic eyes.

And while he watched her with barely banked heat.

Tyler Minor had been watching Zoe, owning her with his damn eyes, since the day she arrived at Three Rocks Ranch over a year ago. The heat behind the liquid gold of his gaze never failed to call up an answering spark low in her belly. He could make her wet with just a look—and as keen as his sense of smell was, the bastard had to know it—but he'd never once acted on the lust burning behind his eyes.

She knew he wanted her. She *knew* it. But he never *touched* her. Just looking. Always looking. Stepping back when she stepped forward. Circling around and dodging her every advance. He would look at her with naked hunger and then just shut it off and walk away. Running hot and cold until she wanted to scream at him to just fuck her already.

It was almost enough to give a girl self-esteem issues.

If anyone else had ever managed to make her half as hot and bothered without so much as a touch, she'd have written off Tyler Minor months ago. But no one else got under her skin and made her writhe the way he did. She couldn't control or contain it. Like the motion of the planets, it just was and there wasn't a damn thing she could do about it.

Damn the man for being the sexiest hunk of masculinity— shifter or human—she'd ever laid eyes on. He practically projected a field of testosterone. And damn if that didn't turn her crank in a big way, though she'd chew off her own tongue before admitting it to him. Even if he could probably smell it on her.

Tyler propped open the hood and bent to poke at something inside. Zoe's eyes locked on the faded denim stretched lovingly over his ass. She licked her lips and wandered over to stand behind him for a better angle on her favorite body part.

"You shouldn't have left the ranch unescorted," he said without taking his eyes off the engine. "You know how things are right now."

Things was a nice way of referring to the epic shitstorm at the pride lately, but Zoe didn't particularly want to talk about the fact that she'd broken The Rule and left without permission. "What are you, my keeper?"

"Honey, you couldn't pay me enough to take that job." Still bent to show off his best side, he flicked a look at her beneath the arm he'd propped against the hood above him.

It was *that* look. The one that made her breath come faster, her heartbeat picking up in a helpless response only this imbecile seemed to inspire. She took half a step forward.

Then his eyes dismissed her, locking back on the engine block. "I'm just here for the car."

Zoe's temper flared like a sparkler on the Fourth of July. Damn but she hated it when he ignored her. Almost as much as she hated it when he made her want him with a look.

She needed a reaction—*any* reaction—to prove she owned him as much as he owned her.

"Anyone ever tell you you're a shitty mechanic?"

"Only you," he grunted. "Repeatedly."

"Well, it bears repeating. Cars are supposed to run. FYI."

Tyler growled without looking up from the engine. "*This* car wasn't supposed to be taken off the ranch until I replaced the radiator. That's why the keys were in my *office* and not hanging on the board with the others."

Zoe shrugged, unrepentant. "Landon padlocked the board. You didn't lock your office."

"A mistake I won't be repeating."

"A smart man would leave a set of keys out so I wouldn't have to break into his office to get them. Or try to teach myself how to hotwire a car on one of his precious jeeps."

"A smart woman would listen to her damn Alpha and stay the hell on the ranch like everyone else until things calm down in town."

Zoe smiled sweetly. "Then I guess neither of us has much in the way of intelligence."

He twisted, his eyes locking on her again. There was a subtle threat in that look, filled with his need to dominate her. Her heart rate accelerated.

"There's a reason none of us are supposed to leave the ranch right now, Zoe. It isn't just your own life you're risking with your recklessness." The muscles in his neck were corded with anger—which, perversely, just made her want to lick them.

Which, even more perversely, made her want to punch him. The constant compulsion to push him until he pushed back couldn't be healthy, but she needed to break through his reserve and feel the reckless heat beneath that calm, controlled surface like she needed to keep breathing. It wasn't even conscious anymore—fighting with him, goading him. It had passed habit and become reflex.

"It wasn't *my* recklessness that got us into this position in the first place," she countered. "I believe that was *your* baby brother and his floor show at the Bar Nothing."

A muscle jumped in his jaw as his gaze retreated back to the engine. "Michael's apologized for that."

"Aw, that's sweet. But maybe Michael shouldn't have gone into a bar and half-shifted in front of two dozen humans in the first place."

The muscles in his shoulders tensed, and Zoe felt a dim flicker of guilt. Tyler's family was his only weak spot—a weak spot she'd been poking at ever since she discovered it. Never let it be said that Zoe King didn't fight dirty.

She wasn't even really annoyed with Michael. Yes, he'd fucked up by showing too much of his animal side in a human bar, but it hadn't been on purpose and as yet the world hadn't come crashing down around their ears.

In fact, not a damn thing had happened.

It had been over a month. A month of battening down the hatches and bracing for the worst. A month of waiting to see if the humans had seen enough to call in the media and the scientists—the media to turn them into a freak show and the scientists to turn them into lab rats.

Humans didn't tend to react well to things that were different and a bunch of men, women and children who could shapeshift into giant predators at will definitely fell into the *different* category.

Zoe was inclined to give their homo sapiens cousins the benefit of the doubt—there hadn't been a witch burning in centuries—but she was in the minority at the pride. The fear of what *might* be done to them if their secret was exposed, as well as the tradition of zealous secrecy, had kept the scattered shifter prides and packs all over the world from revealing themselves to the humans long ago.

When Michael inadvertently let the cat out of the bag—so to speak—Zoe had momentarily thought Landon, her forward-thinking brother, would take the opportunity to come out to the humans. Instead, he'd called in all their nomads and strays, commanded everyone to stay on the ranch indefinitely, and held his breath, waiting for the humans to lay siege.

And nothing had happened.

Tensions had been at DEFCON One for weeks now. After a month of isolating a bunch of cranky lions on the ranch, Zoe wasn't the only one going stir crazy. She was just the only one fearless—or, as Tyler accused, reckless—enough to break the rules.

"I don't see what difference it makes if I go into town to buy tic tacs. What are they going to do? Stone me in the Stop 'N' Shop?"

Tyler straightened suddenly, turning his back on the jeep and facing her, his gold eyes blazing. "Tell me you weren't going to put us all at risk for some *tic tacs*," he demanded. "You aren't that stupid."

Zoe's hackles went up at his icy growl, even as a thrill of victory shot down to her core now that she had Tyler's undivided attention. She dug in her heels as he prowled toward her, holding her ground. Excitement sizzled in her blood, but she rolled her eyes, feigning scorn and an indifference she'd never felt around him.

"I wasn't actually going to buy tic tacs. I was just going to roll into town and see if there was anyone suspicious hanging around. Do some reconnaissance. I'm sick of waiting for the bad guys to strike without even knowing if there are bad guys in the first place."

His golden eyes darkened. "We're being cautious."

"We're being ostriches," she snapped. "It's idiotic. And I for one am sick of being afraid of my shadow. I want to see if the Big Bad Wolf is actually in town before I hide inside my straw house and wait for him to huff and puff at me."

"There's been an increase of trespassers."

"High school kids. Pranks. It's the end of the school year. Has anyone gotten anywhere near the main buildings? No. And even if it is the boogeyman, don't you want to know what he looks like?"

Tyler stopped advancing. He rocked back on his heels, the heat in his eyes cooling. "Huh."

How did he do that? Just shut off all that gorgeous fury from one second to the next. *Why* did he do it, dammit? Zoe narrowed her eyes at him and planted her hands on her hips. "Huh what? What does *huh* mean?"

"You have a point. We should know what's going on in town. Just hiding out isn't going to keep us safe." Then his eyes darkened again. "But you should have told Landon what you were up to. What if something happened to you and no one knew where you'd gone?"

Zoe pursed her lips. "If I told Landon I wanted to check out the town, he would have sent you or Caleb instead. I brought my phone in case I ran into any trouble." She pulled the cell out of her pocket and waved it in front of him. "And even if I did run into trouble, I'm not helpless. I can take care of myself."

He arched an eyebrow toward the broken-down jeep. Damn supercilious bastard.

Zoe glared. "Just because I can't repair a busted radiator doesn't mean I'm a damsel in distress. I could kick your ass any day of the week, Tyler Minor." She put a rumble of a growl into the words, a challenge for supremacy and dominance. *Just try to take me on, big boy.*

The challenge caught something primitive and instinctive inside him. He stepped forward, looming over her, trying to use his size to intimidate her. At five ten in her bare feet, Zoe wasn't the kind of girl who was easy to loom over, but when a man could manage it, it never failed to make her toes curl.

Tyler didn't just manage it. Tyler loomed like an angry Greek god. Mouthwatering and imposing all at once.

His eyes held hers and her heart began to pound. *Do it. Push back. Touch me.* Zoe swayed forward.

And Tyler shut off.

Just like that. Between one heartbeat and the next, Tyler went from looming Greek god to aloof and disinterested. His gaze slid away from her, focusing on some vague point behind her left shoulder for a moment before he turned away.

"Wait over there until I have the jeep on the hitch." He pointed to a dusty patch of grass off the side of the road without looking back at her or breaking stride as he walked back to the tow truck.

Frustration built in her throat, but she managed to keep from screaming. Or roaring her rage. She'd had a lot of practice.

Running away again. In the last year, Zoe had seen Tyler in retreat more than any other sight. Her gaze rolled over the tense muscles in his wide shoulders down to the lean hips and that God-almighty-gorgeous ass. She couldn't seem to stop scaring him off, which sucked a little more every day.

But at least the view was nice.

Chapter Two

Tyler beat a strategic retreat back to his truck. Backing down wasn't in his nature, but it was becoming a habit around Zoe. It was either that or pin her against the jeep and show her who was boss. Kiss her until she couldn't remember her own name, screw her until all she could say was his—which was completely out of the question. The Alpha's only sister was not someone you fucked around with, and the absolute last thing Tyler needed right now was another commitment, another goddamn responsibility.

So he walked away. Every. Single. Fucking. Time.

Because it was the smart choice. The responsible choice. The only choice that wouldn't completely fuck up the rest of his life.

He just had to remind himself of that whenever she was standing there in front of him with her eyes flashing with equal parts lust and anger. She looked like a walking invitation to all his best fantasies, but she might as well have had a neon flashing *Hands Off* sign on her forehead.

So Tyler kept his hands off and focused on the parts of his life he could get a grip on. Cars. Engines never made him feel like he'd jumped off a cliff without a parachute.

He drove the tow truck in front of the dead jeep and jumped out to winch it up onto the flatbed. He could feel Zoe watching him. No surprise there. He could never be around her without being excruciatingly aware of her presence. He couldn't control that, but he could control his response to her. So he didn't respond. He ignored her—as much as anyone could ignore someone who smelled like heaven on a stick—and put his back into cranking the old-fashioned flatbed down at an angle so he could drag the jeep up onto it.

But Zoe, being Zoe, couldn't let herself be ignored for long.

"You know, they have these new handy-dandy mechanical thingies. You just hit a button and zip." She snapped her fingers. "It tilts like magic."

"This one works fine." He grunted, leaning his weight into it.

She muttered something that sounded a lot like "ornery son of a bitch" and scuffed her boot in the dirt, kicking up a mini-tornado.

He didn't bother to explain that he would rather put in the effort to keep up something with some history behind it working than buy a brand-new piece of crap that was just going to be outdated in a few weeks anyway. Too many things worth keeping got discarded when something bright and shiny and new came along. He enjoyed babying the old jeeps on the ranch until they purred for him.

But if Zoe thought he was a contrary SOB, that was simpler for both of them, so he let her think it. She paced restlessly at his side and he pretended not to notice the way the tip of her long blonde ponytail flicked against the small of her back with each step, guiding his eye down to the twitch of her ass.

"You really aren't pissed at Michael? Not even a little?"

Tyler forced himself not to react visibly. *Pissed* couldn't hold a candle to what he'd felt when Michael told him about going half-furry in public.

After twenty years of being the responsible older brother, raising his siblings, living his life for their happiness and their safety, avoiding unnecessary chances and sacrificing his own opportunities so they would have more...after twenty goddamn years, Tyler had been a heartbeat away from seeing all four of them settled—happy and safe. A whisper away from leaving the pride and taking off on his own—who knew for how long, but any time he had would be his and his alone. No responsibilities. No obligations. Responsible for no one's happiness but his own.

Then Michael half-shifted in front of a bar full of witnesses.

Tyler had tried rationalization. Everyone was drunk on a Friday night—they wouldn't know what they'd seen. He hadn't fully shifted—lots of special-effects guys could make claws and fur seem to sprout on people's hands, and who didn't have a pair of fake fangs these days?

But no matter how he tried to rationalize it, the truth remained. The pride was at risk. And Tyler couldn't leave his siblings—the only family he had left—until he knew they would all be safe.

So he was trapped. Again.

To say he'd been pissed at Michael... It was more accurate to say he'd wanted to shred his baby brother's hide.

But there was no way in hell he was telling Zoe that.

Trust her to ask what everyone else was too tactful to say. Trust Zoe to shove her nose in where it had no business. The woman had no goddamn sense of boundaries whatsoever.

His anger with Michael was none of her business. It didn't affect her or the pride or anyone other than himself. The pointless frustration boiled in his gut, but he refused to give it an outlet. He was a lion, not a goddamn dog. He didn't howl at the moon over what might have been.

Life was one shitstorm after another, but there was no changing it, so you sucked it up and played the hand you got dealt with a fucking smile on your face.

Tyler kept his hands working steadily and didn't so much as flinch when her question prodded the embers of frustration burning in his gut. "No," he said flatly, working the winch up higher.

She inched closer, hovering right over his shoulder. "It was gonna come out eventually anyway, right?" She swayed from foot to foot, the constant motion tugging at his peripheral vision as he locked the jeep in place and cranked the flatbed level. "If not Michael, someone else would have been seen. And it's not like he could help it. And who knows, it might be a good thing in the long run, right? If we weren't trying to hide what we are from doctors and scientists, they might be able to help fix whatever imbalance keeps Michael from being able to control his shifting. Landon needs to get his head out of his ass and treat this like the opportunity it is."

Tyler grunted and steered her toward the cab of the truck, careful not to touch her. Platonic touch was traded casually in the pride, but he always avoided putting his hands on Zoe, never entirely certain he would be able to get them off her again if he gave in to the temptation of her smooth, golden skin.

"He picked a hell of a time to go all barbarian traditional Alpha," Zoe grumbled. "Right now is when we need to be taking action, framing the way our debut into the world is going to go. Not hiding out and bracing for the worst."

She bounced into the cab, so caught up in her complaints she didn't seem aware of what her body was doing. Tyler was aware enough for the both of them. He watched her ass in the tight jeans, the movement of her full breasts beneath the too-thin T-shirt. His mouth watered and his palms itched, but he just slammed the passenger door and rounded the hood.

As soon as he opened the driver's door, Zoe started in again. "You could talk to him. He listens to you. If you told him—"

"Not my call," he said shortly, cutting her off before she could get going. "Alpha's decision."

Zoe snorted. "Oh please. That isn't you."

Tyler ignored her, cranking the key until the truck's engine sprang to life with a jagged roar. He shoved the truck into gear and pulled out onto the deserted country road, headed back toward the ranch.

"Caleb is the soldier in your family," Zoe continued. "You're the thinker."

"I'm the mechanic."

Zoe twisted toward him and he tried not to notice the way her legs draped over the bench seat between them, her knee brushing the outside of his thigh through two layers of denim. "You analyze everything," Zoe insisted.

He couldn't argue that. Right now he was analyzing exactly how long it would take him to get her jeans down around her ankles and her knees over his shoulders if he pulled the truck off to the side of the road. Twenty, maybe thirty seconds. That big-ass silver belt buckle she'd taken to wearing lately might slow him down some.

"You have opinions about everything. Typical alpha I-know-best-and-you-must-obey bullshit, even if you shove it all down and try to pretend it isn't there. I bet you always get your way, right?"

Only rigid control kept Tyler from laughing out loud at that. He always got his own way, did he? Whoever Zoe thought she was talking about, it sure as hell wasn't him. He couldn't remember the last time he'd done anything just for himself.

"You're more manipulative than the other he-man lions in the pride though. I bet you're the one who taught Ava everything she knows about diplomacy."

"Something you never learned, apparently."

Zoe's soft laughter rippled out to fill the cab. Not the reaction he'd expected, but Zoe rarely conformed to expectations. The brim of her cowboy hat knocked against the window, tipping it back so he had a better view of her face and the easy warmth of her smile. A knot tightened low in his gut.

"I never did see much point in tact." She linked her fingers over the knee wedged against his thigh, the backs of her fingers pressing into his leg. His jeans suddenly felt tight, but he couldn't remove her hand without acknowledging her touch affected him, so he tightened his hands on the steering wheel, keeping his eyes locked on the road ahead.

"What I don't get is why *you* need to be Mr. Diplomacy. Ava, I get. She's tiny and that's like tattooing *kick me* on your forehead in the prides. But you're one of the biggest shifters I've ever seen. Why weren't you the Alpha before Landon and I showed up? Are you just a really crappy fighter or something?"

His lion sent a growl rumbling out of his throat at the insult before he could swallow it down.

Zoe chuckled and her fingers uncurled to pet his thigh. "Down, boy."

He wanted her hands on him, petting, stroking. Just a little higher. Her skin would be soft, her hands firm and capable. Stroking him from base to tip, wringing need from him in juicy drops...

Tyler grabbed her hand off his leg and flicked it away from him before he gave in to the urge to grind himself against her. "Not everyone wants to rule the world." His voice sounded odd— too rough and low.

She folded her arms across her stomach, tucking her knees in so they no longer pressed against him. He didn't suspect for a second he'd hurt her feelings with the rebuff. With Zoe, a strategic retreat was much more likely. Feint and parry. Retreat and advance. A constant campaign to test for weaknesses in his defenses.

She tipped her head and the cowboy hat slid back farther. "I get that you aren't power crazy, but my impression is that pride life was pretty much hell under Leonus. I'm surprised you wouldn't take him out just to improve living conditions. Seems like that kind of noble shit would be right up your alley."

He could have explained. He could have told her that he was Alpha of his own pride: Caleb, Kane, Michael and Ava. Protecting his younger siblings had been his top priority since his father left. Being Alpha of Three Rocks would have made him responsible for ten times as many lions. He couldn't care for that many and still look after his four the way he needed to, so he had ruthlessly suppressed his frustration at the way the pride was run under Leonus. His family came first. Always.

"I never claimed to be noble."

Zoe hummed her agreement. "Tricky thing, nobility. The more claims you make to it, the less you have."

"So I must be noble because I told you I'm not?"

She shook her head and the cowboy hat gave up the fight, tumbling down over her shoulder. She caught it one-handed and tucked it into her lap, running her long, slim fingers over the brim. "It doesn't work in reverse," she explained. "But if you'd said you were noble, I'd have known you were full of shit. Denial is a good sign."

He flicked her a glance out of the corner of his eye and had trouble looking away. They were on the ranch drive now, so he didn't really need to pay much attention to the road, but looking at it was safer than watching her. Zoe King was a hazard to his senses.

Curled in the passenger seat like the cat she was, her

179

green-gold eyes never wavered from him as her fingers stroked patterns in the hat, teasing him with thoughts of those same fingers branding patterns into his skin with a touch.

God, she was gorgeous. Tall and strong like a Viking goddess, with curves just where he wanted them. Her face was so actively expressive it was easy to miss the sheer beauty of it—the high cheekbones and lush, inviting fullness of her mouth. Tyler often found himself captivated by her constantly changing expressions. He could sit and watch her for hours, sucked in by the way each thought and emotion tracked across her face.

He yanked his gaze away and locked it back on the road.

She was quicksand. She'd suck him in and trap him here so he'd never be free. He just needed to keep reminding himself of that.

"Don't worry. I don't expect you to be gallant and noble." Her voice was low and smooth, a purring invitation to sin. "Virtue is so overrated. I like my knights rough with their armor a little tarnished around the edges."

The scent of her twined around him in the cab, the tang of ginger mixed with something dark and rich. Tyler rolled down the window, taking a deep breath of the dry, dusty air in an attempt to get some more blood flowing to his brain instead of diverting to his crotch.

Her knees inched closer again, brushing against the side of his leg. With every bounce along the rutted dirt drive, she edged toward him. If not for the seat belt keeping her back, she probably would have crawled onto his lap. Tyler's brain began to melt at the thought of her straddling his lap, her lush curves rising above him.

Zoe'd never made any secret of the fact that she wanted him—she wasn't exactly the coy type—but he'd ignored every hint and passed up every not-so-subtle invitation. If he acknowledged that she wanted him, if he gave her any clue that it was the thought of her he jacked off to in the shower every night, she would never give up.

And he needed her to give up. He couldn't take much more temptation from Zoe King.

He didn't need another rock tying him to the ranch. He'd

played Atlas too long to want to shoulder any more responsibilities. And Zoe would be a massive weight on his life if he let her in.

You didn't jilt the Alpha's sister. Especially when the Alpha was married to your own sister. If Zoe got her hooks into him, Tyler would stay here, trapped on the ranch. Forever.

Shit, if Zoe got her hooks in him, he might not even mind the life sentence.

"Tyler?" Her voice was a throaty rasp that did nothing for his calm.

He realized his knuckles had gone white from his grip on the steering wheel and forced them to loosen as he drove the truck through the main gates and toward the garage.

The ranch had gone through several incarnations before it had ended up as the headquarters for the largest shape-shifter pride in West Texas. Since its first life as a summer bible camp, it had undergone substantial changes, but the clusters of cabins surrounding the communal dining hall had suited the lions perfectly. Another previous owner had added the requisite outbuildings and fencing to turn it into a cattle ranch—though the Three Rocks pride owned just enough cattle to provide their own game on the traditional semi-annual hunts.

With the addition of their own schoolhouse, medical clinic, his garage and a massive greenhouse, they'd done what they could to become their own community, independent of the outside world. Everyone contributed in the pride. Many of their members had telecommuted or worked in town to bring in additional cash, but most of those with jobs in town had lost them in the last month.

In spite of the unwritten rule that everyone work for the good of the pride, the pace of life was slower here. Like their feline cousins, the lion-shifters were sensualists who valued their indulgences and relaxation with a European appreciation. They felt safe enough to reveal their true natures here—in spite of the concerns about the town.

This afternoon was no exception, perfect for a hammock and a cold beer. Shifters basked in the sun in both lion form and human.

And Tyler didn't see any of it. Zoe consumed every one of

his senses as he threaded the tow truck along the service road that twisted through the maintenance buildings, toward his garage.

The cab had begun to feel like a cage. His lion chafed at the restriction, pressing against the inside of his skin.

God, the scent of her. It was killing him. How could she tease him to a frenzy with just a brush of her leg and the heady intoxication of her scent?

"Are you in heat?" His voice lashed across the cab, whip-crack sharp.

The unmated pride females were tucked away during their heat for a damn good reason. The scent of them made the males crazed with lust. It was chemical, uncontrollable. A biological imperative for a sexual marathon. He was hard to the point of pain, but it wasn't his fault. She had to be in heat. There was no other explanation.

Zoe made a small choked sound in her throat. It was her uncharacteristic lack of a response that lured his eyes from the road. Her constantly changing expression had stilled, her body tense and motionless. "You can't tell the difference," she whispered, almost to herself.

Too late Tyler realized what he'd just disclosed if she *wasn't* in heat. *Shit.* He'd just admitted she drove him wild. He might as well have told her he wanted to fuck her until she couldn't stand. Which, God help him, he did.

A year of denying himself. A year of unrelenting sacrifice. A year of keeping his damn hands to himself to convince her he didn't want her and he'd just ruined it in one fell swoop.

Give her an inch and she'll take your whole life. He felt like he was trying to put the sand back into a shattered hourglass—like every grain was a piece of his freedom he'd never get back.

"The way you're acting. It's like you're in heat," he said in a fast, desperate attempt to repair the damage.

One of Zoe's brows slid up toward her hairline. "What gave me away? Was it the striptease while you were hooking the car to the tow hitch or my attempts to give you a blowjob while you drove?"

His jean tightened like a vise in Pavlovian response as her

lips formed the words *blowjob* and *striptease*. Tyler winced, drowning in lust and a sensation that wasn't unlike blind panic. His brain was short-circuiting, but he just needed to focus on the task at hand. Turn Zoe over to her brother. End of story.

His judgment was in shreds. He couldn't be alone with her right now.

And he sure as hell couldn't tell her he'd gone hard from just the scent of her and her knee bumping his thigh. It had happened only because he'd been living like a goddamn monk for the last few months, and he'd be damned before he defended himself to her. Zoe might be able to talk circles around him, but he could control the silence.

He'd built a stable environment for his siblings growing up, even when things were shitty and chaotic in the pride, and he did it by always keeping a level head. Always rising above attempts to bait him, always pushing down his own desires for the good of his family. Restraint, control, sacrifice. He'd lived those words until they'd become who he was.

What was it about Zoe that threatened all that?

He spun the wheel, pulling the truck around behind his garage and slamming it into park.

"Tyler—"

"The Alpha's expecting us." He cut her off, killing the engine and jerking the key free of the ignition. He was out of the car and halfway to the back door of the garage before the truck's engine stopped wheezing and rattling.

Tyler didn't wait to see if she was following. He didn't need to. Zoe wouldn't give up so easily. She didn't know how.

Zoe King, gorgeous and unstoppable. His own personal silver bullet.

Chapter Three

Bastard. Tyler was six feet away, the cab still shuddering from the slam of the door, when all of Zoe's year-long frustration crashed over her like a wave.

No way. He was *not* walking away from her. Not this time.

Zoe had wanted Tyler from the first second she'd laid eyes on him and when she wanted something, she went after it with everything she had. So there was no reason why she shouldn't have him by now.

The entire drive back to the ranch she'd been tempted to crawl into his lap. The urge to break through his reserve and stir up the banked heat beneath taunted her. When he'd asked if she was in heat, it had spun her world like a top. It was all the proof she needed. Tyler Minor wanted her. Unequivocal, no two ways about it, sweet, hot *lust.*

And she'd hesitated. For a nanosecond there in the cab, for the first time in her life, nervous uncertainty had spiraled through her chest. And he just left. When the creaking slam of the car door jolted her, the uncertainty flashed into hurt and quickly twisted into its cousin, anger.

This wasn't over. He didn't get to just pretend nothing had happened. Not today.

Zoe launched herself out of the truck. "Tyler!" His only response was the clang of the heavy metal door to the garage slamming behind him after he ducked inside. "*Dammit.*" She stalked after him. Cutting through the garage was the fastest way to the main part of the compound, but they weren't finished here yet and she was going to make sure he knew it.

She ran to the door, jerked it open and surged through, carried on a tide of indignant frustration.

"Tyler!" Her shout echoed in the garage bay along with the ringing clang of the heavy door banging shut behind her. "Stop running and face me, you coward!"

Two yards from the front exit, Tyler's feet took root on the concrete floor. She could hear a growl rumbling in his chest. His lion must not have liked being called a coward. Well, hers didn't much like him running away from her.

Her lioness was ready for this fight, had been itching for it for months.

He turned to face her, his eyes narrowed and hands loose around his hips like a gunslinger. As they faced one another across the length of the garage, she felt that high-noon feeling herself. Tension snapped in the air, the unavoidable sense that *something* was coming. Something that had been bearing down on them for a while now.

Love or war. Whichever it was, there wasn't any middle ground left. They'd burned it all away with the friction of the last year.

"Coward?" he asked, his voice a soft, dark rumble.

"You have another word you'd prefer?" She strolled across the concrete floor, adding an extra sway to her hips as she came to stand directly in front of him. "Chicken? Pussy, perhaps?"

"Don't push me, Zoe." He rumbled the warning.

"Or what? You gonna show me who's boss? Or are you just gonna run away like you always do? Like a coward."

His lips pulled back from his teeth in a snarl and he loomed over her. She could practically feel his lion pushing against his skin, burning with the need to prove to her, once and for all, which one of them would end up on top if it ever came down to a battle for dominance. He might play at being civilized, but Tyler wanted to make her submit. She could see it in the luminous feline gold of his eyes.

"Are you going to kiss me or throttle me?" Zoe tipped her chin back, meeting his eyes with a blatant challenge. "Whichever you're going to do, do it now. Because I'm sick of waiting for you to make up your mind."

"What makes you think I didn't make up my mind months ago and you just can't take a hint?"

"What hint was that? The way you stare at me when you think I'm not looking? How you take the longest possible path between your bungalow and the garage each evening just so you can go past my house? Or maybe the fact that you can't tell when I'm in heat because you *always* want me?"

He turned away, striding toward the door. "That's quite a healthy ego you have there."

"It's all in my head, is that it?" He put his hand on the door and Zoe felt her composure fracture. "Dammit, Tyler! What the fuck is your deal?" He didn't turn back to her, but he didn't open the door either. She shouted at his back. "You want me. I've made it embarrassingly obvious I want you too. So what is the big problem?"

"Your brother..."

"I'm twenty-seven years old. I don't have to ask his permission to fuck whoever the hell I want."

He turned, leaning his shoulders against the door, one hand still resting on the knob. "He's the Alpha—"

"So what? This has nothing to do with him. He doesn't even have to know."

"He'll know."

"Who the fuck cares? Because I'm the Alpha's sister, I'm not allowed to get any?"

"I don't want any more commitments in my life. I'm sick of being responsible for everyone."

"Who's talking about a commitment? I'm talking about *sex*. Fucking. Screwing. Banging our brains out. No strings attached. I never *asked* you for a fucking commitment, dumbass."

"It's never going to be no strings. Not with the Alpha's sister."

"God, I am so sick of being the Alpha's sister. I'm *Zoe*. Can we just have one conversation that doesn't include Landon?"

Tyler thunked his head back against the door. "Look, Zoe, if I wanted to stay here at the pride for the rest of my life and mate with a little lioness who'd give me lots of fat babies, you'd be the first person I'd—"

She cut him off with a solid punch to his shoulder that made him wince. "You *asshole*. Would you listen to me for five seconds? *I don't want to marry you.* I'm not Mara the fucking baby-making machine. If you tried to give me a picket fence, I would rip up the posts and shove them up your ass. So stop trying to put me in that box." She slapped her palms flat on his chest, baring her teeth up at him. "I want sex. And I want it from you. So do you want me or not? Because I'm done waiting. We're deciding this, once and for all. Are you a man or what? Because for someone with the teeth of an alpha lion, you're awfully fucking scared of me."

He grabbed her so fast her back was slamming against the door before she even realized his hands were on her waist. Her hat went flying, landing somewhere on the dirty floor. "Scared, am I?" He gripped her jaw and forced her face up to his. "Does this look like fear to you?"

His expression was harsh and unforgiving, the animal running close to the surface. There was nothing contained or distant about the heat in his eyes. *Who is this man and what has he done with Tyler Minor?* Zoe's breathing quickened.

His claws flexed against her side. Zoe wet her lips. She'd goaded him to this.

A little flicker of misgiving flared in her chest.

"Hasn't anyone told you not to bait lions?" he growled, palming her nape.

Zoe's heart stopped then restarted and accelerated. The nervous sensation got lost in a flood of heat as he took command. *Finally.* This was it. After a year of foreplay, it was finally happening. Quick, rough, one and done. At last, she'd get over this stupid obsession.

Tyler Minor had her pinned between hard and harder, leaving no doubt in her mind exactly how much he wanted her. Then he leaned in and sealed his mouth over hers, and Zoe forgot everything but the taste of him. This wasn't just a quickie to get him out of her system. This was *everything*.

He hadn't expected her to taste so good.

The tang of her went straight to his brain and shut it down. He didn't need it anyway—for the first time in his life, pure animal instinct took control. His lion clamored to claim her completely. After a year of buildup, he craved her, needing nothing more than to dive in and drown in her.

Zoe made a jagged, needy sound and stabbed her fingers through his hair, tilting her head to invite him deeper. She hooked her legs around his waist and he stepped closer, notching his hardness at the apex of her thighs, crushing her against the door. She clutched his shoulders, purring throatily, and Tyler realized, with the distant part of his brain that was still running on auxiliary power, that Zoe wasn't going to stop him.

Dimly, he recalled his master plan. Something about teaching her not to tease him? But this wasn't a tease. This was a full-body erotic invitation.

Tyler caught her ponytail in his fist, holding her steady as he devoured her mouth. Her scent swamped him, clouding his senses until he felt savage, feeling nothing more keenly than the throbbing need to make her submit. Where was his famous self-control?

He shoved her thin T-shirt up above her breasts, barely managing to keep from shredding it with his claws. She released him long enough to yank the shirt over her head and fling it aside, then her hands were fumbling with the buttons of his shirt, her own claws extending and retracting.

Tyler reached over his shoulder with one hand, the other palming her ass. He grabbed a fistful of fabric and jerked the shirt off over his head, sending a couple buttons plinging against the concrete. Zoe made a hungry sound and her hands stroked his chest, petting and kneading until he leaned into her and she had to move them or get them caught between their bodies. The feel of her, pressed hot against his skin, was sheer perfection. He ground his erection into her heat and she cried out as the friction hit her clit, her green-gold eyes dark with need.

Zoe clutched his shoulders, moaning, "*More*," against the shell of his ear.

Didn't that just figure? He owned her body right now and she was still making demands. The woman just didn't know how to stop pushing.

Luckily, he was inclined to give her what she wanted.

He held her steady with a hand on her ass and ground into her again, gently biting the curve of her shoulder as his other hand slid up her side to cup the fullness of her breast. Her strong thighs squeezed his hips as her own began to move against him. She moaned his name, then whispered it brokenly, repeating it until it became a mantra, a rhythmic plea and exultation rolled into one.

Tyler fumbled with her belt, cursing softly, until Zoe shoved his hands aside and unfastened it with quick, deft fingers. He had no trouble with the row of buttons on her fly, flicking them loose and sliding his hand inside beneath the thin silky scrap of her panties.

At the first brush of his middle finger on her clit, Zoe's back arched and a jagged cry ripped from her throat, her head thrown back as an orgasm shuddered through her body. Tyler continued to work the tiny bud, rubbing his finger in a fast, tight circle until she went off again in his arms. He stroked lower, thrusting a single finger into her moist channel and curling it inside her. She was so hot. Wet and tight. The way her inner muscles clenched around his finger, she'd feel like a fucking fist gripping his cock. His vision nearly went black with the thought.

He needed to get inside her. Now.

She rode his hand, panting his name, as Tyler struggled to unzip his jeans over his aching erection one-handed without success. Realizing that wasn't going to happen, and Zoe was too close to climax to be any help, Tyler gave up on his jeans for the moment and pulled down the cup of Zoe's bra, cradling the weight of her breast in his palm and plucking the tight bud of her nipple. Zoe catapulted into another orgasm with a shattered cry, and he eased his finger from her sheath, determined to get them both out of their clothes while she was enjoying a little afterglow.

"Tyler? You in there?"

Tyler froze with his hand down the front of Zoe's jeans at

the sound of his brother's voice on the other side of the door. He cursed low as Zoe's eyes met his, a spark of amusement kindling in hers. She bit her lip, a smile fighting its way past her attempts to keep a straight face. Of course *she* would think this was funny. She wasn't the one about to break the world record for bluest balls.

"Tyler?" The doorknob rattled.

Tyler's hand shot out and slammed flat against the door as it began to move behind Zoe, banging it shut before Kane could push his way inside. "What is it, Kane?" he called, then cleared his throat raggedly.

Tyler removed his other hand the rest of the way from Zoe's jeans and braced it against the door as well. She eased her legs to the floor and tucked herself back into her bra, her eyes twinkling with wicked enjoyment.

There was a moment of silence—if he didn't count the soft, panting laughter coming from Zoe—before Kane replied, "Have you seen Zoe? Landon wanted to see both of you as soon as you got her back to the ranch, but Caleb said he saw the tow truck pull in fifteen minutes ago."

"I know where she is," Tyler called through the door, choking on the last word as her fingers brushed across his fly, flicking the button open. He caught her wrist, but her fingers were hooked in his waistband and he couldn't pry them free. "This isn't funny," he whispered harshly.

One golden brow arched upward as a smile overflowing with mischief quirked her lips. "You look tense." She twisted her wrist free as Kane called through the door again.

"Can you tell her to get her ass to the Alpha's? Landon's wearing a groove in the floor with his pacing."

Tyler hissed as Zoe took hold of his zipper and began dragging it down, with one hand tucked inside his jeans to caress each inch as it was released. "Tell him she's—*Jesus*—fine." *More than fine.* The zipper had hit bottom and so had Zoe. She gripped the base of his cock with one hand and gently brushed a thumb across his glans with the other. "We'll be right there. In a—" She dragged her hand up his shaft, the slow milking pull knocking the top right off his head. "*Fuck.* In a minute."

"More like five," Zoe purred, wetting her lips until they glistened as she slid down the door to kneel at his feet. All his blood and good sense rushed south with her.

When her mouth closed over his cock and liquid suction pulled him deep, Tyler would have corrected her if he still had the powers of speech. He wasn't going to last five seconds.

As primed as he was, it was a miracle he hadn't come in his jeans before she got him unzipped. Tyler braced both palms flat on the door, focusing on the feel of the sun-warmed metal beneath his hands to distract from the smooth, moist mouth pistoning on his shaft.

"Okay, but hurry up," Kane—the brother he'd forgotten he had—called through the door. Tyler was vaguely aware of footsteps fading out of range, then Zoe did some swirling thing with her tongue and his last few brain cells evaporated.

He closed his eyes and let his head fall forward, far too heavy for his neck to support anymore. Her hands peeled his jeans down until she could cradle his balls with one hand as the other grasped his hip, holding on tight, her claw tips pressing into his skin. His own claws sank into the metal of the door, his fangs cutting the inside of his lip as he fought the urge to pump his hips and shove himself deeper.

His existence narrowed to a few square inches of flesh. He opened his eyes, hoping to distract himself from the monopoly touch had on his senses, but with his head bowed, the sight that greeted him was Zoe's golden head bobbing, plunging his ruddy, veined cock repeatedly into her mouth. He watched her take him in, eagerly swallowing every inch, humming her pleasure against his shaft. The vibration from deep in her throat thrummed up his spine, and Tyler's last shred of resistance snapped. His roar echoed off the ceiling as he came into her mouth, hips jerking with hot jets of come, his claws digging grooves in the metal door until he was wrung out, a dazed and empty shell.

Zoe released him, rocking back on her heels. She rubbed a thumb across her softly swollen lips and flashed him a bright, flirty smile. Breezy and casual, as if she hadn't just sucked him off like a fucking Hoover Energizer Bunny.

"Landon's probably given himself a stroke by now," she said

as she rose gracefully to her feet. She turned away, wandering over to collect her shirt where it dangled from a fender and buckling her belt as she walked.

Tyler's brain came back online with a jolt, jarred by the easy conversation of the woman who'd just had his cock balls-deep in her mouth. It was disconcerting. He'd done casual sex before, but never with a woman who treated it so...casually.

He tucked himself back into his jeans and refastened them, feeling inexplicably irritated by Zoe's notable lack of pillow talk. She'd said *no strings*, hadn't she? So why was her stringlessness so vexing?

She pulled on her shirt, smoothing the soft, stretchy cotton over her flat stomach. "He's probably dying to tear me a new one. God knows he's been freaking out at the drop of a pin lately."

"He's responsible for a lot of people," Tyler grumbled as he crouched to grab his own shirt, untangling the twisted fabric. "You'd be stressed too."

She snorted. "That's why you don't throw yourself in the path of responsibility."

Tyler straightened, catching Zoe in the act of staring at his bare chest. He'd never thought of himself as vain, but the hungry little smile curving her lips stroked his ego.

"Has anyone ever told you how mouthwatering you are?"

Tyler considered lying just to feign modesty and continue the flirtation, but he was still annoyed enough to be truthful. "Yes."

Her eyebrows flew up and she laughed as she bent to scoop up her hat, smacking it against her thigh to dust it off. "Well, whoever she was, she had good taste." She popped the hat on her head, angling it back. "Thanks for the preview, Tyler. Can't wait to see what you can do when we have time for the feature presentation."

Tyler yanked his shirt on, stupidly bothered by her presumption that there would be a *feature presentation*, even though he knew there would be. Even frustrated with her I-got-what-I-wanted-from-you attitude, he still wanted her down to his bones. And as long as they kept it quiet...just between them...

But how could they?

Even if Kane hadn't heard them, he had to know something was up. The most tactful of Tyler's brothers, he wasn't likely to say anything—certainly not to Landon—but how many people saw Kane shouting through the garage door? How many people had seen Tyler drive onto the ranch with Zoe in the passenger seat twenty minutes ago? How was he supposed to explain the delay? They needed to get their stories straight. They needed—

"Relax, Tyler." Zoe strolled over to stand inches in front of him, resting her hands on his sides. He couldn't help thinking of the last place she'd put her hands, and his cock stirred. "Stop freaking yourself out. It's just sex. No ball and chain. I promise."

The amusement in her eyes grated even more than her cavalier dismissal. "If Landon finds out—"

"Then he finds out. Who the fuck cares? Cat shifters were horny even in Victorian times. It's in our nature. People have sex without getting married all the time. You need to learn a little carpe diem, Tyler. There's more to life than the shoulds."

"I think I just proved I have plenty of carpe diem."

"Oh? Was that you? I thought I was the one who jumped you."

"I have restraint, unlike some people. But, for the record, the jumping was mutual."

"You just keep telling yourself that, sugar. And let me know when you're ready to seize something." She ran her hands across his stomach, her eyes dark with invitation, then pivoted and strutted out the door, her gait liquid with satisfaction. The kind of walk that made sure anyone who saw her knew exactly what she'd been doing.

Tyler cursed and followed his doom out the door to the Alpha's place, hoping Landon didn't have some kind of sex radar that could tell that Tyler had just had his cock in his sister's mouth.

Chapter Four

Ava *knew*.

Zoe sat at the large round table that took up half of Landon and Ava's bungalow, convinced her sister-in-law had been shooting her funny looks ever since Tyler walked into the room. It probably didn't help that Tyler refused to sit down and kept circling back to her like he needed to mark his territory.

Ava had to know. She was too perceptive by half, though she was too diplomatic to say anything. Petite, gentle, malleable, Ava was all the things Zoe wasn't. And tonight, for the first time, her sister-in-law's quiet gaze was making her a little bit crazy. Zoe fidgeted guiltily, even though she didn't have a damn thing to feel guilty for. Tyler's paranoia must be contagious.

She'd avoided getting too close to Landon and Ava, knowing Tyler's scent would be all over her, but his behavior was effectively negating her attempts not to rub her sex life in her brother's face.

Luckily, Landon seemed oblivious to any suspicious undercurrents. He was too busy being pissed at her for trying to go into town without permission.

"Goddammit, Zoe, are you even listening to me?"

Not a bit. But she knew the gist. *Obey me, blah blah blah. Think of the pride, blah blah blah.*

She met her brother's eyes calmly. He may be the Big Bad Boss, but he hadn't been able to intimidate her since she was ten. "Don't you think I'm a little old to be called into the principal's office, Landon?"

"You aren't independent anymore," he roared. "Your actions affect more people than just you. Especially the stupid ones."

"The stupid people?" she asked with false sweetness, batting her lashes.

"Zoe." Her name was growled as a guttural reprimand, but it was Tyler's voice checking her for her impudence, not Landon's.

Zoe stiffened. *You give a guy head and suddenly he thinks he owns you.*

Ava shuttled a gaze back and forth between the two of them, a frown furrowing her brow.

Zoe shoved down the urge to smack Tyler, hoping to avoid further attention from Ava, and focused on her irritation with her dictatorial brother. The same brother who had touted himself as *different* from all the other dictatorial Alphas. The distraction almost worked. She barely noticed Tyler prowling the room behind her, taking up too much space with his broad shoulders and bounce-a-penny-off-it ass.

"I don't suppose you'd care to explain why you felt the need to directly disobey my order to stay on ranch lands until things had quieted down."

Zoe shrugged, leaning back in the chair. "It was a stupid order."

"This is our home now, Zoe." Landon's voice was a rumbling growl, betraying how close his lion was to the surface. "You've made it very clear you don't want to accept this pride as your own, but while you're here, you're a part of us. Protecting our family is never *stupid.*"

"It is when we don't even know what we're protecting against."

"That's no excuse for going behind my back," Landon snarled. "You aren't a nomad anymore, Zoe. Your actions affect all of us."

"So do yours, dumbass! You're the Alpha. You can't afford to be a reactionary dipshit, jumping at shadows and imagining the boogeyman around every corner."

Startled silence hung in the room.

Zoe had made a point never to publicly defy Landon in the

year since he'd been made Alpha. The last thing he needed was his own sister undermining his authority while he was trying to find his feet as the leader. But today the only people there to hear her little rebellion were his wife and Tyler, one of his staunchest supporters. She had no doubt where Tyler's loyalty would fall in this fight. Not that she wanted his loyalty.

"Watch yourself." Landon swelled with an air of command, but Zoe didn't play at subservience.

A year of obedience and biting her tongue in public hadn't sat well. It wasn't in her nature to keep quiet. It had only been a matter of time before she bucked his authority and asserted her independence. No time like the present. And it certainly didn't hurt that she was still riding the hormone high of three mind-bending orgasms. She felt invincible.

Zoe bared her teeth, feeling her fangs sharpen with the tingling pinch of a partial shift.

"We don't know what's going on in town," she growled. "We don't know whether we need to be getting ready to fight or run. We can't do damage control if we don't know what the damage *is*. And no one is telling you to get your head out of your ass because you're the fucking *Alpha*, and we've all been raised since birth to either fall in line with every damn thing the Alpha says or fight it out to take control from him, and no one wants to depose you because in all ways other than this you've actually been really good at this. Where's your head, Landon? I know you aren't this big an idiot, so why are you acting like one?" Zoe was leaning across the table as she challenged Landon. She twisted, turning her rant on Ava. "And why are you letting him? Aren't you supposed to be the voice of reason around here?"

"I— Caution seemed—" Ava broke off, blushing so guiltily Zoe knew instantly it was Little Miss Diplomacy who had suggested the ostrich approach to begin with. And of course Landon had gone along with it. *Idiot men, getting led around by their dicks.*

"Leave her out of this," Landon snarled, rising from his chair to loom over her, hackles high and teeth bared.

Zoe reined in her own reckless snarl, not stupid enough to tweak her brother's protectiveness toward his mate. "Landon, use your brain, I'm not going to touch Ava. I just want you to wake up."

"I am awake, but I refuse to jeopardize our home by poking a hornets' nest."

"You don't know it's a hornets' nest! You could be making everyone stir crazy and paranoid for *nothing*."

"I'd rather take that chance than risk the pride—"

"She's right."

Tyler's voice, low and filled with calm certainty, cut across their shouts. He stood, literally at her back. Even knowing he was there, she was still startled to feel his hand grip her shoulder.

Her hackles rose under his palm.

This was his definition of no strings? This was how he kept things under the radar? By interfering? By butting his nose in and playing the big man like she wasn't even capable of fighting her own battles?

"Tyler?" Ava's gaze lingered on the hand that felt like an anvil on her shoulder.

Landon took a step closer, a growl rumbling up in his throat as he faced Tyler over Zoe's head. "Are you challenging my authority?"

"Landon," Ava said, rising to her feet, her naturally husky voice calm and soothing, ready to diffuse the situation.

But Zoe was closer and she didn't do calm. She surged up to stand between Tyler and Landon—as much to shake off Tyler's lead-weight hand as anything. She knocked her brother back a step with a jab. "Get a grip, Landon. No one's challenging anyone." She turned, shoving Tyler back with a hand to his chest. "Are you?"

Warning and something more dangerous gleamed in Zoe's amber eyes as she stared him down. Though she had no goddamn excuse for being so pissed at him. He had taken her side. Trust Zoe to take offense at that.

Tyler had been on edge since they arrived at the Alpha's bungalow. He felt like a live wire, stripped of all his usual controlled insulation. He tried to stay away from Zoe, to play things casually, but his lion kept urging him to protect her, to mark her—his animal side refused to understand that she didn't belong to him. Every time Landon raised his voice to her, it was a battle not to snarl at the Alpha.

But even through the haze of his own conflicting instincts, he knew nothing in the world could make him want Landon's job.

He took a deep breath and a step back. "No," he said, continuing back as Landon stalked in the opposite direction, like prize fighters returning to their corners after a draw round. "I have no desire to be Alpha."

"See?" Zoe flung the word at Landon, doing nothing to lessen the aggression hanging thick in the air. "We're all friends here, right?" she snarled.

Ava went to her mate and fitted herself to his side, bringing Landon back to reason with a touch. She rested her head on his chest and the tension visibly eased from his shoulders. A part of Tyler envied the mated pair's bond. His hands itched to smooth over Zoe's back as she nestled against him, but that was just his lion's misdirected instincts.

"Everyone's been on a hair trigger lately," Ava spoke to Landon softly, "wondering when the shoe's going to drop. Maybe Zoe has a point. It might be good to do a little reconnaissance."

"We can't plan until we know," Tyler agreed. He leaned against the far wall, arms folded across his chest as a reminder to keep his hands to himself. "Someone needs to go into town—cautiously, and with your knowledge, Landon—to see whether Michael's incident has raised any alarms."

"Exactly," Zoe said, mimicking Ava's rational calm. "I'll go into town—"

"No." The word jumped out of his mouth without his permission. Zoe shot him a look that would have killed a lesser man on the spot. "I'll go with Caleb and Kane."

"I'm sorry, Tyler." Zoe's tone was sickening in its sweetness. "I didn't realize you were the one making decisions. I thought that was Landon."

"I haven't agreed to let *anyone* go." Landon's mild protest cut across Tyler's standoff with Zoe.

"But you will," Zoe said without looking at her brother. "You won't put your stubbornness ahead of the good of the pride. And the good of the pride means finding out what we've been missing in town. And you're going to let me go, because you know I'm right. And I have more experience looking for threats than they do." She waved toward Tyler, the gesture somehow encompassing all his brothers.

"We have more experience handling threats," Tyler insisted.

Zoe's spine snapped straight. "You did *not* just tell me I can't handle threats."

"Zoe." Landon's voice stopped her before she could go for Tyler's throat. "You'll both go. As soon as possible." A growl rippled up Tyler's throat, instinctive rejection of any plan putting Zoe in harm's way calling his lion to the surface, but Landon wasn't done issuing orders. "And you'll take Caleb and Shana with you."

"Shana's insane," Zoe grouched, but the complaint didn't have much heat since she'd just gotten her way.

"Shana goes. She can handle herself in a fight, she's lived outside the pride, and if I try to send Caleb without her, we'll have to lock her up to keep her from following. Just try not to kill one another until you're back on pride land."

"No promises."

"Zoe."

"Fine. I'll play nice." Zoe snatched up the cowboy hat she'd left on the table and started toward the door. "I guess I'll go tell the Bitch Queen the plan."

Tyler knew he should probably go along to referee that encounter, but he had more pressing matters—like keeping Zoe from throwing herself in front of every oncoming train. As Zoe strode to the door, shooting him one last glare he was sure he hadn't earned, Tyler shoved away from the wall, stalking toward where his sister was still pressed up against the Alpha's side. "Landon. A word?"

Ava went up on her toes to kiss her mate and then slipped out of his arms. "I'll just go make sure Zoe and Shana don't kill one another."

Landon waited until the door shut behind Ava before he

spoke, keeping his voice low even though both women should be well out of earshot. Shifter hearing was notoriously acute. "I don't want to get in the middle of whatever is going on with you two."

"This isn't about that. She doesn't need to go into town. Caleb and I are more than capable—"

"If Zoe wants to go into town, she's going." Landon shook his head ruefully. "I've never been able to control her, and I suggest you don't try to."

Tyler grimaced, knowing he wouldn't be able to take that advice. Landon might not be able to control her, but God knew Zoe could use a keeper. And Tyler knew just the man for the job. If Landon wouldn't check her, he would. For her own good.

Chapter Five

"It's too quiet."

"It's a weekday."

"It's still too quiet." Zoe flicked a glance around the Bar Nothing—the seedy honky-tonk where the shit had first hit the fan. It looked like the kind of place well acquainted with shit.

Shana had called dibs on investigating the town proper, hauling Caleb with her to do some shopping. Which stuck Zoe with the ass who thought he had the right to dictate her life just because she'd let him get to third base, trolling for clues at the high-class joint where Michael Minor had half-shifted defending his mate from a drunk. The Bar Nothing was filthy enough to be a health-code violation and probably a biohazard, smelled of beer and less savory things, and still managed to draw a crowd of hopeless hopefuls every weekend.

Zoe dragged a fingernail through the grime coating the chipped wood bar. "I do not understand the appeal of this place."

Tyler shrugged, leaning one elbow against the bar at her side. She ignored the way his biceps flexed beneath his fresh shirt—she was too pissed at him to notice how mouthwatering he was right now. He'd been hulking over her protectively, shadowing her every move since they walked out of Landon's place. And from the way he avoided looking at her, he was still pissy because he hadn't been able to leave her home, chained to the stove.

"Beer's cheap, music's loud, and everyone looking to get laid comes here, male and female."

Jealousy spiked, an unwanted jab in Zoe's gut. "Know this from experience, do we?"

"I've lived twenty miles from here my whole life. So yeah, I know from experience. Doesn't mean I've been here recently."

Zoe refused to ask what qualified as *recently*. They didn't have that kind of relationship, where they talked about past lovers. She reminded herself that she didn't *want* that kind of relationship. Tyler Minor was just an itch to scratch.

And from the appetizer she'd gotten in the garage, he was pretty damn good at scratching.

But right now, he was the last thing she needed to be thinking about. She'd lived outside the prides long enough to know distractions could get you caught or killed.

Zoe studied their surroundings as the bartender ambled in their direction. His slow pace didn't appear to be due to caution, just his natural rolling gait—which made no sense. Michael going part-furry was bound to leave an impression. Tyler and Michael had drastically different coloring, but their features and build were so similar the bartender should have reacted. Caution, wariness, *something*.

If he'd been working that night. Though he seemed like the kind of guy who was a fixture in the bar, working every night. Fifty-something and heavyset with a face like a bulldog and a wedding ring embedded on one fleshy finger, he spat on the floor and folded his arms over the barrel of his chest. "Getcha somethin'?"

"Whiskey sour, please." Zoe put a little extra oomph in her smile to make up for the behemoth glaring at the world next to her.

"Bud," the behemoth grunted.

The bartender nodded, keeping the same lazy pace as he reached under the bar. Out of the corner of her eye, Zoe saw Tyler's shoulders tense then relax slightly when the bartender came up with a bottle of Jack. She knew he was remembering Michael's description of the pump shotgun that also lived underneath the scarred wood.

But her new buddy the bartender didn't seem inclined to drive them out at gunpoint. *That's a start.* He just mixed her drink, popped the top off Tyler's beer and slid them across the bar until the glass caught on a crack in the wood and stopped itself. Tyler laid a ten next to the trail of condensation. The bartender nodded to Zoe with a "Ma'am", scooped up the money, and ambled back toward the regulars shooting the shit at the opposite end of the bar.

"That was anticlimactic," Zoe commented, sipping her sour. "I expected threats and pitchforks at least."

"Maybe they only do lynchings every other day."

Zoe frowned, scanning the room and examining every drunken patron in turn. "They aren't even staring at us. Shouldn't they be staring at us?"

"I had no idea you were so vain."

Zoe glared at him. Under other circumstances she might have been amused, but right now she was concentrating on holding a grudge.

"A bunch of people live on a secluded compound outside of town and almost never leave their own land. I know this is Texas where the unofficial motto is *mind your own damn business*, but you'd think there would at least be a few whispers and stares at the possibly cultish people when we show up on their turf. So why aren't they staring?"

"I thought you'd be happy you were right." Tyler tilted the bottle for a long draught. "There's no danger here. We were wrong. The ostrich approach was unnecessary. So why aren't you celebrating?"

"I wouldn't jump right to unnecessary. There's something weird here. It's too quiet."

The Bar Nothing bordered on abandoned. The diehard drunks who filled the stools at the other end of the bar all gave them a wide berth, but Zoe's instincts told her that distance had more to do with the fact that the two of them radiated *lovers' spat* than fear. After a month of rumors flying with no damage control, there should have been more of a reaction. Something was definitely wrong.

"I've never met a woman so reluctant to be right," Tyler bitched.

"I've never met a man so determined to be wrong all the

time. I guess we're even."

Tyler bristled. "You wanna tell me what you're so pissed about?"

That was all the invitation Zoe needed. "Do I look like I need a babysitter to you?"

"You look like you need a fucking keeper, and I don't see anyone else lining up for the job."

"A *keeper*?" Zoe saw red. "Who do you think I am? All this time I thought we've been friends—or whatever you wanna call it—and you don't know me at all. I'm not a fucking damsel in distress, Tyler. I take care of myself. Always have."

"I'm sorry I dared try to protect the invincible Zoe King."

"That's your idea of an apology? God save me from alpha males."

"What do you want me to say? Go on, have fun, get yourself killed?"

"I'd be thrilled if you could say you'll trust me to look after myself and mean it, but that's probably too much to ask. You're the big bad lion, right? And I'm the helpless little kitten who needs to be wrapped in cotton for her own *protection*."

"No one could mistake you for a helpless kitten."

"No? So that isn't what you're trying to do?"

"Wanting to keep you out of harm's way isn't the same as thinking you can't handle yourself."

"Of course not. So if a bar fight started up and we were swarmed on both sides, you'd let me fend for myself?" She could practically hear crickets in the Bar Nothing today, but Zoe enjoyed the idea of her hypothetical brawl. She could do to blow off some steam. "No," she said, "we both know you wouldn't. You'd be so busy trying to defend me, you'd probably get your head split open."

"Another reason you shouldn't be here. You're a distraction."

"I'm only a distraction because you don't trust me to hold up my end. If you could just accept that I'm tough enough to take care of myself, we could be a great team, but until you do, you're going to slow me down with this *protection* nonsense."

"I'm going to slow *you* down?"

"That's what I said." Zoe polished off the last of her drink and shoved the empty glass away before swiveling on her stool to face Tyler. "You don't think I can keep up, so you slow us both down playing nursemaid to me. I know you're trying to be all noble, but the interference is a problem. And I don't need it. You can ask Landon. He never tries to take a bullet for me."

"I'm not your brother," Tyler growled, looming over her.

"No, you aren't." *And thank God for that.* "So you don't get to play big brother and boss me around."

"Big brother?" He coughed, a jagged leonine sound of irritation. "That's what you think today was?"

"I don't know what today was," Zoe snapped. "I thought it was chemistry and need and the build up to a good hard fuck, but then some asshole tried to tell me how to live my life. Even if I needed looking after, you don't have the right to protect me just because you finger fucked me and I sucked you off."

Chairs creaked at the end of the bar as the other patrons took a sudden interest in their conversation. Zoe's face flamed as she leaned toward Tyler, hissing the next words just above a whisper.

"I. Don't. Belong. To. You."

Something dark and possessive sparked in Tyler's eyes. He loomed closer, his body crowding hers aggressively. "Yes. You. Do."

Zoe wanted to be indignant, but her insides liquefied in a girly rush, heat pooling at her core.

"Not forever. No commitment. But as long as you are with me, you are *mine*, Zoe King. And I protect what's mine."

No one had ever said anything like that to her before, especially not with the fire of angry possession leaping in his eyes. *Wow.* Words abandoned her. Tyler bent over her, pressing his mouth against her ear, and delicious shivers chased one another down her spine.

"That's the deal you get when you take me on. So make up your mind. Do you want me or not?"

That wasn't much of a question. Right now a hard thought would tip her over into a climax. "I want you," she whispered.

"Then let's get out of here."

"Reconnaissance..." Her protest was halfhearted at best.

"Maybe Caleb and Shana found something." He guided her off the barstool with a hand on the small of her back. "And we've already found out they aren't going to lynch us on sight. That's something."

Zoe scanned the bar one last time. Now that they weren't arguing loud enough to draw an audience, the heavy drinkers at the back had stopped paying them any attention. Again, she was struck by the oddness of that. No one was even glancing in their direction. No curiosity. It was almost like the town residents thought they already knew everything there was to know about the Three Rocks Ranch.

The thought was disconcerting to say the least.

"Come on." Tyler slipped his arm around her waist, tucking her against his side. Zoe tried not to bristle when she realized he was shielding her with his body. It wasn't going to be easy, taking him on his terms, letting him protect her. But his arm felt good, so she leaned into him.

She could use the comfort. Something was very wrong here.

Chapter Six

"They're onto us."

Zoe had only stepped across the threshold of Landon and Ava's place for the debriefing when Shana's words stopped her in her tracks. The redhead had been sullenly silent the entire drive back to the ranch, but now her opening words caused a sudden uproar in the small crowd. Kane and Michael Minor were there with Ava and Landon. Shana had been the first into the room, alongside Caleb. Behind Zoe in the doorway, Tyler nudged her on the back to get her moving again, then stepped across the threshold and shut the door behind him.

"Calm down." Landon's voice cut across the hubbub. He waved them all toward the table, but there weren't enough chairs, so Zoe leaned against the wall, Tyler taking a position at her side, though he didn't touch her. "Shana, what did you see?"

Caleb folded his massive arms on the table. "She didn't see anything."

"Shut up, Caleb. He didn't ask you." Shana sent an icy glare at her mate, but considering it was her usual expression, Zoe couldn't be sure whether she was angry with him or if this was their warped idea of foreplay.

"Did anyone say anything suspicious to you?" Landon asked, interrupting the mated pair's staring contest.

"No," Shana admitted.

"Were you followed? Was someone watching you?"

"No." The redhead shook her head sharply. "Nothing like that. It wasn't that they were suspicious of us, it was that there wasn't even a single odd glance tossed our way. They didn't even seem curious. After Michael wigs out in the bar and then the entire pride stops leaving the ranch for any reason for a month, any normal person would at least be curious enough to look, but they all looked at me like they already knew my secrets."

Zoe hated to agree with Shana on anything, but in this case she had to. "That's exactly it. They were too comfortable with us. We weren't even interesting." Except when she was shouting about blowjobs.

"That's what we want, isn't it?" Tyler pointed out. "To be below the radar?"

"We aren't below the radar," Shana insisted. "We're on it. They just think they've already identified our dot."

Landon looked to Zoe and arched a brow. "Zo?"

"Yeah. I agree. Someone told them something, cleared things up with some story."

"But no one's been off the ranch," Kane protested.

"Are we sure about that?" Zoe countered. "I would have been to town and back again without anyone the wiser if the jeep hadn't broken down."

Ava shook her head. "We knew you'd gone," she said, her soft voice a contrast to the tense tone around the table.

"And you're positive no one else has?" Zoe asked, not wanting to voice the other possibility—that someone outside the pride had stepped in to cover their tracks. That an outsider knew enough to know *how* to cover their tracks.

Landon was obviously thinking along the same lines. He met her eyes and then his gaze slid away. "Caleb, Tyler. Can you find out if there were any other unauthorized trips?"

Without a word, Caleb and Tyler moved toward the door, purpose in every step.

Zoe kept her eyes straight ahead, refusing to watch Tyler leave, but she felt every step he took away from her. The two of them had unfinished business, but the pride came first. If there was one thing she knew about Tyler, it was that family duty trumped everything.

"Zoe?" Landon said and she refocused on him.

Reading the question in his eyes, she shook her head. "I don't think just one of us sneaking into town could explain it, Landon. If someone covered for us, they were thorough. These people, they looked at us like every question they'd ever had about us had already been answered."

"But not with the truth?"

"No pitchforks and lynch mobs, so I'm guessing whoever is covering our tracks can lie like the devil himself."

"Why would they do that?" Ava asked.

Landon looked away from his mate. It was clear he didn't want to say it, so Zoe did. "They can't use our secret to control us if everyone knows."

The Alpha shook his head sharply, the picture of denial. "We don't know that—"

"Is this about that cougar in Colorado?"

All eyes flew to Shana. Zoe's mouth went dry to have her fears voiced. "How did you hear about that?"

"What cougar in Colorado?" Ava reached blindly for Landon's hand, not even seeming to realize she was doing it. The Alpha's larger hand engulfed hers completely.

"It's an urban legend," Landon said. "A shifter boogeyman."

Shana snorted. "It's a rural legend, but it's more than just myth."

Zoe took pity on Ava and explained. "Cougars are solitary. They don't have the protection and resources of a pride or a pack. Without anyone watching your back, it can be a lot harder to stay hidden. There's a story of a mountain lion living in a small town in Colorado a few years back. The locals started to suspect things and he thought he was going to have to move on, but then suddenly it was like all their suspicions had been wiped away. He decided to stay, but three weeks later he vanished, never to be heard from again."

"He could have just gone into the wild."

"There was no scent trail." Shana took up the tale. "He'd been writing letters to his sister, explaining about his fears of discovery and subsequent relief at having been concerned for nothing. He'd invited her to visit and disappeared the night before her arrival. It hadn't rained. If he'd gone wild, there should have been some scent trail for her to follow after less than twenty-four hours, but there was nothing. He'd just disappeared. Everything in his cabin was as he left it. His car parked in the driveway."

"So who's the boogeyman? Who took him?"

"They say a group had arrived in town just before the suspicions around him were cleared. And they left within a day of his disappearance. I guess they were there to survey the mountain pass, but their equipment was all wrong. The townspeople just called them the scientists."

"So the scientists took the cougar?"

"His sister thinks so. She's been trying to find him for years. Trying to rally the other cougars to help her, but that breed is so independent, she hasn't had much luck."

"But even if they did take him, what makes you think this is the same group? We haven't heard about any surveyors in town, have we?"

"No. But we haven't exactly been in town a lot to hear. And someone is covering our tracks. Someone who has a vested interest in making sure no one is looking too hard at this ranch."

"We have the pride. They can't make all of us disappear."

Landon held his mate's hand between his own, but he was the one who gave her the harsh truth. "Until we know who they are and what they want, we don't know what they can and can't do."

Zoe sighed. "So I guess the ban on going into town holds?"

"Alone? Hell yes."

She cringed, but being trapped at the ranch didn't sound like the same punishment it had this morning. Tyler had changed that. She didn't want to think about what else he might have the power to change in her.

They went over the trip into town in minute detail and discussed possible strategies for learning what the townspeople thought was going on and who might have told them. Around the second hour, Shana declared herself bored with it all and left. Shortly after that, Kane and Ava slipped out, speaking quietly. Leaving Zoe alone with her brother.

Her brother who looked like he'd been through the wars. He raked a hand through hair streaked with the thousand different blonds and browns of a lion's mane, worry lines that hadn't been there a year ago creasing his familiar face.

"We could go," Zoe said, the words slipping out of her mouth before she realized she'd thought them. "If we took off tonight—"

"*Zoe.*" Landon's voice was harsh. The disappointment in his expression shamed her.

It was instinct, the urge to run with Landon when things went bad. For so many years he had been the only one she relied on—and she'd been the same for him.

Growing up depending on one another for sanity in the Florida pride, then leaving the pride as teenagers to live as nomads for years—that kind of bond was unshakeable. And it was the only reason Zoe had stuck around Three Rocks as long as she had.

Landon loved the community he'd found here, but Zoe'd never been the hearth-and-home type. She'd been fantasizing about the freedom of the road since the day they got here. But Landon had needed her, so she'd stayed. Did he really need her now? She wasn't the only one he relied on anymore. He had a whole pride now. She wasn't his home anymore. Ava was. Fifty lion-shifters young and old had taken up pieces of his heart that used to belong to only her.

It was stupid to be jealous of a community, but for all their solitary lifestyle, Zoe had never felt alone until she came here, where she was surrounded by people.

She turned away from the disapproval on her brother's face, staring out the window into the black night.

She heard movement behind her, then Landon spoke from just over her shoulder. "I thought when you left today that this was it. That maybe you..."

"That I wasn't coming back?" She'd thought of it. Too many times to count.

"You could have talked to me before stealing a jeep and breaking the rules."

Zoe shrugged. "Easier to beg forgiveness than ask

211

permission."

They'd modified that saying growing up. Zoe knew he would be remembering the same words she was. Better to take your licks afterwards than get smacked for even thinking of it. At least then you get to enjoy what you're being punished for.

Life hadn't been fair then. Landon had reacted by becoming fixated on justice. Mr. Nobility and Equality. Zoe's response had been more self-serving. You took care of yourself because you couldn't count on anyone else. Except Landon. She'd always been able to count on him. Before they came here. Three Rocks had changed everything.

"You could be happy here," Landon said softly. "If you let yourself be. This is a good place. It's different."

"It's exactly the same as all the others. The only difference is you're in charge. And how long will that last? Until someone younger and stronger walks up and kills you for the right to be Alpha? Or maybe until scientists raid the place and turn us all into lab rats?"

"I won't let that happen."

Some things even you can't stop, big brother.

She lowered her eyes, studying the old claw marks scarring the hardwood floor. "I can't stay here, Landon. I never planned on settling here, you know that."

"Right now..."

"I'll stay for now. Until things are stable again. I won't leave you when you need me."

His hand closed on her shoulder, tugging her away from the window and into a hug. "I'll always need you, Zo."

She smiled and pulled away. "No, you won't. The pride follows you now. You've got this. We always said you were born to be Alpha. You were going to change the world one pride at a time. And you've started something here, even if it's still rough and there are still bumps. You're going to be great whether I'm here or not. Changing the world was never really my thing."

His expression solidified like concrete setting.

Zoe forced a smile. "Come on, Landon. You know I don't fit here."

He shook his head sharply and began to pace, stalking

across the floor. "You haven't tried to fit. You never gave this pride a chance. Playing dress-up in cowboy boots isn't the same thing as trying to fit in. I know you too well to believe you aren't mocking this place with those clothes."

She couldn't deny it so she joked instead. "You have a problem with the way I dress?"

Landon didn't laugh. "Give it a chance, Zoe. A real chance."

She huffed out an exasperated breath. "I don't want to. I'm not you. I'm not looking to settle down somewhere. I didn't leave our old pride because I wanted to find a better place to plant myself and pop out a few dozen cubs. I left because I felt like if I couldn't get out into the world and see a bigger piece of it, I would lose my mind. I was going crazy trapped inside that pride just like I'm going crazy trapped in this one." She gripped the edge of the table, concentrating on the feel of the wood beneath her palms so she didn't have to think about how she knew she was disappointing him. "I always wanted to be a nomad, even when it was forbidden for females to leave Twelve Oaks. I'm glad we left together, but I would have left even if you hadn't. I had to get away."

"If you could just see how a real pride feels—"

"Landon, you aren't listening. It has nothing to do with the pride. I would hate the Garden of Eden if I thought I had to stay there forever."

He stopped pacing, shoving his hands into the pockets of his jeans. "Does this have anything to do with Tyler?"

Zoe's face heated. "I'm going to pretend you didn't say that."

This wasn't about some guy. Though if she was honest with herself, Tyler was part of the reason she'd stayed as long as she had. There was something addicting about him, even when he'd been driving her crazy. She'd been enjoying the game, in a way.

"I don't know what's going on between you, but he might have something to say about you leaving."

"Tyler Minor doesn't get a say in my life," she bit out, hating the fact that the words felt like a lie.

Chapter Seven

Tyler crouched in front of the bony, shivering teen who looked like he was one harsh word away from pissing himself. "Relax, Cory. You aren't going to be punished," Tyler assured him, reining in all his impatience and trying to remember what life was like at fifteen. Of course, his life at fifteen probably didn't bear a strong resemblance to Cory Berg's. He'd been taking care of four younger siblings, not sneaking off into town to climb a tree into a human girl's bedroom. "We just need to know what you saw and heard in town."

"I just went to Hailey's and came straight back. I swear." Cory's teeth began to chatter, even though it had to be pushing ninety in his parents' bungalow.

The kid was going to give himself a heart attack.

"Anything you remember can be helpful," Tyler said, gently gripping the boy's shoulder in what he hoped was a comfortingly paternal way. It had been a while since he'd grilled a teenager—Michael and Ava were in their twenties and beyond the need for a firm hand. Hopefully he hadn't lost his touch.

Cory shook his head, a quick, jerky movement. "I didn't see anybody. Honest."

"Nothing was different? Any change, no matter how small, could be significant."

"No. I mean, Hailey seemed more, you know, *into* me." His eyes flicked to his parents hovering on the opposite side of the room, and his face flushed a deep red. "But I never told her a thing about the pride. I know better, Tyler. I swear, man."

"Did she give you any idea why she was suddenly more into

you?"

"Dude, I don't know. I mean, I'm not a total idiot. I know Hailey Winters is out of my league, but when the head cheerleader asks you out, you say *yes*, you know? I didn't want to screw things up with her just because we'd been yanked out of school and restricted to the pride land. And she never asked about the pride or coming out to the ranch until last night. I thought maybe she, like, really liked me."

"And last night?"

"I guess it was weird, looking back now. She said something about how cool she thought it was that I lived on a federally funded secret research facility or something. I thought she was fishing so I, uh, distracted her. You know?" His eyes flicked to his parents again and Tyler would have grinned if the situation hadn't been so serious. *Little Cory got some action.*

"You didn't ask where she'd heard that?"

"No, I thought she was guessing—but yeah, I mean I guess she seemed pretty certain."

A federally funded research facility. It was a convenient lie—accounting for their heightened security and secrecy. And if that was the story going through the high school, it would explain the recent increase in teenage trespass attempts.

Unfortunately they had no idea how widespread that belief was in town because their only source had been too focused on getting to second base.

"Thanks, Cory. If you think of anything else, let me know."

"You really aren't going to kick my ass for sneaking out?"

Tyler glanced over at Cory's parents. His father gave a slight nod. They had disciplinary action covered. "I'm not on ass-kicking duty tonight. Maybe tomorrow."

Tyler let himself out of the Berg bungalow and loped down the path to Landon and Ava's place. It would have been faster to call in the information, but cell phones and radio frequencies were too vulnerable to eavesdropping, so their use was restricted on the ranch.

Tyler mounted the Alpha's steps, checking his watch. Almost midnight, but Landon hadn't taken the Alpha position because he wanted a lot of quiet, undisturbed nights.

Twenty minutes later, Tyler slipped out of the Alpha's house, the weight of the day descending on him. His eyes were half closed already as he trudged through the darkened compound on autopilot. It wasn't until he was dragging his feet up the steps that he lifted his head and realized where instinct had taken him.

He stood on Zoe's porch, listening to the cicadas and the hum of his own midnight insanity urging him inside.

The lights were off in her house, all the windows dark. He knew he should walk away. Let her sleep, but he needed to see her, just for a minute. Then he'd be able to rest.

Tyler knocked softly, telling himself if she didn't hear that, he would walk away.

He'd been holding Zoe at arm's length for months. He tried to keep her from becoming important to him. The lines in his life were carefully drawn—family on one side, everyone else on the other. One mattered, one didn't. His philosophy was simple—do anything for family, everyone else is on their own.

Zoe fell very clearly into the *everyone else* category. But on some instinctive level, a level ruled by the lion in him more than the man, he had already begun treating her like she belonged to him. Like she was part of his pride within a pride.

All this time, he'd been dreading adding another yoke of obligation to his neck, but without any conscious decision on his part, Zoe was already there. The man could fight it, but the lion knew. The animal side of him wasn't as practiced in denial. The inevitable had happened months ago, maybe even the first day they met, but the human piece—the piece that hated change and didn't trust easily—that part had taken a lot longer to cop to the reality.

Something had shifted today. The last of his denial falling away until he was forced to face the truth. She meant something to him. He just didn't want to think too hard about what that might be.

Tyler raised his fist to knock again when the door opened.

Zoe stood in the doorway, wearing only a faded T-shirt that fell to her hips. Suddenly the heavy feeling lifted and Tyler was wide awake. His gaze raked her from her bare toes to the golden curls tumbling around her shoulders. Arousal stirred to life.

She blinked blearily up at him, shoving a lock of hair out of her eyes. "Tyler?"

His heart stuttered. Zoe wasn't only something. Right now, she was everything. "Can I come in?"

She swung the door wider and he slipped past her into the room.

Zoe had gone to bed alone, feeling lost in the expanse of her empty bed. She'd always liked having her own space before, but tonight her cabin felt like a cavern.

She'd expected to feel a sense of freedom when she told Landon about her plans to leave. Now she could slip off whenever she wanted, as soon as the pride was secure. She'd thought it would feel like a cage springing open, but tonight she felt even more penned than ever.

Ever since leaving Landon's, she hadn't been able to think for all the restless energy running under her skin. She should have been exhausted. It was after midnight and her day hadn't exactly been uneventful, but Zoe hadn't even been able to contemplate sleep.

She'd shifted to her lioness form, hoping that would quiet the white noise cluttering her human thoughts, but her unease had shifted with her into an itch beneath her hackles, an agitation that had her pacing back and forth in her room like a feline in a zoo.

She'd heard Tyler step onto her porch and shifted back to her human figure, grabbing the nightshirt she'd discarded in an instinctive defense against what she was feeling. What he was making her feel.

As soon as she opened the door, she wished she hadn't. Tall, muscled and weary, he looked far too good standing on her porch, something dark and needy in his eyes. Her soul felt like it was trying to reach out to him through her skin. She told herself it was just her animal side's need for the reassurance of touch, but the words felt like a lie.

When he squeezed past her into the cabin's single open room, the scent of him teased her, inviting her to press her face against his neck and breathe, urging her to rub against him until their scents were tangled around one another and everyone who came near him would know who he belonged to.

Zoe shut the door, pausing to stare at the worn wood until she could evict that instinct from her thoughts. Even her feline side wasn't usually possessive. She didn't need to mark her lovers and resisted all their attempts to mark her, so why couldn't she stop imagining branding Tyler Minor with her scent?

"Nice," he commented behind her, and Zoe turned, realizing as she did that he'd never been inside her place before. He was careful about boundaries, careful never to be alone with her anywhere there was a bed handy.

Zoe's gaze slid to the large, low mattress, the only piece of furniture in the room. The austere lack of furnishings and decorations weren't really her style, but she'd never seen the point in making a place feel homey if it wasn't going to be her home.

Now the lack made her uncomfortable. Watching Tyler survey her bare walls and impersonal furnishings, she wished she'd bothered to do something with the place. At least it was dark. He couldn't see much. Maybe he'd just think it was charmingly minimal without the light to show it was barren.

Not that it mattered what he thought. She refused to let it matter. He was just a guy. This was just a house. Shelter and nothing more. It filled a need. Just like he did. A physical need. Zoe took care of her own emotional wants.

Those emotional wants had nothing to do with the need to touch Tyler that burned under her skin. Nothing.

She didn't know why he was here. To finish what they'd started in the garage? To fight about her tendency to speak for herself rather than play the meek little woman? There was a restlessness in him that matched her own, but she didn't know how to soothe it. She wasn't the soothing type.

Zoe opened her mouth to ask him why he'd come, what he wanted from her, but didn't get a syllable out before he answered both questions in a way that left no doubt in her mind.

Tyler crossed the distance between them in two long strides, speared his fingers into her hair, cupped the back of her head and sealed his lips over hers in a searing, toe-curling kiss.

This afternoon had been about heat and chemistry and impersonal lust, but this was something else. The intensity in his touch, the raw, almost desperate way he held her, as if at any second she could be pulled from his grasp. This felt personal.

Zoe clutched his arms, using him as the only fixed point in her existence as the world seemed to melt beneath her feet like a Dali painting.

Her hands found his shirt—once as neat as the man himself and now hopelessly wrinkled by the day. Zoe had always marveled that a man who spent his days rolling around under cars could look so put together, but now she couldn't think about his pristine façade. She just wanted to peel away the last traces of civility.

She fisted her hands in the fabric and backed toward her bed, dragging him with her until her calves hit the mattress. She knelt on the bed and knee-walked back, pulling him forward with fistfuls of shirt, never breaking the hungry kiss. Tyler leaned over the bed, propping his fists on the mattress as he pressed her back to sit on her heels as he explored every corner of her mouth. As decadent as the kiss was, as complete and deliberate, it wasn't enough. She couldn't get to the good stuff fast enough. Zoe had never been the patient type.

Hoping to spur Tyler to speed things up, Zoe dropped his shirt and grabbed the hem of her own, breaking the kiss long enough to whip it over her head and fling it away. Tyler groaned, his hands going instantly to the full curves of her breasts. Zoe put her own hands over his, holding them to her as she lay back on the bed.

Tyler eased down on top of her, still fully clothed, his head level with her breasts. He plumped and shaped them, grazing his lips over them too gently to satisfy her craving for *fast* and *hard*. Sensation escalated with each teasing touch. She raised her knees, bracketing his waist between them, and threaded her fingers through the golden mane of his hair. Half of her wanted to press him close and demand he get a damn move on, but the other half hesitated, enjoying the slow, intimate pace he

219

was setting. Zoe let her head fall back to the mattress, closing her eyes, and gave herself up to the deliberate, tender seduction of his touch.

He worshipped her body with his mouth and hands, taking nothing for himself and yet taking all of her, more than she'd ever allowed anyone else. Her prized distance was falling away with each caress. Zoe squirmed beneath him, uneasy from the mix of desire and intimacy, writhing with the discomfort of this foreign vulnerability. But she didn't stop him. She didn't know if she could.

It was all in her head. She was imagining the tenderness in his kiss—the idea that it meant anything more than a satisfactory release was a fantasy of her own making. And as long as he didn't notice her preoccupation, she was still safe, the most vulnerable places in her soul still hidden, even as he managed to stroke them.

But some of her unease must have communicated itself to him. Tyler braced himself on his elbows and looked down into her face, his gaze dark with hunger but penetrating. "You okay?"

Panic shot through her bloodstream. She hauled him down for a forceful kiss to avoid answering the question. She wasn't okay. She was too exposed, but she couldn't let him see. Tyler let her kiss him, calming her with the dragging strokes of his tongue even as she tried to amp him up until he wouldn't try to peer into her soul anymore.

Then he pulled back and frowned down at her. "Zoe," he said softly, her name a gentle scold, as if she should know better than to evade him.

Why couldn't he just be a guy and play through without paying attention to whether she was with him?

"I'm good." The words sounded forced, too rushed, and Zoe winced internally at the crack they exposed. *Distract him.* She stroked her hands down the corded strength of his neck and pushed open the collar of his shirt. "Why are you wearing so many clothes?" she purred, half-veiling her eyes behind her lashes.

Suspicion flickered in his eyes—*why did he have to see so much?*—but then Tyler grinned. "Clearly an oversight."

He rolled away from her to take care of the clothes issue, and Zoe sat up, turning her back on him to collect herself.

What was wrong with her? This was what she wanted, wasn't it? What she'd wanted for months. So why did it feel like she was getting more than she'd bargained for? She tried to remember what comfortable flirtation felt like.

She needed to get control of the situation. She wasn't a fainting virgin or the kind of girl who assigned nonexistent significance to sex. She was a predatory cat, not the meek, sheltered prey. *Get a grip, Zoe.*

She turned back to Tyler, her breathing quickening at the sight of his golden, muscular body wrapped only in moonlight and shadows. His cock rose between them, swelling further as she watched, in silent invitation. A feline smile curled her lips. She crawled across the bed and knelt on the edge, feeling a surge of power and control at the way his gaze tracked her every move.

"C'mere," she demanded. He obeyed instantly and she felt every step he took toward her like a magnet being drawn toward its match. By the time he was within a foot of her, the press of his skin against hers was inevitable, a scientific law.

She twined her arms around his neck and hauled him to her for a kiss, but this time it wasn't desperate and defensive. This time it was pure, sweet need. Clean, simple lust. She burned.

Tyler responded with gratifying ferocity. He bore her back to the mattress, the scalding heat of his bare skin making her feel like she'd been dropped into a furnace, inside and out. They fell in a tangle, but he found his way naturally between her thighs. He kissed her deeply, slicking a finger between her folds until she was twisting beneath him with pent-up desire. "Tyler," she groaned, "now, *please.*"

At her plea, Tyler's vexing patience evaporated. He tugged her hips down the mattress until she was tucked beneath him at just the right angle. Thrusting into her, he filled her in one deep, smooth stroke. Zoe clenched her inner muscles, her breathing reduced to ragged gasps. He took up a steady rhythm, muscles clenched with the effort, sweat slicking the muscles of his back as she clutched them.

That caged feeling was back, but this time she knew exactly how to find the release she needed. Digging her heels into the mattress, Zoe canted her hips and moaned, *"Harder,"* into Tyler's ear, her lips caressing the lobe. Tyler grunted an unintelligible reply and his hips began pistoning faster, intensifying the delicious drag of each withdrawal and jarring spike of pleasure at every pounding return.

Her orgasm built like the electric tingles in the air before a storm, an ominous anticipation. Zoe twisted her face away from Tyler, pressing her cheek into the mattress, startled by how cool the sheet felt against her skin. She squeezed her eyes shut, focusing every particle of her being on the storm rising inside her.

But then Tyler's lips caressed her jaw, his fingers cradled her face. There was a roughness, almost a violence in their mating, but his touch was so gentle, so damn tender, she couldn't resist it when he turned her face back to his for a startlingly chaste kiss.

Her climax burst through her, not like a storm, but like the sudden radiance of the dawn, light spilling through her. She opened her eyes, startled by the sweetness of it, and his gold gaze was directly above her. Eyes like the sun bore into hers, illuminating every corner of her being, and she flew. *This is the freedom I've been missing.* Tyler roared, his claws digging furrows into the mattress as his own release took him, but the sunrise in his eyes never wavered from hers as aftershocks in pinkish hues sent pleasure down to her bones.

Zoe wrapped her arms around Tyler and pulled him over her, loving his weight pressing her down into the mattress, but also needing his cheek beside hers so he couldn't look into her eyes right now. She felt...disoriented, like some small piece inside her had shifted, changing its purpose, and all the rest of her had to figure out how to operate around the change.

She couldn't face him right now. *God, please don't let him try to pillow talk me.* Zoe closed her eyes and let the muscles in her arms loosen, falling lax and slipping off his shoulders. She made the rest of her body boneless and gave a soft, breathy sigh. Feigning sleep wasn't the most mature approach to handling the aftermath, but the alternative was too intimidating.

Tyler lifted his weight away from her and she fancied she could feel his gaze on her, checking to see if she really slept. She kept her breathing even and her body still—which would have been a warning sign if he knew her, since Zoe was a distinctly restless sleeper.

She half-wondered if he would leave—just slip out as no strings seemed to imply—but Tyler settled himself against her, one strong arm wrapped around her ribs beneath her breasts. He pressed along her right side and her body quickened for him, but Zoe forced herself to remain still.

She focused on the deep in and out of her breath, concentrating on the details of the lie, until the exhaustion of the day aided her and she slipped off into a genuine slumber with the scent of Tyler Minor and the feel of his strength surrounding her.

Chapter Eight

Tyler couldn't sleep.

The lithe lioness curled against his side consumed his thoughts, keeping him awake even though it had to be nearing five in the morning. His body felt heavy and dull even as his mind buzzed like a hornets' nest.

He shouldn't have come here tonight. It was the final nail in the coffin of his unfettered lifestyle. But even knowing that, he couldn't regret it. He wouldn't have traded the last twenty-four hours for anything, but that didn't mean he was ready to surrender just yet.

He'd had twenty years of responsibility. Twenty years envisioning the day he would walk off the pride lands with no one depending on him but himself.

Ava and Michael had been so tiny when their father left and their mother withered into a shell of herself. They'd needed him so badly. Kane had gone from being a bright, quick-to-laugh kid to a quiet, solemn teen almost overnight. Caleb had always been more withdrawn, always so self-reliant. Shana, obnoxious as the rest of the world found her, had kept Caleb from pulling too deeply into his own reserve, but he'd still looked to Tyler for guidance. For strength. They all looked to him. So he'd learned to be the man they needed him to be.

When Kane's sexual preference had become apparent, Tyler had kicked the shit out of anyone who dared suggest he ought to be sent off as a nomad, as some prides liked to do with their so-called *deviants*. When Ava was picked on for her diminutive size, he made sure anyone who touched her knew they were taking on the entire Minor clan. And when the bastard Alpha who'd ruled before Landon had threatened to geld Michael to help him control his erratic shifting, Tyler had promised to repeat the procedure on the Alpha himself if he dared touch his baby brother.

For twenty years he'd been their champion. His responsibility for them had defined him, but now they didn't need him anymore.

Ava, for all her diminutive size, had learned diplomacy and developed a quiet strength of character that had won her the love and respect of the Alpha himself. No one would ever dare harm her again.

Caleb and Shana had finally managed to find the middle ground in the constant battle that had been their decades-long, on-again-off-again affair. Recently, his most reticent brother seemed happy in a way Tyler had never seen him before.

Michael, too, had found love and a sense of peace—though he still couldn't contain his shifting. Logical, pragmatic Mara was the last person Tyler would have expected an impulsive, willful soul like Michael to love, but she grounded him in a way Tyler had never been able to do, no matter how he'd tried to help.

Independent Kane had carved out his own happiness. Under Landon's rule, Kane and his partner Tom weren't just grudgingly tolerated, they were actively accepted by the rest of the pride. With Tom, Kane's laughter had returned, lightening his solemnity.

And now...Zoe. It was a romantic epidemic.

But he wasn't ready to join the ranks of happily-ever-afters.

She was his—that question had been decided already. If tonight had proved anything, it was that Zoe was inevitable.

Just another example of the universe yanking choice out of his life.

He needed a little time to come to terms with tying himself to her forever. And it *would* be forever. No strings just wasn't going to happen.

Tyler rolled silently out of bed, the lion's instinctive need to stay with her warring with his all-too-human wariness of commitment. Wariness won.

Finding his clothing in the dark seemed an impossible task, so Tyler shifted to his feline form, the feel of his fur a comfort to his restless thoughts, though the senseless circles of his reservations chasing one another around his mind were no quieter in this form.

He padded quietly to the door and nosed it open, batting it shut behind him with the flat of his paw, the well-oiled hinges never making a sound. He leapt off the porch, concentrating on the bunch and spring of his muscles and the feel of the earth beneath his paws as he landed. He wove through the compound, paws silent on the dusty ground. The garage loomed unlit in the darkness, a black box against the starry sky.

He'd locked it behind him earlier and his keys were back with his clothes, but he'd left his "back door" open. He circled the building to the rear where the loft window was open wide, high above the ground.

Gathering himself, Tyler crouched and sprang to the roof of the nearby parts shed. The corrugated metal rang dully like a muted tuning fork even though he tried to land softly. From there he leapt into the oak tree that shaded the area, timber groaning and creaking ominously under his weight. Lions were among the heaviest cats and the high branches bowed and cracked as he ran lightly across them and launched himself across the space to the open window.

He tucked his body tight, trying for an aerodynamic grace that his bulky cat form naturally lacked. His front legs and shoulders made it through the open window, but the ledge caught him hard on the ribs and his back paws scrabbled against the exterior siding for purchase. He muscled his hindquarters through the window and flopped onto his belly on the cement floor of the loft, panting softly.

Not the best secret entrance, but the height of the window discouraged the cubs from trying it.

Tyler shifted back to a form with opposable thumbs and pulled on the spare coveralls he kept stashed in the loft. His bare feet were silent on the metal stairs leading down to the garage bay.

The world made more sense when he was elbow-deep in

engine parts.

The shop had always been his refuge. He could take something run down and cast aside and bring it back to life. He could keep everything moving smoothly, all the pieces interacting together just as they should. There was justice in that, satisfaction and worth.

Tyler knelt next to the engine he was rebuilding, and his brain fell into silence as he concentrated on his task.

The other side of the bed was empty and cool when Zoe woke. With the first few rays of dawn streaming in through her window, her fears of the night before seemed ridiculous.

They'd had sex. Nothing earth shattering in that. For the life of her she couldn't think why she'd been so paranoid. Why she'd been so stupidly convinced they wouldn't be able to keep things no strings.

Zoe rolled out of bed and grabbed a pair of jeans and her snug *Bigger in Texas* T-shirt, propelled by the urge to talk to Tyler. She wanted to smooth thing over with him and make sure they were still on the same page. Make sure he hadn't read anything—accurately—into her awkwardness the night before.

She hurried down her porch steps, following the scent trail Tyler had left. She was so tuned to his scent, she probably could have found him even after a rainfall, but the morning was dry and hot, the sun already gearing up for an early summer scorcher, and his scent remained fresh.

She wove between the buildings, grateful there was no one about this early to see her. The garage bays were all closed when she arrived, the main door locked, but his scent circled the building before disappearing and there wasn't another trail leaving. He had to be in there.

"Tyler?" Zoe called, tapping on the metal door. She smoothed her palms over her hips and fidgeted, agitation bubbling up inside her.

This was stupid. For all she knew he was sleeping in there. She'd seen a cot in the loft. That didn't explain why he would have gone to the garage rather than back to his own place...unless he was trying to avoid her. He'd expect her to check his place first, wouldn't he? Was he hiding from her?

Zoe hated this insecurity. She felt like such a *girl.* She reminded herself that she was here only to make sure he knew they were still no strings.

Which, now that she thought about it, was a really freaking stupid reason to be here. Dammit. What had she been thinking?

She took a step back, pivoting on her heel, when the door creaked open behind her. "Zoe?"

Shit. She turned back, a fake smile plastered on her face. "Tyler. Hey."

"Were you looking for me?"

Yes, because I was being a total freaking moron. "Yeah, I..." *Shit.* She needed a reason to be looking for him. What the hell kind of reason could she make up?

"Is this about the clothes?" he asked. "I was going to come back for them. I just needed to work on some stuff."

For the first time, Zoe noticed he was wearing a pair of greasy grey coveralls open to the waist rather than the clothes he'd worn to her place. She hadn't even noticed that he'd left them behind. She latched onto his excuse eagerly. "Yeah. Your clothes. But you look like, you know, you found some."

And damn if the man didn't look edible in the uniform of his trade. The shapeless coveralls seemed to accentuate the breadth of his shoulders and the large, capable size of his hands. Hands that had been all over her body only hours ago.

"You wanna come in? I'm about done here."

Did she want to come in? Why did that question seem like the Riddle of the Sphinx? This was a casual visit, right? She wasn't asking for strings if she accepted his invitation to go into the garage. The garage where they'd hooked up only yesterday— but also where they had first discussed the no-strings plan. There wasn't anything hidden in his invitation. He was a guy, for fuck's sake. They didn't see the minefields in conversations that chicks planted there. They could still talk without having it complicate their sexual relationship, couldn't they?

"Zoe?"

Oh, Jesus. She'd been standing there gaping at him. "Yeah.

Yeah, sure. I'll come in."

Tyler opened the door wider and she slipped past him, reminded of when she'd let him into her place only hours earlier. But if she hadn't put her mark on her house, the garage was all Tyler. His scent saturated every surface, but even more than that, the neat efficiency and small, personalized touches made it a space that was uniquely him.

"How long have you been the pride mechanic?" she heard herself asking, even though she'd sworn she would keep things light and impersonal.

"Seventeen years." Tyler wandered over to a sturdy table where a mass of unidentifiable metal cluttered the surface. She trailed along behind, careful not to touch anything.

"You never met Tobias," Tyler commented as he picked up a piece and adjusted it in some mysterious way. "Cranky bastard. He was my mentor, taught me everything he knew about cars and then sent me to trade schools to learn more. He used to run the garage, even when he could barely lift a wrench anymore, but he retired when I was eighteen and handed it all over to me. He died...I guess it was five years ago now."

"I'm sorry."

"He was eighty-six years old and he died with the help of a box of Viagra." Tyler grinned fondly. "I wouldn't be too sorry."

"Eighteen's pretty young to be responsible for keeping the whole pride in wheels."

He grimaced. "One thing I'm used to, it's responsibility. You deal with it. No one else is going to."

Zoe shoved her hands in her pockets, knowing she shouldn't ask the next question if she wanted to keep them impersonal, but driven by a need to know. "Ava said you pretty much raised her and your brothers."

Tyler grunted. "No one else was going to," he repeated, but something cold had crept into his voice. "Our father left and our mother was useless."

"My sire was banished too." Zoe scuffed her toe over an old oil stain on the cement floor. "I don't really remember him." She'd been raised more as part of the pride litter than by her actual parents, but with Landon as her partner in crime she hadn't felt bruised by the lack.

"Our father wasn't banished. He left," Tyler said harshly. "Just decided he didn't want his responsibilities anymore and walked away. Headed for greener pastures."

Zoe struggled for something to say that wouldn't sound patronizing. *He would be proud of you?* Because how could he not be? Tyler was an amazing man. He was tempered steel tested by a lifetime of burdens. He was the man every father hoped his son would be, but she didn't think saying that would help. She didn't want to imply that Tyler needed his father's approval. He was better than that.

And besides, who was she to talk? She avoided responsibilities like the plague and she was an old hand at greener pastures. She knew better than most that they were almost never green.

Arriving in a new pride wasn't easy as a nomad. She and Landon had visited their share in their years of wandering before they'd come to Three Rocks.

Zoe cleared her throat self-consciously. "Can I ask you something?"

Tyler shrugged consent, his focus centered on the parts in his hands.

"That first day, when Landon and I arrived here at Three Rocks. The old Alpha Leonus and his thug Kato tried to gang up on Landon, but you didn't let them. I would have fought with him. I remember how surprised I was when I didn't even have to shift. But Leonus was even more surprised than I was when you stepped in, like you'd never interfered before. I've always wondered why you didn't. And why, that day, you did."

Tyler's hands stilled on the engine components. "Why do you ask?"

Because that was the moment I started falling in love with you.

She shook her head, in denial of the thought. This wasn't love. She wouldn't let it be. She hadn't needed a hero then, but having him step in with his armor shining had linked them somehow.

"I have a theory about why you didn't," she said. "Landon's

always had big sweeping ideas of changing the whole world, but you strike me as more focused. Ava... Michael... You only fight personal battles. I think Leonus was betting on you not lifting a finger for a stranger, but for some reason that wasn't a good bet." Zoe wet her lips, unaccountably nervous. "I guess I was just wondering if that reason had anything to do with me."

She was able to ask only because he wasn't looking at her. When he raised his eyes to hers, the words turned to sawdust in her mouth.

"Doesn't that make me less noble? If I wasn't doing it for the justice of it, but only to get laid?" Tyler slowly advanced on her, and Zoe found her feet retreating without any direction from her brain.

"But you didn't get laid. If you were only doing it so I'd feel indebted to you, why didn't you ever come to collect?"

"Isn't that what I did last night?"

"You waited over a year to claim your prize? I don't think so." Her back bumped against an SUV with the side paneling shredded by some lion's claws.

Tyler kept advancing until his chest brushed hers, using his superior height to loom over her in that way that never failed to make her internal organs melt like butter.

"Why, Tyler?"

He bowed his head and buried his nose in her hair, inhaling deeply next to her ear and then whispering the words into it. "I didn't want you to get hurt." He rested his hands on the SUV on either side of her so his forearms brushed the sides of her waist. "I've had this compulsion to protect you since the second you walked through that gate."

"I don't need you to protect me."

"*I* need to. You belong to me, Zoe. And you drive me mad when you put yourself at risk. I thought I could control it. I thought if I didn't give in to it that I would stop wanting to claim you, but it never worked."

Her breathing accelerated, fueled by the mix of arousal and panic his words inspired. "I don't want a protector."

"Tough," he growled against her ear, his body leaning into hers until she could feel his strength pressing her back into the door panel. "We don't always get what we want. I wanted to be free of my obligations and leave here for good, but I stopped thinking that way the second I realized you were mine to protect."

"You can't have it both ways," she said, her argument slightly less effective due to the breathy gasps that were all she could manage with his hands sneaking under her shirt to her braless breasts beneath. "You can't be both the big, strong protector and the no-strings lover. It doesn't work that way."

He lifted her, guiding her legs around his hips and pinning her hard against the SUV. "We both know no strings was never an option."

His mouth slammed down on hers, driving any protest she might have made out of her mind. He consumed her with the kiss. He shrugged out of his coveralls, and Zoe lowered her legs long enough to help the stiff cloth drop to his ankles. As he kicked it off, she quickly stripped out of her own jeans and T-shirt. Then he fell back on her in a hungry frenzy. His hands were filthy with engine grease, but Zoe didn't care. She wanted them on her everywhere, smearing tracks of dark grease across her skin.

Tyler was forceful, commanding. He spun her away from the side door and bent her over the table he'd been working at earlier, her ass raised like a gift. He nudged her feet wider and stroked a calloused hand over the curve of her buttocks as Zoe gripped the table for balance. She felt his thick cock probing at her entrance, impossibly hot like all the heat in his body was being redirected there, and then he plunged inside and she screamed raggedly as sensation ratcheted to an unbearable pitch, her cries echoing hollowly in the garage bay.

He drove into her again and again, hard enough that the heavy table began scraping across the floor with each pounding thrust. Zoe held on tight, aware of nothing but the knot of pleasure building in her blood. Tyler reached around and found the heart of the knot, rotating a single finger on her clit. The knot unraveled like a slingshot, flinging her into the stratosphere as her climax shook her body, and Tyler rammed into her one last time, holding tight and deep as he came hard inside her.

As she floated back to her body, Zoe concentrated on the sound of their uneven breathing. Everything else was too big, too much to contemplate.

Whatever this thing was between them, it had just gotten a hell of a lot more complicated.

Chapter Nine

Zoe snuck into the back of the mess hall, hoping to go unnoticed at Landon's mandatory defense summit. Flying under the radar wasn't something she had much experience with, but she'd been practicing it diligently for the last forty-eight hours. Ever since Tyler tossed no-strings out the window.

She'd fled the garage, throwing some lame excuse she couldn't even remember over her shoulder. Tyler hadn't stopped her, either smart enough to know she needed space or cocky enough to be certain she was coming back.

The world felt like it was squeezing in around her like a vacuum pack, sucking all the oxygen out of her lungs. She'd needed some breathing room. Some time to evaluate. Just a few minutes when her hormones weren't running on overdrive and insisting she absolutely must stay with that walking aphrodisiac of a lion. She couldn't think when she was with him.

Unfortunately, after two days apart from him, she was no closer to knowing what she wanted.

She'd avoided Landon, Ava, the entire Minor family, but especially Tyler. She knew what *he* wanted—what they all wanted. For her to decide she really did want to settle down.

Settle. The word tasted like rust on her tongue. If she stayed here, she'd be close to Landon and Ava. She'd have Tyler, and probably a few cubs and an extra thirty pounds of baby weight she couldn't shed.

She'd be domesticated. A house cat.

The thought made her physically ill, so much so she'd

actually considered going to the pride doc and asking him to give her a pregnancy test even though she *couldn't* be pregnant without going into her heat cycle. Wouldn't that be just her luck? If Tyler knocked her up, there'd be no denying him.

She didn't want her claws pulled. She could handle it for a little while—being surrounded by people you cared for wasn't exactly torture—but eventually the wanderlust that was so deeply embedded in her soul would start pressing against her heart again, begging for an outlet. Independence. Freedom. Adventure. Would her soul just wither and die without them? Could she be a house cat? And on the other side, could she even make herself leave Tyler?

He already felt like the cornerstone to the foundation of her happiness, like it would all crumble without him. But was he too grounded? He might profess to want to leave the pride and see the world, but he would never be able to leave his family. His siblings meant too much to him. And knowing what she now did about his father, she knew he would never let himself be the kind of man who abandoned those he loved. Tyler was even more caged than she was here at Three Rocks. But if she put herself in that cage with him, would they soothe one another or rip each other to pieces?

Zoe shuffled along the back of the room filled with every able-bodied adult in the pride. She didn't need to scan the room for Tyler. She spotted him right away, leaning against the base of the stage they never used. Landon stood on it now, Ava at his side, the Minor siblings and their mates arrayed at his feet. Zoe felt a twinge of guilt that she wasn't up there with them, presenting a united front, but that would only reinforce the illusion that she was part of this pride, and she wasn't. Not really. *Not yet*, a small voice whispered in her mind.

The mess hall was crowded. Meals were communal but rarely attended by all pride members simultaneously. Full-pride gatherings, like the ritual hunts, usually took place in the amphitheatre on the edge of the compound. Holding the meeting here was doubtless an attempt to keep the cubs from listening in, but Zoe would bet there was a cluster of small, furry ears pressed to the walls outside, trying to pick out stray words through the timbers. Curiosity was a feline trait, after all.

Landon raised his hands above his head, and the rumble of conversation in the hall instantly quieted. Zoe realized she was holding her breath and forced herself to let it out. Whatever they'd discovered in the last couple days, it couldn't be good, judging by the grim set of her brother's jaw.

Guilt jabbed again. She should have been with them. She should have been on the front lines, investigating and planning, but instead she'd been hiding. Taking care of herself first, like a true nomad outside a pride. So why did she feel like she'd done something wrong?

Landon cleared his throat and tipped his head back in his master-orator mode, projecting the charisma that made him a natural leader. "Since the incident at the Bar Nothing, a trio arrived in town, claiming to be government research scientists investigating the geological properties of this land. Two men and one woman, young by all accounts, they have been telling the town that we are operating under a similar government research grant, but that our funding is set to expire soon and they will be taking over the ranch when it does."

Sounds of unease momentarily rose, cutting Landon off until he raised his hands again for quiet.

"We haven't been able to determine yet where these so-called geologists are staying, though it is somewhere outside of town, and we have no way of knowing if there are more than just the three who've been seen by the townspeople. We don't know what they know about us. This could be nothing more than a misunderstanding. At this point, until we know more, our best strategy is to be always on guard defensively. Patrols will be doubled and run in pairs who will be in constant radio contact with the central security team. We'll be working to upgrade the sensors at the perimeter as quickly as possible, as well as beefing up security around the cubs. In the meantime, stay close to the compound, try to avoid going anywhere alone and report anything suspicious, no matter how insignificant it may seem."

Ava slipped her hand into Landon's, and the anxious tension in his shoulders seemed somehow to shift into a sense of power and strength.

"With luck we'll be able to face our enemy directly soon." A predatory growl rose through the room. Landon bared his teeth, nodding as if satisfied by the bloodthirsty response. "We will win this hunt. Until then, come up and get your new security assignments."

Zoe wrapped her arms around her stomach as the shifters in the room stood and shuffled toward the pride leaders to collect their new duty rosters. There was a sense of solidarity as the pride banded together to face the common enemy. Zoe knew she should feel motivated and a swell of camaraderie with her fellow lions, but all she felt was the intense urge to leave.

Lions rarely hunted alone, but Zoe wanted nothing more than to leave the group behind and go hunting, to test the sharpness of her claws against the flesh of those who threatened them.

The line to get assignments would take a while to clear out. Zoe slipped out the side door, striding quickly away from the building. She would talk to Landon later about whatever he wanted her to do. Now the lioness stirred restlessly within her, scratching to be let out. Zoe stretched her stride, loping down the path toward her place.

"Running away?"

The deep voice behind her brought her up short. Zoe paused, unfamiliar indecision slithering through her. Turn and face him? Or run like hell?

"It's a lot for me to adjust to too," Tyler said, closer this time.

Zoe turned. "It?"

Damn, he looked good. The sight of him so close was a salve to an ache she hadn't known she had. Tall and strong, a golden god gazing down at her with an expression of such possession it should have had her sprinting in the opposite direction, but all she wanted to do was throw herself against him.

"Taking a mate," he said. "It's a big adjustment for both of us."

Her breath left her in a whoosh. "Who said I was taking a mate?" *Presumptuous bastard.*

"Zoe."

"Tyler," she mimicked, a growl sneaking into her voice. "Before you grab a shotgun and start wedding planning, maybe you should check to see if the bride is willing."

"This isn't exactly how I pictured my life going either," he said, the words sharp.

"Oh, well done. That's the way to convince me we should get married. Bitch about how I'm screwing up your life plan. Bonus."

"That wasn't what I meant and you know it. We're both stuck in this, so we might as well—"

"I'm not stuck in anything, Tyler Minor. So you can just cram your *make the best of it* speech up your ass, okay, sweetie?"

"Dammit, Zoe! What did I do to get you so pissed at me? I thought we were good and then you bolt on me with no fucking explanation and avoid me for days. What did I fucking *do?*"

You wanted me. Zoe knew it was messed up, but him wanting her had scared the shit out of her. She was allowed to pin all her emotion on him when he was running hard in the opposite direction, but she hadn't been prepared for his about-face. When he wanted her, when it was real and she had to choose between a real life with him here and the life she knew on her own, suddenly everything she felt was bigger and scarier than she could handle.

But she couldn't tell him that.

"You didn't do anything. What do you want?"

His jaw locked and his hands fisted at his sides, but he lowered his eyes, visibly restraining himself from the urge to dominate her. Zoe was more impressed than she cared to admit by the effort.

"Landon wants you to take a look at the perimeter security. You know more about that techno-spy shit than anyone else on the ranch. I'm supposed to escort you."

"Babysit me, you mean. I can do it myself. I'll be on pride land the entire time."

"You'll be on the border and *everyone* is using the buddy system, so stop whining and get any gear you need. We're going as soon as you're ready."

Zoe stiffened, itching for a fight, wanting to take out all of her frustration and confusion on someone. "Is that an order?"

Tyler stepped forward until he was looming over her, but he didn't touch her, just saturated the air around her with the weight of his presence. "Zoe," he growled low. "We can play all the dominance games you want later, but right now you have a job to do for the pride, so get your ass moving and fucking *do it.*"

If she'd needed it spelled out for her that his family would always come first to him, Tyler had just done that. Pride first—even if his definition of pride was narrower than Landon's. Zoe didn't want to be another person he protected and bossed around. It wasn't in her.

Suddenly the picket fence looked more like bars. He would keep her safe, even if it meant building a cage around her with his own two hands. The two of them chafing against their restriction together she might have been able to handle. Tyler as her jailer would be unbearable.

"I'll get my things," Zoe said, her voice soft and expressionless.

Tyler rocked back on his heels, a flicker of satisfaction at the victory showing on his face. Zoe didn't bother telling him he'd lost something bigger than this argument. He'd lost her.

"Three more and we're done."

The truck rumbled over the cattle guard fifteen feet from the outer perimeter. Zoe sat in the passenger seat with a laptop open on her legs, ignoring him with a businesslike concentration that was starting to make him crazy.

For days he'd tried to give her space, even as his lion fought against the restriction, urging him to prove to her he was strong enough to be her mate the only way the animal in him recognized—through dominance. He'd nearly ripped Landon's head off for no good reason, just because he was another male in Zoe's life and Tyler couldn't stand the idea of anyone else having a claim on her. His human side refused to be ruled by his instincts. He knew Zoe would be as resistant to the idea of spending forever with him as he initially had been, but she didn't have decades of bending to Fate's will to prepare her as he did.

Strangely, the more time he'd given her, the more certain he'd become that he didn't need any more. The more she'd resisted, the faster he'd adjusted. He would never find anyone else who suited him the way Zoe did. It was her or no one, and now that he'd been with her, no one wasn't an option anymore.

But her rigid silence in the passenger seat couldn't be classified as encouraging.

They'd been replacing and updating the electronic monitors at the perimeter for the last four hours, and other than instructions, she hadn't said more than two words to him.

With only three more points to work, he realized he was running out of time when she'd be forced to be in his presence. He'd already wasted hours he could have been pleading his case. Whatever the hell his case was.

Tyler cleared his throat as he pulled up next to a fencepost that concealed motion sensors and a tiny infrared camera. "Zoe—"

She was out of the truck, the door slamming on her name. Tyler scrambled out after her and circled the bed. He scanned the horizon for threats automatically, even as he tried to figure out some way to convince her being his mate wouldn't be too horrible.

His lion insisted he dominate her. His human side urged him to reason with her. But on one thing the man and lion were in perfect accord. Zoe was his. Which made his priorities clear. Keep her safe, no matter what.

Which would have been easier if she wouldn't insist on throwing herself toward every hint of danger just to prove she could.

"Zoe," he began again, trying to make his voice sound reasonable rather than frustrated. "Would it really be so terrible to be my mate? You know you can always depend on me to watch your back."

"What about your back?" she asked without looking up from the tiny device she was fiddling with on the post. Her tone was hard and ruthless. "Do I get to watch it?"

Tyler hesitated, knowing his instinctive response of *hell no* wasn't going to get him the reaction he wanted. "If it were necessary to have someone watch my back..."

Zoe's head snapped up and her eyes narrowed at the evasion. "Bullshit. If I tried to do anything to defend you, you'd probably tie me to your bed for a week."

Tyler couldn't deny the idea held some appeal.

"*If* I were to mate with some lion—*if*, mind you—it would have to go both ways. Equals."

"It does go both ways." He protected her body, and she protected his heart. If anything happened to her...

"God, Tyler, you are such a crappy liar."

He flinched, feeling his future with Zoe slipping away at the distance in her voice. "You have to understand—"

"Oh I get it. The idea of me being hurt makes you feel sick and you're convinced the only thing that will keep me safe is you standing there ready to take any bullet aimed at me."

His breath left him. "Yes. That's it."

"Did you ever stop to think that I feel exactly the same way? That your complete lack of trust in my ability to watch *your* back is as frustrating as it is insulting? How would you feel if I left you chained to the stove while I went waltzing off into God-knows-what? I'm not asking you to stop protecting me, Tyler. I know that would go against every alpha instinct you have. I'm just asking you to let me protect *you*. We have to be equals in this or I'm going to end up trying to kill you someday—and it'll be self-defense because you couldn't stop smothering me. I'm not like Ava. If you want to date some delicate flower, you need to look elsewhere."

He didn't want to look elsewhere. He wanted Zoe *because* of her strength, the fight that was a part of her down to her soul, but he'd been denying her that part. He'd admired her fierceness, her power as a lioness, but then he'd tried to bind her spirit.

And he didn't know how not to. If her definition of compromise put her in danger, he didn't think he could do it.

She must have read the truth on his face. Her hands fisted,

her expression locking down to a flat, emotionless mask that looked so wrong on her expressive face.

"It isn't going to work," she said softly. "We have to end this now, before things get any more complicated."

"*No.*" The word sprang out of him with the same force as his claws that suddenly unsheathed. He never shifted involuntarily, never lost control, but the thought of Zoe just giving up and walking away pierced right through his shields and stabbed his heart.

"You don't get to dictate to me," she retorted. Her eyes were bright with anger, the vivid expression back in her face, but her hands were deft and gentle as she handled the sensors, never pausing in her work. "I never agreed to take you as my mate and even if I had, it wouldn't be a free pass for you to run my life." She snapped the cover closed on the post sensors and swept her tools up. She stalked toward him, challenge in every line of her body. "I'm never going to be the meek little woman who sits obediently by with her fucking *needlepoint* while you ride off into battle." She flung her tools through the open truck window onto the bench seat, but didn't move to climb in, turning to snarl up at him, "And I am *never* going to take orders from you."

Tyler started toward her, intending to give the words *kiss her into submission* new definition, when something sharp jabbed into his shoulder. He hesitated, raising a hand to the sting, blinking as the world slowed and the colors of the pasture bled into one another before his eyes like an impressionist painting. *What the hell?*

"Tyler?" Zoe's voice sounded like it was coming from an out-of-tune radio, soft, then suddenly loud then soft again, and all battling against the static that filled his ears.

"*Run,*" he grunted, as his knees gave way. Whatever drug they'd shot him with, it was fast working.

His cheek smacked into the ground hard. He couldn't lift his arms to brace for the impact. His vision was still functioning—blurred though it was—as all the rest of his motor functions shut down one by one. He saw Zoe's boots running away from him—obeying him for once in her life, thank God— but the steps were slowing, staggering, and she didn't make it ten yards before she slumped to the ground.

No.

A surge of something vicious and powerful ran through his blood. His vision cleared. He still had no feeling in his arms, but he managed to move them even though they felt like they belonged to someone else. Rolling slightly to the side, he shoved himself up. Half-crawling, half-dragging himself, he inched toward Zoe.

Protect your mate.

Another sting pierced his neck. Tyler lifted his dead-weight hand and yanked the dart out before the tranquilizer could find its way into his bloodstream. But enough of the damn poison had gotten in to send him crashing back to the ground.

Zoe, Zoe, Zoe. His eyes stayed locked on her unmoving form in front of him as he willed his body to fight the drug. She'd become his mantra, his reason for being. They could take him, but he had to get her out of here.

His eyes were still open, his hearing still staticky but functioning, when a pair of footsteps approached.

"Jesus, he's still conscious."

"Hit him again."

"Will that damage him? I already gave him enough to take down an elephant. He said a breeding pair is no good if one is damaged."

"Do you want this big fucker waking up before we get him back to the lab? Hit him a-fucking-gain."

"Fine, but you get to explain it to the boss if he's sterile or brain-dead."

The second man snorted. "Just don't aim for his junk. Brain-dead isn't a problem."

Tyler didn't feel where the next dart hit him. He only knew it had when a yellow fog swamped him and the world faded away.

Chapter Ten

The voices were the first thing that infringed on Zoe's consciousness. Long before she was awake enough to move, she heard them, broken riddles that faded in and out and meant nothing in her fuzzy cotton-candy world.

"...can't keep him under. Nothing in the data suggests a male of his size should be able to..."

"...responding to the hormone yet? Check her temperature again."

"...don't think the wall will hold if he attacks it again..."

"...shouldn't she be shifting? The data clearly states within four hours of injection..."

"...you wanna try putting him in restraints, be my guest. I'm not going in there..."

"...running out of sedative..."

Sedative. That explained the IV she could feel in her arm. She was drugged. Was she in the hospital? Lying on her back, she could be in a hospital bed. Had she been in an accident? Emergency surgery? The voices didn't sound like the pride doctor. If she wasn't at the pride, where was she?

The last thing she remembered...huh. What was the last thing she remembered?

Tyler's face pushed to the front of her fuzziness. *Tyler.* She remembered the shock on his face as he told her to run, the sickening dread and fear that had hardened in her stomach as he'd collapsed at her feet, the sting in her upper arm. She remembered running for help, though everything in her screamed to stay and guard him. Then nothing.

Chills shot through her blood, but Zoe couldn't let terror freeze her. They'd been taken. Were they being held together? Was he all right? Was she?

She flexed her muscles as much as she could without moving, careful not to alert their captors that she was awake. She tested her extremities. Everything seemed to be working, but she felt...odd. Achy, hot, and like her skin had been stretched too tight.

"I can tell you're awake." The voice was feminine and high-pitched, young. Not one of *the* voices.

Zoe opened her eyes. The room was tiny and poorly lit, the walls and ceiling corrugated metal, like a container from a cargo ship. But they were in west Texas, or at least they had been when they were captured, not exactly close to a port. The room barely fit the narrow twin bed Zoe was strapped to and a pile of unidentifiable medical equipment.

The girl who'd spoken stood in the corner, as far as she could get from Zoe without leaving the room. She was older than Zoe'd guessed from her voice, but still couldn't be much more than twenty-five. Thin and nervous, she clutched a water bottle against her breastbone, her wide eyes fixed on Zoe as if she might leap from the bed and eat her—which she would, if she weren't strapped to the bed tight enough to restrict circulation.

"Where am I?" Zoe tried to say, but her voice came out a ragged croak. Her throat was raw, as if she hadn't swallowed for days. How long had she been out? She felt nauseous. From lack of food? Or the aftereffects of the drug? She hadn't completely shaken it off. The room still seemed to lurch and sway around her.

"Are you thirsty?" the girl asked, though she showed no inclination to give Zoe the water.

Zoe ignored the question as beyond idiotic. "What do you want?"

She fidgeted with the bottle. "I'm not supposed to be talking to you. They only let me check your vitals."

A low growl and a shuffling thud sounded through the wall. Zoe's heart rate quickened. *Tyler.*

The girl made a keening noise and scuttled away from the metal barrier. "You need to get him to calm down," she whispered urgently. "They want him alive because they've never been able to capture a breedable pair before, but if they can't keep him sedated, they'll kill him. You have to make him stop."

"Untie me and I will."

She shook her head frantically. "I can't."

One of the voices filtered through the wall. "...half dose should do her. Use the rest on him."

The girl shuddered. She was terrified. Of Tyler, of Zoe, but also of *them*.

"I'm not even supposed to be talking to you. You need to use your mate-link thingy to tell him you're okay, or they're going to shoot him with something other than a tranq."

Mate-link thing? "We don't have—"

"Candice!" A piece of the wall slid open and a slim, dark-haired man with a ponytail appeared in the opening, holding a syringe. "Out. Now."

The girl sucked in a sharp breath and darted past the ponytail guy.

He advanced toward Zoe, never looking at her face, his eyes flicking over her body like she was nothing more than an animal or a specimen on a table. Which to him, she probably was. Zoe jerked against her restraints, baring sharp teeth and releasing her claws in a partial shift, but it didn't do any good.

The plunger on the syringe pressed down. The world blacked out.

The last thing Zoe heard was the unmistakable roar of an enraged lion. Numb lips twitched in a smile of vicious satisfaction. They'd messed with the wrong lion.

Tyler was coming for her.

Tyler swam up through a yellow haze, desperately clawing his way to consciousness even though he couldn't remember why he felt such violent urgency. He knew only that he needed to be awake. To be strong.

He heard a snarling roar and realized dimly that it was coming from him. His fur felt sticky—blood?—and his claws were extended with the awareness of a threat. He scented the air, trying to identify the danger.

Metal, chemicals, human sweat, a fading scent of onions. And beneath it all, familiar as his own heartbeat, *Zoe.*

Protect your mate.

There it was. That's why he needed to be sharp. Why he needed to fight. He had to keep her safe. His mate, his life.

And they'd dared touch her.

Tyler launched himself at a wall already heavily gouged, the metal yielding like warm butter beneath his claws. He heard voices shouting on the other side, frantic and panicked. *Good. Let them piss themselves with fear.* Tyler roared again, pushed beyond reason and violence into blind carnage.

The room jerked. Only when it slammed to a stop, throwing him sideways against the far wall, did he realize the entire structure had been moving. As his lion leapt again at the sides of his cage, savagery in every swipe of his paws, the small part of him, buried deep but still capable of rational thought, picked up on the telling details.

The room was claustrophobically tight, no room for a running start. They had to be in a trailer of some kind. If the bastards had been dragging a camper all over, it would explain why the pride hadn't been able to track their movements to any one spot. It also meant he had no idea where they were and only instinct telling him he hadn't already been separated from Zoe. Instinct and scent. She was either near or they'd doused the trailer in the scent of her distress just to send him into a frenzy.

Dimly he heard panicked voices seeping through the holes his claws were punching in the metal.

"...used the last of the sedative an hour ago. He's shaking it off at four times the rate the research suggests," a tenor whined.

"I don't give a shit. Get a hold of the situation!" a dark, authoritative voice barked. "I can't drive with a thousand pounds of enraged lion rattling around back here. Put him under or fucking put him down, but get control, dammit! We can always catch another male, but I refuse to jeopardize the female. We've never been able to experiment on one before—"

Tyler stopped listening. The female. *Zoe.* Like hell they were going to experiment on his mate. His humanity receded under the crushing need to reach Zoe. To protect her, no matter the cost. Adrenaline coursed through his blood, thickening it until each heartbeat was heavy with angry purpose.

He coiled back on his haunches and sprang at the door. Jagged metal edges screamed against one another, more piercing than nails on a chalkboard, as the frame gave way. The deadbolts held, but the frame ripped out of its moorings. The heavy metal panel fell into the room beyond, a feral lion riding it down.

Tyler spun in a circle, his tail lashing out behind him as he scanned for threats. He'd fallen into a compact office of some kind, tightly packed with filing drawers and locked cabinets. It was empty, but held two additional doors. The one next to where he'd been held smelled sterile, with distinct human scents—*lab.* That's where the men behind the voices were hiding. But the door on the opposite side of the little office smelled so familiar the fur on his shoulders stood on end. *Zoe.*

Anger called him toward the lab, but need drove him across the room. The deadbolts holding Zoe's cell shut required thumbs, but for a moment he couldn't shift. Rage locked him in his lion form. Tyler planted his paws on the metal floor, struggling to calm himself enough to change. There wasn't time to waste. The scientists must have heard the crash. They would know he was loose. They'd be coming.

But his body refused to obey. Tyler, who never lost control, was at the mercy of his lion and the lion wouldn't rest until he'd ripped out some throats and lapped up the warm blood that spurted out.

The small part of him that still possessed some shred of human awareness appreciated the catch-22. His feral need to protect his mate prevented him from freeing her, but the man's frustration was a dim echo of the lion's obsession.

The sound of the lab door opening behind him spun him snarling to face the new threat. Time was up. The lion roared his pleasure. He would have blood.

Zoe came awake to the same sound that had followed her into darkness—a familiar ragged roar. But much closer now. Tyler was right outside the door. He'd gotten loose.

He's coming for me.

The sharp comfort that thought inspired was disconcerting. Was she a damsel in distress? Did she just lie there and wait to be rescued? Tyler would always come for her, her certainty of that fact was unshakeable, but she refused to be declawed by that certainty. She was a lioness, dammit. She didn't wait for a white knight.

Even if she was still dopey from sedative and strapped to a bed. She wasn't without resources.

Zoe tested the restraints, but they were no looser than before. She was going to have to shift. It would destroy her clothes and hurt like hell—changing the shape of her body while restrained felt like her joints had been repeatedly jerked out of their sockets and rammed back in again. But she wasn't afraid of pain.

Zoe reached for her lioness form. There was a minute delay, thanks to the sedative still slowing her reflexes, but when it came, the change ripped through her hard. The force of the shift shredded the leather of the restraints, and she gave a feline hiss of pain. Shaking off the remnants of leather, she sprang to the foot of the bed on four paws then abruptly shifted back again, coming to her human form with her arms wrapped around her middle like she could hold the broken pieces of herself together.

"Shit." *Yeah, it definitely hurt.* Lurching to her feet, she staggered from the wave of dizziness that always accompanied changing form twice in quick succession. She groped at the door, fumbling with the knob for several seconds before her fuzzy thoughts cleared enough for her to realize it was locked. *Brilliant, Zoe.*

She was doing a pretty shitty job of rescuing herself so far.

She didn't know how long it had been since she'd eaten, but it was too long to risk another shift—she'd just pass out in lioness form. Helplessness churned sickeningly in her gut. Then a pair of gunshots echoed loudly in the room beyond her cage.

"Tyler!" she screamed. Claws sprang from her fingertips,

her teeth sharpening to fangs as she barely stopped a full shift from incapacitating her.

A fraction of a second later the door sprang open, and Zoe saw the blood.

It wasn't the pain of the bullet punching through his shoulder that brought Tyler back to humanity. It was the sound of Zoe's voice screaming through the door.

The pansy-ass science geek who had fired wildly into the room retreated behind the shut door to the lab again. Taking advantage of the cowardice and his own sudden clarity, Tyler shifted back to human form. Blood gushed from the hole in his shoulder, running faster with the reconfiguring of his body. It streamed down his torso in thick rivulets, but he didn't care. He threw back the bolts on Zoe's cage and yanked the door open, his heart jerking spasmodically at the sight of her, clothing shredded, claws sharp, fangs bared. She was an Amazon warrior ready for battle.

Sweet Jesus, she was gorgeous.

He reached for her, needing to touch her, but though she rushed forward, it wasn't into his arms. "God damn, you're bleeding a ton. No spurting, that's good. Not arterial, then." Her hands slapped his shoulder over the bullet hole, bearing down on the wound. Tyler made a sound that wasn't remotely human, and Zoe's wild eyes jerked up to meet his. "Who shot you? How many are left?" Her words were choppy, efficient and emotionless—crisis mode.

As gratified as he was by her confidence that he'd already eliminated some, he couldn't live up to her expectation. He shook his head as he pulled her behind a filing cabinet so they'd have some cover if the bastards opened fire again. "I've heard two men and one girl."

Zoe nodded once. "The girl's scared shitless. She shouldn't be a problem. The one guy I saw was sort of thinnish, but if they're armed—" She broke off, her eyes scanning every surface of the tiny office even as she applied pressure to the wound in his shoulder. "D'you see anything I can use as a shield? Kevlar would be nice, but I doubt they left a flak jacket lying around for me."

Tyler wrapped his fingers around Zoe's wrist to get her attention, focused on the one part of her statement that scared him most. "You aren't going in there."

"You want to wait 'em out? I gotta say that's a pretty crappy plan, Tyler, since I'm pretty sure the exit to this tin can is through that room. Unless you're feeling up to tearing through another wall."

"I'll go."

"You're bleeding. A lot. There's macho and then there's dumbass. Don't be a dumbass."

The animal rose up inside him, fast and violent, and he ground his teeth against the primal urge to shift. He'd probably die of blood loss if he did, but instinct didn't care. "I can't watch you get shot, Zoe," he growled. The sight would kill him faster than a bullet.

"Yeah, well, I can't stand here and watch you get shot *again*. The one who isn't injured gets to take on the bad guys. Those are the rules."

"Together." The word was painful to push out, but Zoe was right, he wasn't much protection shot up and unable to shift to his more powerful form.

"Together? Bonnie and Clyde style?"

Tyler winced. "Maybe pick a couple who didn't die."

"Can't think of any. Butch and Sundance... Thelma and Louise..."

"Zoe. Stop."

"Together is good," she said, a catch in her voice.

He squeezed her wrist gently, looking away from the door to study the curves of her face he'd long since memorized. Dark circles smudged the smooth skin beneath her eyes, lines of stress bracketed her mouth and her eyes were glassy, but her hands were steady. "*Zoe*," he whispered.

She swallowed thickly, looking up to meet his eyes. "Yeah, I know. I love you too."

His heart lurched. He'd run from her, from this, for months. He'd known from the second he laid eyes on her that Zoe King was *his*, and he'd done everything he could to keep from falling for her. He'd seen her as another duty, another

251

weight of responsibility, but Zoe wasn't an obligation, she was his whole heart. He didn't just need her or want her, he loved her with an intensity that made the rest of his life small by comparison.

What kind of fool saw that truth only when their life together might last only a few more minutes?

Tyler wrapped his uninjured arm around Zoe and held her against his chest, pressing a kiss on her forehead, breathing in the scent of her—even if it was overlaid with the thick tang of his own blood.

A muted thud from behind the door to the lab called them back to the task at hand.

Zoe pulled away, straightening to stand on her own. "Let's do this."

Zoe crouched on her haunches beside the door, trying to shake the woozy feeling that had accompanied her latest shift. Tyler hunched to the left of the doorway, ready to throw it open so Zoe could leap through—a plan she'd feel much more confident with if he didn't look like he was about to pass out from blood loss.

They made a great team. Dizzy and dizzier. If surviving came down to a race to see who could lose consciousness first, they were set.

But the situation wasn't going to get better if they waited. There was nothing in the office to stitch Tyler up and nothing for her to eat to get her energy level up. They were never going to be in better shape than they were in right now.

Zoe nodded once—the gesture always feeling oddly foreign in her feline form—and Tyler reached for the doorknob.

She darted through the opening as soon as it was wide enough to fit her body, belly low to the ground, teeth bared, claws out—and drew up short, paws scrabbling to stop her momentum on the smooth tiles of the lab.

Two bodies lay prone on the floor, unmoving, white foam dribbling from their mouths and a sickly sweet smell rising off them. Zoe hissed, instinctively backing away from the too-sweet death scent.

Ponytail guy and a younger, even thinner man with a military-style haircut weren't going to be a problem anymore.

"What the hell?" Tyler stood in the doorway, frowning at the bodies on the floor.

A clicking sound brought Zoe around sharply, and she saw the girl, huddled in the corner between an exam table and a metal cabinet, sobbing silently and shaking so hard her teeth were rattling against one another. "I c-c-couldn't," she moaned, holding something clutched tightly in her fist. "Please don't h-h-*hurt* me."

Zoe closed her mouth to hide the sharpness of her fangs, rising out of her hunting crouch.

"A suicide pill?" Tyler bent over the bodies to check for pulses, his nose wrinkling at the sweet-and-sour scent. He turned his head toward the girl. "Why?"

"B-B-Ben said the bullets didn't stop you. We didn't have s-s-silver," she explained, somewhat calmer now that she wasn't being snarled at by a few hundred pounds of pissed-off lioness.

Silver bullets. Thank God for superstitious idiots.

"Ben was a lousy shot," Tyler grunted. "Why not just run?"

"They knew too much to be captured and tortured by weres."

Tyler's eyebrows arched speculatively. Zoe could almost see him assuming the mantle of a pride lieutenant. "And what do *you* know?"

The girl's teeth began to chatter again. "I don't know anything! I'm new. They only brought me in a couple months ago in San Antonio. Long after they broke off from the Organization. I don't know where any of the research bases are, I swear. Just don't hurt me!"

The Organization. Zoe's ears pricked forward. The girl didn't know how much she did know. The shifters had never even had a name for their boogeyman before now.

"We aren't going to hurt you. What's your name?"

"C-C-Candice. Candice Murphy."

"Candice. Where are we?" Tyler asked her.

Her face screwed up in concentration. "New Mexico? We couldn't make very good time because Dr. B couldn't use the main roads with you making the truck swerve all over, throwing yourself around back there."

Zoe eyed the two men on the floor, wondering which of them was Dr. B. Her stomach rumbled noisily, hunger from her multiple shifts stabbing into her gut. If she didn't eat soon, she'd be tempted to take a bite out of one of the bodies. Just a small bite. A little nibble from the calf maybe. Did it even count as cannibalism if she was in her lion form?

The room dipped and swayed around her and Zoe sneezed, shaking her head sharply to try to get the world back to rights.

"Zo? You all right, babe?" Tyler came toward her, digging his fingers into the fur behind her ears. She leaned into his touch, steadied by his presence.

When the wall behind him began to slide to the side, she thought it was just her eyes playing tricks on her again. Until the muzzle of a gun lowered into the opening, aimed at Tyler's broad back.

Dr. B wasn't on the floor.

Zoe roared, throwing her weight against Tyler's legs to knock him to the ground and leaping past him toward the opening as the gun fired, deafeningly loud in the enclosed space. Zoe didn't have time to see if the bullet had struck Tyler. She landed hard on the heavy-set man behind the sliding panel which led to the cab of a truck. Her claws ripped through flesh, her teeth sinking deep into the soft tissue of his throat, cutting off any attempt at a scream. Warm blood gushed in a sweet rush into her mouth.

This man had tried to kill Tyler. He'd kidnapped her and experimented on her. Who knew how many other shifters he'd harmed? She basked in the last feeble beats of his heart before dropping his body with a thud. She swayed over him, dizzy from expending the last of her energy, and felt Tyler's hands on her, steadying her.

She looked up, seeing only that he was whole—no new bullet wounds marking him. Then the world flipped upside down and whooshed away from her like a train through a dark tunnel, and Zoe collapsed into blackness.

Chapter Eleven

"Ben and Andy worked for the Organization for like six months, but they weren't being given any responsibility, see? So they decided to go it alone. They'd heard about Dr. Busey getting kicked out of the Organization for trying to, you know, breed the weres in captivity, which went against the Organization's, erm, mission statement, I guess? So they went to find Dr. Busey and get some hands-on experience. When I met them, they'd all been together for a couple months, hunting weres. Dr. B was definitely the boss, but he let Ben and Andy have, like, responsibility, right? They were more like equals. I mean, Ben barely even got in trouble with Dr. B for telling me about the weres. I almost knew already. I'd read a lot of werewolf books, right? And I told him I really wanted to see one up close, see? So Ben convinced Dr. B to let me come along as a research assistant. That was when we heard about this town."

"So the Organization doesn't know about this pride?" Landon's sharp question cut across Candice's rambling recital.

She sat on a chair in the mess hall, her hands wrapped around a cup of cocoa, surrounded by the pride's war council. They hadn't needed to torture anything out of her, though Zoe thought they might need to apply thumbscrews to get the girl to shut up about how cool it was to be around "weres".

"I don't think so. I mean, Dr. B was always saying how the Organization had their heads up their you-know-whats cuz they were ignoring all the signs of were activity south of the Rockies. He says they were dumb to fixate on the wolves. Said," Candice corrected after a moment, her eyes flicking sideways to Zoe before scuttling back to gaze worshipfully at Landon.

So the pride was safe. For now. As safe as they'd ever been. And more informed than they'd ever been.

Zoe shoved away from the wall she'd been propping up and slipped out the side door, restlessness driving her feet. She was halfway up the path to the infirmary before she realized where she'd been headed. Tyler was up there, getting patched up by the pride doc. He'd insisted Zoe be looked at first, idiot man, and after a nutrient shot and eating her weight in red meat, she was fine and dandy. While he still had a hole in him.

Zoe rubbed a hand against the pressure in her chest, turning and walking down the path away from the infirmary.

The jumbo-sized camping backpack that had traveled with her across the country was dusty when she pulled it out of her closet. Zoe brushed off the thick fabric and unzipped it, flopping it open on her bed. Packing wouldn't take long. She didn't have much she wanted to keep. Travel light. That was her motto. Easier to run that way.

When a soft tap came at her door, Zoe flinched, her hands freezing in the act of stuffing her rain poncho into a side pouch. She half-expected Tyler, though it was early yet for him to be released from medical. Her other instinct was Landon, but he must still be interrogating the prisoner.

She didn't want to see anyone else. She didn't particularly want to see those two either. She just wanted to go. And she didn't want to think about or talk about why.

The knock came again, accompanied by "Zoe?" in Ava's distinctive husky rasp.

"Shit," Zoe muttered. Ava would look at her with those big, eerily ice-grey eyes, all wounded and shit that Zoe hadn't planned on saying goodbye. Guilt rose up like bile and Zoe swallowed it down. One thing she wasn't was a coward. "Come in."

Ava opened the door just enough to slip her slight frame inside and shut it behind her, leaning back against the wood. "Hey."

"Hey." Zoe didn't stop packing—a silent reminder to them both that she wouldn't be talked out of going.

"I didn't expect to find you packing," Ava said softly. "Not after the way you came back."

Zoe didn't need the reminder of their dramatic return. She'd been dipping in and out of consciousness, but even she knew what it must have looked like. Tyler driving through the gates in the truck with the researchers' trailer hitched to the back, kicking open the door and carrying Zoe to the infirmary, even though his shoulder was bleeding through the makeshift bandage Candice had rigged for him. The message had been clear to everyone who saw it—Tyler had saved her, saved them all. But instead of sending her swooning into his oh-so-heroic arms, Zoe couldn't face him. She had to get out of here.

"Pride's safe now," she said shortly. "You have Candice and all the files those nutjobs collected on us. Landon doesn't need me anymore."

"Landon was pretty upset when the two of you vanished like that. We all were."

"Tyler's popular."

"*You* are popular, Zoe. Sticking around for a few days to reassure your brother wouldn't kill you. But I don't think Landon is the only one who's going to protest your departure," Ava commented. "Zoe, I haven't interfered in the past—"

"Then don't start now."

Ava ignored her. "I always figured whatever was between you and my brother was your business, but—"

"This isn't about Tyler," Zoe interrupted sharply. The words were only half a lie. It wasn't entirely about Tyler. A lot of it was about her. Who she was when she was with him.

"At least talk to him before you go," Ava urged. "He deserves that courtesy, don't you think?"

"Tyler doesn't want a mate any more than I do," Zoe said harshly. "He'll understand."

Ava grimaced. "Maybe you're right. He probably will. God, if two more commitment-phobic people ever existed on this earth..." She sighed, turning to go, but stopped to deliver one last blow to Zoe's willpower. "If you guys weren't so busy trying to prove how independent you are, you might just find that you're perfect for each other. If you would just let yourself be."

Zoe waited until the door clicked shut behind Ava to slump

down onto the bed. Ava was right. Tyler was perfect, but more than that. He was perfect for her.

But perfect didn't change anything. Zoe grabbed her toiletry bag, zipping it up and shoving it into her pack.

Tyler trotted down the steps of the infirmary, ignoring the doc's order that he take it easy. One thought drove all others right out of his brain. He needed to find Zoe. Now. He hadn't seen her since the doc had taken her out of his arms, and his heart wouldn't slide down from the place it had lodged in his throat until he could see with his own eyes that the reports that she was *good as new* were true.

He needed to touch her, to feel the texture of her skin beneath his fingertips so he could breathe again.

The path to Zoe's bungalow felt a million miles long, like it had been stretched since the last time he walked it. He moved faster, half-jogging and then running. His shoulder ached like the devil, little jabs of hot pain spearing into him with each jolting footfall, but he didn't slow. Mara was coming up the path, but stepped out of the way as she saw him coming, a knowing smile quirking her lips.

He didn't care who saw him. Didn't care who gave him that smug *must be newly mated* look. He just ran.

The door was open when he got to her bungalow. The room was usually so bare it took him a moment to realize it had been stripped even further. The only item that was Zoe's left inside was the cowboy hat someone must have collected from the perimeter where they'd been taken. It sat lonely and abandoned on the bed.

She was gone.

Tyler didn't waste time searching her place. He scented the air and took off after her. He'd be able to track her more easily in lion form, where his sense of smell was sharper, but he wasn't quite panicked enough to rip his stitches by shifting form. Yet.

Rounding the corner of his garage, he saw her. She stood at the door where he'd pinned her only days ago, a piece of paper in hand, her backpack resting against her ankle. His heart eased its panicked seizing at the sight of her. But his voice was gruff with the aftereffects of fear and anger when he spoke.

"A note?" he growled. "You weren't even going to wait until I was released from the infirmary?"

Zoe spun toward him, her eyes widening in a way he would have thought was pleasure to see him and something like relief—if not for the fact that she was clearly leaving him. "Tyler."

"Going somewhere?"

Her expression hardened, firming with resolve. "Yes. I have to go."

"You don't have to. No one wants you to leave, Zoe."

"I want to." She made a face, turning away from him then turning back before he could take a step toward her. "I don't like who this is making me," she said, waving between them to indicate the *this*. "If I leave, at least I'll be me again."

Tyler felt his expression softening, even as his chest ached with remorse. This was his fault. He'd failed her. "I'm sorry about what happened in the trailer," he said, fighting to keep his voice low and steady. "I shouldn't have let you be put in that position. You shouldn't have to feel guilty for killing that man."

Zoe's snort cut him off. "God, Tyler, that isn't it. You think I feel bad for killing that bastard? He was trying to shoot us. Put us down like animals. I'd kill him again in a heartbeat—and I'm sorry if I'm a little too bloodthirsty for you, but I figured you of all people would understand why I had to do it."

"Of course, I—Zoe—if not that, why are you...?"

Her shoulders sagged. "I was the damsel in distress," she muttered toward her feet. "I expected you to save me. Yeah, I got over it and kicked some ass, but there was this moment when I just *waited* for you. I can't be that person, Tyler. I don't like that part of me. The part that wanted to just sit back and let you rescue me. It feels too much like I'm losing who I am, if I become that girl." She looked up, meeting his eyes for the first time during her speech. "I can't be with you."

"It isn't weakness to rely on someone else, Zoe," he said, approaching her, needing to touch her, feeling that if he could just get his hands on her, she wouldn't be able to slip out of his life like smoke on the wind. "I've spent my entire life protecting everyone around me, doing it all myself, being the rock. You were the first person I depended on. I wouldn't have let you watch my back if you were weak." Close enough to touch her now, he gently brushed a hand across her jaw, cupping it. "I wouldn't love you if you weren't a warrior."

She started to speak, but he could see on her face it was going to be denial, so he spoke over her, willing her to believe him. "I thought we made a pretty good team. You kept me from getting myself shot a second time. Turns out having someone to watch your back isn't such a bad thing. So who's gonna do that if you leave me?"

"I know you, Tyler. I don't want to be another obligation, another person for you to protect."

"You won't be," he vowed. "It isn't easy for me to let you put yourself at risk, but I don't ever want to hurt you or hold you back. I'm going to fuck up sometimes. I'm going to try to protect you, no matter what, but I'll try to listen when you tell me I'm being a complete dipshit. And those obligations..." Tyler shook his head, trying to find the right words, unused to pouring his heart out. He swallowed thickly and tried again, not caring if the words were pretty as long as they were true. "My siblings are my life."

"And you deserve a life of your own—"

"No, let me finish. My life wouldn't be anything without my obligations. Without Ava and Michael and Caleb and Kane. They make it... They give my days reason and happiness. And you...my life would be empty without you, Zoe. I need you. I love you. Could you please say something and stop looking at me like that?"

Her lips quirked in a small smile, but he couldn't celebrate yet. The smile was too sad. "I don't want to stay here and raise a bunch of cubs."

"I don't want that either. Maybe kids. Someday down the road. But I want to leave Three Rocks too. Just you and me."

She was already shaking her head. "You know you won't abandon your siblings, Tyler. It isn't in you to walk away from your responsibilities."

"They're grown now. And I won't be abandoning anyone.

Landon will need an ambassador to go to the other prides and packs, warn them about the Organization, make a plan for the future. Hell, maybe even talk about coming out to the humans." He grinned. "I seem to remember someone thought that was a good idea."

Zoe's expressive face had stilled, a thoughtful light kindling in her eyes. "Ambassador?"

Tyler brushed his thumb over the fullness of her lower lip, marking his place. "We need to band together, all the shifters, if we're going to have any chance of survival, but not all the prides are going to come easily. A trusted, persuasive emissary to travel around the world, acting on behalf of our families and our people... It would have to be a pair. So there's always someone there to watch out for you..."

Tyler bent and pressed a soft kiss onto Zoe's lips.

"It's okay to rely on me, Zoe. I will always be here for you." He kissed her again, longer this time, lingering in the warmth of her mouth. "It's okay to need me," he whispered against her lips. "I need you right back." He kissed her a third time, deep and drugging, putting everything he felt, everything he hoped for into each caress. "It's okay to love me..."

"I do."

He dared put his arms around her. "Just don't leave me."

"I can't. I won't," she promised, tugging him down for another kiss, fiercer and more passionate than the last. That single vow lit a fuse in his soul, sending him up like a firecracker exploding in the sky. When she finally pulled back, they were both breathless, clinging to one another to stay upright. They stood in front of the garage, in full view of anyone who cared to walk by, but Tyler couldn't care less.

Zoe was his. Finally, irrevocably, perfectly *his*.

About damn time.

About the Author

Vivi Andrews lives in Alaska when she isn't indulging her travel addiction. She's currently hard at work on her next paranormal romance. For more about her books or the exploits of a nomadic author, please visit her website at www.viviandrews.com or stop by her blog at viviandrews.blogspot.com. Vivi also loves to hear from readers and invites you to email her at vivi@viviandrews.com.

HOT STUFF

Discover Samhain!

THE HOTTEST NEW PUBLISHER ON THE PLANET

Romance, fantasy, mystery, thriller, mainstream and
more—Samhain has more selection, hotter authors, and
everything's available in ebook.

Pick your favorite, sit back, and enjoy the ride!
Hot stuff indeed.

WWW.SAMHAINPUBLISHING.COM

Discover eBooks!

THE FASTEST WAY TO GET THE HOTTEST NAMES

Get your favorite authors on your favorite reader, long before they're out in print! Ebooks from Samhain go wherever you go, and work with whatever you carry—Palm, PDF, Mobi, and more.

CPSIA information can be obtained at www.ICGtesting.com
Printed in the USA
BVOW04s0016300315

393710BV00001B/62/P